AUTOMATON
NATION

CYNTHIA **KUMANCHIK**

author HOUSE®

AuthorHouse™
1663 Liberty Drive
Bloomington, IN 47403
www.authorhouse.com
Phone: 1 (800) 839-8640

Published by AuthorHouse 06/03/2020

ISBN: 978-1-7283-6326-4 (sc)
ISBN: 978-1-7283-6325-7 (e)

Library of Congress Control Number: 2020909604

Print information available on the last page.

This book is printed on acid-free paper.

encounter

CHAPTER 1

Dat's sensors nearly overheated, and his circuitry was on high alert. He stood among his coworkers, waiting for the Gala to begin. They stood by him in stoic deference. He fidgeted and sighed. Being a Sous Chef both excited and terrified him. But it was the young woman with the auburn hair and jade-green eyes in bright blue, seated at the head table that caught his attention. His acute vision zeroed in on her delicate features and slender figure. His right eye twitched with a signal to his brain waves.

Who's that? Big eyes and long hair equals beauty, according to my highly developed sensations. Need to be near her to see for myself.

The reflection from the chandeliers sparkled on the tables with plates of Mushroom Risotto with Truffles, Chinese Kung Pao grasshopper entree, and Rat Snake soup that Dat had prepared. His chest heaved with pride, and he wondered if the governor knew that these dishes were his specialties with the shortage of meat. Dat believed, after this night, that it would be announced that he had become the Chef for the Grand Old Capitol Hotel, the favored place for the governor and her high-level constituents.

I must live up to Tony De LaFleur's name, my mentor. They tell me my talents come from him.

The hotel's ballroom shimmered with vintage elegance and bustled with the sounds of excited guests. A robotic harpist and violinist played softly in the background. Five hundred people gathered today by invitation only, their names known in elite circles.

Dat felt honored to be a part of this celebration, having just emerged from conception. His perfect French and upscale manners added to his pedigree. Dat smirked and realized he had nothing to worry about.

A hush fell over the room as Governor Thompson stepped up to the podium, her blunt cut chestnut hair and stern gray eyes behind opaque glasses added to the severity of her stance.

"Good evening. I'm Governor Andrea Thompson. I would like to take this opportunity to welcome our guests from all over the world to our beloved Capitol City, once called Sacramento, in California and its surrounding island communities.

"Second, be aware that security is tight, and everyone's eye prints have been scanned before entering the building to protect you from rogue robots. Even though our curfew's intact, our intel has instructed us to be aware of increased tension due to our recent robot protests. As you know, an employee of Robot International was attacked last Monday evening at ten p.m. after leaving the building. It could be a coincidence…but don't be alarmed, your safety is our priority.

"Everything tonight was prepared by our special team of Model 500 robots, created by the chief scientist, Dr. Rod Tate of Robots International. His Genealogy Project paved the way for these human-like androids to perform even greater tasks than previous models. I will let Dr. Tate explain this project."

Dat shifted his eyes toward the table in the middle of the room, where the young woman clapped vigorously. She beamed as her father spoke in commanding tones.

"Many celebrities, scientists, and leaders have supported this project by donating their actual brains at death. Yes, offered up for RI to infuse them into these robots to preserve their legacy and talents. That makes these Model 500s able to take on their donor's traits and idiosyncrasies. One even told me…."

The words faded from his brain as he watched the young woman whispering to her mother and laughing at the joke. Then she turned toward him and smiled brightly. His power supply jolted, and his circuitry went a little haywire. Dat found it hard to contain himself. His legs felt like mush, and he needed to sit down. But he kept himself upright alongside his other coworkers who seemed unmoved by anything going on around them. Their stiff postures and expressionless faces unnerved him.

Can't they see what I see? She's looking at me now.

Dr. Tate continued and gazed upon the group with pride.

"We have lined up each of these unique Model 500s to be inspected. You will see that they are the top of the line. More human than the Model 100 domestics and Model 300 technics with softer skin and emotional capabilities due to their sensitivity tracks. Each one is different and available for purchase. Their complete profiles and photos have been provided to you. Does anyone want to bid?"

Their gazes turned toward him and his cohorts. Horrified, Dat looked at their longing stares. His knees weakened as many pointed at him.

Can't move. Why are they staring?

"Model 500s, please circle around the tables," said the governor.

She gestured for the robots to move forward and pressed a button on her com watch.

Dat hesitated as the others marched past him. But a twitch in his brain activated his sensors, and he quickly followed the group. His legs propelled him around the room, and he heard the crowd's gasps and cries of surprise. His instincts told him to stop, make eye contact, and smile broadly.

I'm not sure what's going on, but now I can check out the girl.

A couple took his arm and asked him a question.

"Enough of this vegetarian stuff. Can you make Chateaubriand? It's a favorite of mine. It says you speak French. Can you speak a few words?" the man in a black tux and teal shirt asked.

He blurted out the words, trying to impress the couple.

"Bien sûr, Monsieur. J'adore cuisiner Chateaubriand."

"Honey, that sounded good, but what did he say?" said the man.

"Babe, he said, 'Of course, sir. I love cooking Chateaubriand.' And he's so adorable with his big brown eyes and politeness. And he has the sculpted hands of a chef," said the woman, in a matching teal gown, her numerous rings sparkling as she held up her bid sign.

Dat was ushered around the room, stopped by interested parties, prompted by questions, touched mostly by females, and asked about his specifications (weight, height, age, and even IQ). The combination of strong chiseled features, olive skin, and curious eyes gave him an advantage. Soon he passed the young woman, Dr. Tate's daughter. Their eyes locked, and voltage sparked through his circuits. She touched his arm.

"Hey, guy. What's your name? You seem so real to me," she said. Her jade eyes penetrated through him.

What do I say to her? Talk to her now.

"I'm…Dat. Vous aimez les cupcakes au chocolat? Je peux les faire pour toi."

Where did that come from? Am I French?

The young woman laughed.

"Mom…he knows French. Wants to make chocolate cupcakes for me. Let's bring him home with us."

His eyes sparkled, and he managed a smile as Dat gazed at the mother and daughter. He could barely hear the bid process in the background. But his precious moment was interrupted by a bid. His acute hearing perked up.

A spotlight appeared on Dat.

"$100,000 for the French-speaking chef, Dat," said a man.

"Any other bids? Going once, twice…"

Dat turned to see who wanted him. He hoped the scientist would bid higher.

The young woman nudged her father.

Dat's circuits became electrified.

"Honey, I can't bid on my creations," whispered Dr. Tate.

Dat picked up his comment.

"$150,000 for the chef who makes chocolate cupcakes," said an older man with thick black glasses, sitting at Dr. Tate's table.

Everyone laughed.

"$300,000," said the woman with the rings.

The room became silent.

"Anyone bid higher? Going once, going twice. Sold for $300,000. Largest bid yet. You can claim Dat at the end of the evening," said the auctioneer.

He whirled around to see the couple in teal, their eyes glazing over at the sight of their new possession. His chest tightened, and his sensors lit up inside him. Immobilized, he stood in the middle of the large room, fear and anxiety overtaking his sensitivity trackers. Dat's dream of being the Chef for the Grand Old Capitol Hotel was now gone. And the girl… never to see her again. She glanced at him with a slight smile on her face.

A crash alerted the guests, and Dat ran for cover. A slight humming caught his attention, and he glanced out a side window to see what seemed like a series of metal birds whizzing by. He sensed danger, but no one else did, even the other Model 500s. The loud chatter and laughter of the guests muffled the incoming buzzing that intensified as they hit the large skylight in the middle of the room.

Like a swarm of bees, tiny drones dropped from the chandeliers and began firing at the tables below. A lady sipping her champagne slumped in her chair upon being hit. Suddenly the laughter was now replaced by the continual buzzing and shooting. Another woman screamed as the patrons were being picked off one by one. Many ducked under the tables. Cries and shrieking echoed throughout the massive room.

Lights clicked off. Shattered pieces of nanocrystal rained down from the ceiling as the demolished skylight opened up to reveal a metallic army with their silver armbands and gear as they touched down on the ground. Shots fired. Tables turned over. The dark army, shrouded in jet black, blended into the background, shooting at the terrified guests as they tried to flee. A stampede of people rushed to escape.

"Activate the weapons. Secure the building. Move to kill," the governor screamed.

From his place behind a column in the room, Dat's x-ray vision focused on the mayhem surrounding him. Many of the police force fell like timber as the army's shots picked them off one by one. Their blood splattered everywhere, and the stench of death and urine flowed through the once beautiful room with its stained carpets, broken chandeliers, and toppled tables of uneaten food.

Dat dropped and crawled along the ground, sensing danger. Many of his coworkers rushed toward the exits. The couple who bought him had vanished. He heard moaning. He sensed a female presence. Dat searched for the young woman with the illuminating jade-green eyes and found her under the main table where he had been a few minutes earlier. She was crying softly, her small hand covered in blood, and there was a jagged cut on her forehead. He sprinted over to her in thirty seconds.

"Help me …please. I can't find my parents," she said.

The lens in Dat's eyes zoomed onto the white cloth napkins from the table. His right brain signaled the word bandage, so he wrapped her hand and applied another to her forehead. Her frightened eyes looked to him for comfort.

"Got to go now. Help you get out of here," he said.

Dat shielded her from the chaos around them, guiding her toward the exit. They tripped on a body of a woman in a white lace dress, now turning a dark shade of rose. He felt the young woman shake, and she moved in closer to his protective embrace.

"Keep moving. We're almost there…to safety," Dat said.

His sensors activating as electricity surged inside him. He rushed past, brushing the sleeve of another. Dat's eyes widened as the figure now rammed into his shoulder.

Keep going…must save her. Move on.

It seemed like hours, but it was only minutes as they trudged along in the darkness, stepping over bodies, hearing the wounded's moans, the roar of ambulances and their labored breathing.

Dat ignored his new danger impulses. People bumped into them, pushing them forward. Someone stepped on the young woman's heel, and she stumbled. He grabbed her free hand and guided her along as she limped toward the exit. His laser eyes cut a path before them in the room's darkness. Only a ray of light from the skylight illuminated a portion of the room. They pushed through the last of the crowds, the ones who made it from the horrors of the mechanical army.

He heard her sigh as they reached the doorway to the front lobby. The young woman spotted her mother, standing against the wall.

"I thought I lost you. So sorry, Val…we got pushed out by the crowd. So glad you're safe, but…" said her mother. They hugged, and tears flowed down their faces. Then her mother smiled at Dat.

"He helped me get out…saved me. Where's Daddy?" cried the young woman.

Her mother slumped as she started to fall to the ground. Dat ran to help her up.

"He was shot multiple times and taken to the hospital. Think it was a drone. He could barely talk, but told me to stay here for you," her mother said.

Val clung to her mother and Dat as her sobs grew louder.

The couple in teal, their clothes marked in blood spotted him and waved. They stumbled toward them, their faces drawn and bodies trembling.

"Dat...you're okay. We're the Landers...we purchased you and want to take you home with us. Let's get out of here; we've *barely* escaped with our lives," said the woman, running toward him.

"Happy to know you're in one piece, buddy," shouted the man in the tux.

Val and her mother turned toward the couple.

"Your...he saved my daughter's life."

Dat looked at them sheepishly. His circuits burned, and his sensitivity trackers fired up, making him feel embarrassed.

"That's our Dat. We certainly picked a good one. I'm Elise Landers, and this is my husband, Arnold. I'm sure we'll be in touch when this is over. I'm so freaked out. What a nightmare this has been...it's like a warzone here. So much bloodshed and a ton of ambulances. It's rumored to be caused by some robot terrorist group, heard from a governor's source, right here on my com watch. They let all the big donors know."

Bad robots? Not logical. Must be something else.

Val's mother gave Elise a quizzical look. Then her com watch vibrated.

"Got to take this incoming message from the governor...my boss. Nice to meet you both. Rod is at the hospital...Val is fine. About this latest attack—here is my strategy..."

Val's mom walked toward the entrance, showing her ID. Val lingered and gave him a quick squeeze.

Maybe, there was a chance I'd see her again or not.

"Dat, we've been cleared, and it's time to go before..." said Elise. They pulled him toward the entrance.

I'm theirs? Wait, I'm a chef.

A swat team in battle gear rushed past them. Dat's sensitive hearing picked up their conversation.

"We had this locked up tight. Must have been an inside job. Heads will roll if the governor finds out."

Dat's sensitivity trackers told him to act like his guardians, and he would get out of here alive. He needed to blend in and be human in order to survive.

CHAPTER 2

Her head was spinning as they raced through the city in a space cab toward the hospital, her mom still communicating with the governor. "Escaped through the skylight, picked up by a helicopter?" Val heard the incredible snippets of their conversation, and she felt like it was her fault the incident happened.

That insect buzzing…Her dad's bloody tux…people dropping dead on the ground…screams…shattered glass and the governor's cries for help— the premonition that Val had in a dream the night before.

"Darling…you know you're highly sensitive and that your intuition sometimes gets you into trouble. Now we don't want to scare anyone with a dream. Better keep this one to yourself, not to upset your dad. Or worse yet, cancel this important event. No…not this time," said her mother when Val relayed the warning.

Val glanced at her clumsily wrapped hand, remembering the comforting touch of the boy who rescued her. Hard to believe he is… her mind could not go there. Only back to his warm brown eyes and the dimple in his bronzed cheek when he smiled. But the night's terror of the shooting drones, blood splattered everywhere, the high-pitched screams, and tragedy of her father would haunt her dreams forever. She should have ignored her mother and given her dad the heads-up.

"We've just arrived at the hospital, governor…to check on Rod's condition," her mother said, her voice cracking.

Val followed her mother through the emergency's automatic doors and was immediately transported fifty floors to her father's room. As they rose, each floor revealing a higher level of care. She bit down hard on her trembling lip and choked back sobs when the doctor reported the unfortunate news about her dad's condition. Her mentor and rock. Now he was lying in a hospital bed, unable to move or talk.

Her mom nearly hyperventilated at the sight of her dad's bloodied, broken body. Her chest heaved up and down as she gasped at her dad's injuries. Val stood numb by her side, glimpsing at his ashen face, torn limbs, and massive wounds. His immobility and shallowed breathing filled her with panic, wondering if he might die right there. Val had never seen a wounded body before, let alone someone she loved. Val knew her mother was trying to be strong in the face of adversity.

"Is he going to make it?" Val whispered.

Her mother looked up, holding back tears.

"I don't know. It's impossible for me to understand. The night seems like one big blur. We need to have a doctor check out your hand and look at that cut on your head," said her mother.

Val pressed a hand to her forehead and realized it was still bleeding. And her other hand started to throb.

"Not now, Mom. I'll be fine—don't worry about me...it's more important that we find out who did this and why," said Val, giving her mom a hug.

She bumped into Nurse Dolli, who stopped abruptly and stared at the robot that was part of the medical team. Val gulped, never coming close to a Model 300 that looked semi-human and handled technical and medical functions, only the Model 100 domestics that cleaned floors and dusted shelves.

"Need to fix you up—bandage that hand and examine that cut on your forehead," Dolli said.

Her eyes blinked, and her mouth moved simultaneously, then her hands worked quickly to suture Val's hand and clean her wound. Dolli then advanced to her mother, checking her vitals and to see if she had any minor injuries while the doctors attended to her Dad's serious issues.

"Clear...for...now, unless you want the doctor to examine...you," said Dolli.

"Umm...fine. Thanks to my husband acting as a shield, I would have been in worse shape. And because of me...he almost died," her mom said as they left the hospital room.

Her eyes teared, her mother heaving a big sigh. Val watched her mother sink down onto the lobby's stiff couch and close her eyes. She wanted to tell her how much she loved them both, but Val felt helpless now that her world was broken. Just hours ago, their family unit was intact, and Val was excited about supporting her father's major design—the Model 500's debut. And her mom's role working as the governor's publicist made her proud. The minutes dragged into hours as Val sat by her mother's side, rubbing her back as they waited for news. Her watch pinged—two a.m.— call from Lucy.

"I'm sorry, Mom, but I have to get out of here…will bring us some food," Val said, happy to hear from her best friend.

"OMG, what happened to you? Are you all RIGHT? Tried calling, but you wouldn't answer," said Lucy. Her hologram screamed at Val.

"Yeah, …it's been…so hard…It's was horrible," said Val, her voice trembling.

"Wish I could be there…can't because of the curfew. Saw the news— it's everywhere," said Lucy.

Val found the elevator, pressing the lobby button, but still listening to Lucy. It arrived in under sixty seconds, causing Val to right herself.

"Really? Can't believe this is happening to me…but got one of my visions," said Val.

"Geez…freaky…what are you going to do now?" said Lucy.

"I'm exhausted, but I'm starving. Got to get some food. Talk later… okay?" said Val.

She stumbled toward the food court.

"Cafeteria is closed," said the mechanical clerk, standing guard.

"Where are the vending machines?" asked Val. Her stomach started to growl, and she also desperately needed some caffeine. Its robotic arm pointed to a corner glass cubicle.

"Welcome. Burger? Pizza? Grilled Cheese? What do you want to eat?" a voice greeted her from the cubicle.

"Uh…grilled cheese, breakfast bar, one black coffee, and a café au lait," Val said, sliding her watch over its surface.

A mechanical hand dispensed the bar and black coffee into a container as a melting, hot sandwich ejected on a plate, followed by a toffee-colored coffee. Then the hand neatly put everything together into a large plastic bag with handles.

"Thirty-five charged to your account. Anything else?" said the machine.

Val blinked. *Pretty steep for hospital food. And no chips. What a rip off.*

A hologram appeared, and Val's eyes lit up.

"Darling, are you all right? I'm watching the news now, and I was so worried. Are you okay? How's your dad and mom? Were they hurt?"

"I'm fine, grandma, but Dad is here in the hospital, and I'm in panic mode. Mom looks so tired. Dad looks like he's going to die and all for what?" she blurted out, telling her grandma all the gritty details.

She looked up to see the wall monitors rolling with late-breaking news. Images of the break-in at the Grand Old Capitol Hotel popped on the screens. There she was crying and hugging her mom in the lobby with Dat in a group hug for all the world to see. The security cameras captured the tragic scenes, and the Government Network or GNet broadcasted it. Her heart beat faster, and her legs felt like mush.

Val gasped, spilling her coffee after reliving it again.

"Don't worry, your dad is in good hands. Robots rebelling and one that rescued you? That's why you can't judge all mechanix the same. Live through many crises like this," said her grandmother.

"How did you survive? What should I do?" said Val.

"Listen to your gut. You've inherited the traits from me. Be aware of everything around you, and it will guide you," she said.

Val backed into someone who tapped her on the shoulder.

"Thanks, Grandma...I will keep in touch. Got to go."

Val turned to see a young man with the long sapphire strands of hair and pale green skin. His wire-frame glasses magnified his astonished eyes with ultra-long lashes as he moved closer to retrieve the bag that slipped from her shaking hands.

"Hey, miss, let me help you with your coffee and food. I'm...Whit Green from GNet. You're...you're the girl there on the monitor. How did you escape? Any reason why the robot terrorist group attacked and disrupted the Model 500 introduction?"

Val steadied herself and stared at his curious eyes. She wasn't ready for any grilling right now. All she cared about was ingesting some caffeine, and finding out how her dad was doing.

"Please…I'm fine, really. Got to get back to my family. It's been a terrible night, and you look so familiar," she said, checking out the monitors.

The monitors continued with the story, showing Dat then being discovered by his guardians and taken away. Footage of the National Guard and SWAT team rushing past streamed on.

"Yeah, I'm the only survivor of the V-parasite disease. I was in the news constantly, and now I want to get the story, not be it. I'm the college intern for GNet. You were actually rescued by a Model 500 android? Such a killer story," said Whit.

Val stared at the reporter who nearly died and was miraculously cured. I guess she should be happy she didn't go through something so extreme. But still, her family didn't need all this publicity. Not now. She needed an excuse to get out of here, away from his questions.

"Yes…I remember now, and I'm glad you're alive. But it's really important that you find out who was behind this and almost killed my Dad. I would love to know why they targeted him…hate him for creating robots? I'll certainly help you with that angle. It makes me sick to my stomach."

She clutched her middle as a sharp pain went through her. Her watch vibrated.

Who was calling? Lucy, again?

The nurse was calling…Dolli. Her hologram made her jump.

"Hey, got to take this…it's an emergency," said Val.

"Come back, Val. Your mom fainted. May need to admit her. Your Dad's in stable condition," Dolli said.

Val felt numb, and her legs wobbled. Her mother had collapsed under the strain. Her father had been wounded. All because of this special Gala to honor her father and show off all those Model 500s and her mind-boggling premonition.

Please don't fall. Get it together. Your parents need you.

The reporter followed closely behind. She stopped, turned around, and looked directly into his questioning eyes.

"Are you okay? You look stressed. Let me come with you, and we'll figure this out together."

"Whit…we need privacy. If you want to talk to Dat, he's with the Landers. He may be able to fill you in. But mostly it's been a nightmare I want to forget. As you can see, my parents need me."

Whit nodded and blushed.

"I understand, and thanks for the info. I'm new and eager to get this story. It's my job to pursue the truth. If you ever want to talk…you can reach me." He brushed his com watch with hers.

Her watch vibrated, and she felt electrical impulses from Whit's watch.

But there's got to be a reason for a robots' revolt and why I was rescued by one. Counterintuitive!

Dat's face popped up in her mind, that tender smile and warm brown eyes. It took her mind off the horrors of tonight. Grandma told her not to judge, so she needed to figure out the truth. But first, she had to focus on her family. It was rough being an only child.

As she entered the ER, Val saw her mom stretched out on a gurney and hyperventilated.

CHAPTER 3

The Landers hurried out of the damaged building with Dat close behind and then stepped into the self-driving Turbo space van. They avoided speaking with the police, having contacted their neighbor and friend, the Police Chief Turner. He eliminated the need for their statements, knowing their extreme need for discretion.

Their self-driving space van whisked them away and cruised above the rooftops of the 1,000-foot lightweight 3D-printed carbon graphene buildings and the unique 500-foot Grand Old Capitol Hotel, a historic landmark, built of self-healing concrete. Another pyramid building stood out among the rest, soaring to 1,500 feet. As Dat looked closer, he noticed the glowing words, *Robot International,* against a rainbow background. The building slowly switched from red to blue, purple, then black. He gazed out of the gold leather interior of the eight-passenger van, equipped with fruit and flavored waters as his guardians chatted nervously.

"We could have almost been killed and our new bot here as well," said Arnold.

He looked Dat up and down.

"Yeah, our huge investment was taken away. Luckily, he was smart enough to escape without a scratch," said Elise.

She patted Dat's arm, and his sensors slowed down. He hardly realized that he was in danger just an hour ago. Tonight's terror seemed like a short-term memory, now erased as they climbed above the clouds near a large golden orb. Dat viewed it with awe for a brief second, before landing on the vast rooftop of the Metro Apartments. Faux palm trees and deck lounges lined the outdoor pool. A cabana and full bar were nearby.

"Here's your new home. I'm sure you will enjoy living with us," said Elise.

As the van doors automatically slid open, a robot in a black uniform bobbed his head in greeting and helped them out and into the transporter.

"Thanks, Rad. Park the van," said Arnold.

Dat nodded to a mechanical butler who stared at him blankly and never moved.

"That's a Model 100, not as sophisticated as you are, and lacks talents or feelings," said Elise.

Arnold's eyes darkened, and he prodded Rad toward the van's open door.

"SPACE 33," he shouted.

"See—he just needs a little direction," Elise said.

Dat's left brain did a doubletake. His sensitivity trackers surged, and he watched for any reaction from Rad, who appeared emotionless. As Rad entered the van, his mechanical arm touched the starter and maneuvered the van toward the garage. The Landers then motioned for Dat to get into the transporter.

"Ha—and they say machines will take over someday," said Arnold as he pressed 33.

Elise laughed, and Dat smiled at the seemingly harmless joke.

Dat viewed the twinkling stars and clear night through the transparent glass transporter as it rose to level 33. His new life was about to begin.

Arnold used his eye imprint, and the doors to the apartment opened slowly.

"Security—has anyone tried to break in? Are we safe to enter?" said Arnold.

Elise shivered, and her hands started to shake.

"All clear, Mr. Lander…no one has tried to break in. You may come in now," a woman's monotone voice answered.

The couple entered the apartment reluctantly and motioned for Dat to wait outside. The apartment lit up, and the monitors came on to show the latest news of the RRG attack.

"The Grand Old Hotel erupted in gunfire tonight. Fifty killed, one suspect captured, others still on the loose with reports of a group called the RRG, the initials sliced into the floor."

Dat wondered when he would be allowed to step inside.

"It's so creepy…I feel violated tonight. Please turn off the news. It's too painful to see right now," said Elise, stepping out of her shoes.

"Dat, come inside. Everything's fine. Nothing to worry about," said Arnold, shutting down the monitors.

The spacious apartment matched the colors in the space van—gold and white. Dat's eyes lit up at the size of a grand room that contained a modern tech kitchen with a huge oven and stove, a quaint dining area and immense living room with white leather couches and gold brocade furniture, with a view overlooking the dazzling city below.

"Quite amazing for a chef who can cook and serve his guests from the kitchen bar, isn't it?" said Elise.

Dat was speechless. He touched the panels, and they became transparent, revealing a built-in refrigerator that spoke to him.

"Are you the new chef? Just smile, and I'll remember you."

Dat's face reflected onto the refrigerator, and his smile opened it to find it neatly organized with fresh herbs, exotic fruits and vegetables, cream and butter, and an assortment of cheeses and breads. Inside the freezer were frozen venison, duck, various cuts of beef, and fish.

Isn't there a meat shortage, or is it artificial? Where'd they get all this stuff?

"Press the menu of items on the side to order any stock item to be delivered at any time."

Dat jumped back in surprise.

"And buddy, we have a wine cellar and drink fridge. Elise wants me to diet, but I have my own snacks stashed away. I can show you later," said Arnold.

Elise rolled her eyes and grinned at Dat.

"I stocked it just for you. Most of it is imported from the Euros, and some has been in the deep freeze for several decades. The 2020 Drought killed many trees and plants forced us to live on separate island communities.

Now how about whipping up something before we retire? And of course, we need a little bubbly to celebrate," she said. She retrieved two bottles of Dom Perignon from the cellar.

Dat surveyed the refrigerator and cupboards filled with dry goods. His mind shifted to the many recipes in his brain. He had been programmed to cook, and here was his chance to create something.

Start simple to see what they like.

"Give me eggs, spinach, ham, and cheese. Also, need instruments for cooking," Dat said.

The fridge's mechanical hands picked out the correct items and transferred them to the counter. Shelves flew open, and the items were stacked neatly on top of one another and placed into Dat's hands. He clicked off mentally the steps necessary for his creation.

His hands worked methodically as he whipped the eggs, cut the ham, and shaved the cheese. As the frittata cooked, he tossed the spinach leaves, added the vinaigrette and sprinkled bacon bits on top. The smell of fresh oregano, sautéed ham, and buttery eggs filled the room. He prepared a simple brioche pastry that looked like it had a little hat and a fruit parfait of papayas, pomegranates, and kiwi. In less than ten minutes, Dat placed the food before the couple on white, rose-embossed china plates, and poured each of them a large mimosa.

"Goodness, we are going to be spoiled now and forever," said Elise.

She had changed into her kimono and gold velvet slippers and was seated at the breakfast bar.

"And there goes my diet now. Merci butt cups," said Arnold, gobbling up the frittata and slurping down the mimosa.

I guess they liked it. His French sucks.

"Dear, it's beaucoup," said Elise, downing her mimosa and handing her glass back to Dat.

He took it from her and examined it.

Does she want more?

Arnold ignored her for a moment and pressed the wall monitors back on. The governor appeared on the screen, calm and dressed in a somber black suit. She spoke slowly and deliberately.

"Such a tragedy tonight at the Robot International Gala. Fifty people died tonight at the event who were dedicated to the creation of a new robot race. We are saddened at the loss of these fine people…and also horrified at the terrorism by the so-called Robots Revolt Group. The RRG must be stopped before they strike again. The perpetrators have not yet all been caught. We believe that Grace Noble is behind this action.

"Dr. Rod Tate was shot and is in critical condition. His wife, Meredith, has been admitted for observation. Their daughter, Val, is with them now.

She barely escaped and was helped by a Model 500. We commend this android for his bravery."

The monitors showed the hotel mayhem after the room was emptied and Dat's back as he assisted Val and reunited her with her mother. His sensors vibrated, and his sensitivity track pinged as Dat relived the devastating scenes once again. He didn't understand why he felt scared.

"You were very courageous tonight, and we're so proud of you. We're all a little shell-shocked right now," said Elise.

Why? I wanted to be near her, that's all.

"And your cooking is fantastic, certainly takes the edge off tonight's tragedy," said Arnold, shoveling more food into his mouth.

Elise's watch vibrated.

"I'm getting an urgent call. It's from the governor. I'll be in the other room—monitors are too loud to hear," said Elise.

Dat continued to watch the news, and his right brain realized that he must have helped her. His circuits electrified at the sight of her photo.

How do I know if she's okay?

"What's wrong, buddy? You look sad. But it was pretty scary tonight. And those damn bots—I mean that RRG. They'll be banished if they're caught and thrown in the junkyard. Sad state of affairs," said Arnold as he clicked off the monitors.

"Uh sorry…what can I…get you?" said Dat.

He struggled to get the words right, even though his French was perfect. He just needed more time to pick up their language.

Elise appeared back into the room with a huge smirk on her face.

"Guess what? We're going to throw a dinner party here. Governor Thompson wants to meet with key leaders in the business and tech sectors regarding the RRG. Preferably those with money and influence…like us. I suggested that we host the first meeting here. What do you think, Arnold? Oh, look Dat, he's snoozing."

It was 3 a.m., and Arnold had drifted off to sleep. His head lay on the counter, and his glass was empty. She patted Arnold on the shoulder, but he started to snore.

He makes funny sounds when he sleeps.

Dat's laugh came out as hiccups.

"Well, I guess he will have to find out tomorrow. This is your big chance to make a huge impression, just like you did at the Grand Old Hotel. We'll work on a menu and logistics tomorrow, and you'll get to meet Tron and Mora."

Cook for the governor? Like Tony De LaFleur? One of the most famous chefs of all time? It's time to be exceptionelle. There it popped out again. Tony lives in me. Be that chef that Tony wanted you to be.

CHAPTER 4

Val awoke stiff and exhausted on a cot in her mother's hospital room. Her eyes wandered to her mother, who was still asleep. Meredith's blood pressure had soared to almost stroke levels and was then immediately instructed to spend the night. That left Val with two parents in the hospital, both at critical levels. Her stomach growled, and she desperately wanted to check on her dad. Val quietly slipped into the bathroom to freshen up.

Ugh…look at those dark circles. And that cut on my forehead. OMG…I hope I don't run into anyone I know. This make-up better work.

She splashed water on her face, applied a little concealer, mascara, and lip gloss. Then she combed out her long hair, so it lay flat on her shoulders. Val tiptoed out of the room so as to not wake her mom and headed to her dad's room.

Her dad's body remained immobile, so still that Val leaned in close to see if he was breathing and noticed the Model 300 nurse at his side.

"As for your dad…Not to worry. Breathing rate is 12 breaths per minute. Heartbeat is 60 beats per minute, and his temperature is 97.8 Fahrenheit," said Dolli.

Dr. Gates nodded in agreement as he walked into the room, his eyes blank, and his tone rigid. His stiff movements mimicked his coworkers.

Val wondered if he was a robot but noticed the bandage on his finger. *Guess not…robots never bleed.*

"First, I'm sorry for all that you have to deal with, and I'm happy to see Dolli attending to your injuries. It's been a shock to your whole family. You're very brave. Val, let me be honest…your dad needs surgery. He was shot in the chest by a drone, but it missed key arteries. Nurse Dolli is attending to his daily needs, and my operating tech, Mobi, will be assisting me with the surgery. I, of course, will be directing the operation, but it will be Mobi's precise movements with the scalpel."

Val wanted to cry, maybe scream at the unfairness of it all. This was all too much to deal with. It was bad enough to spend the night with her mother, but now her father needed to be taken care of immediately. She gulped, blinked back tears, and looked directly at the doctor's passive face.

"I'm not sure about this set-up…he's so weak and anything could happen. Are they ready to handle this?"

She looked helplessly at the doctor.

"Val—you're in a rough position with both parents in bad shape. Is there anyone we can call to assist you? I know you're concerned about his condition and their skillset, but let me introduce you to Mobi."

Val stared at the incoming contraption. Mobi had numerous mechanical arms attached to a monitor and base. She watched Mobi demonstrate his dexterity in picking up the delicate instruments.

Unlike Dolli, Mobi has just an extra set of arms and hands. It seems skilled and from what Dad said about the Model 300s…

Val needed to handle this situation—her parents expected more from her. Besides, she called in sick today and didn't have to worry about school. She glanced at Dad's pale face with grave eyes and a furrowed brow. Val sighed deeply.

"I could call my grandmother, but she can't get around very well."

"I do see your parents gave you the authority to make health decisions. Personally, I think lowering the age was not right, but…get some breakfast, dear…I'll call you when we have some news," said Dr. Gates.

Since Dolli was still attending to him, Val decided to slip out to the front lobby to get some fresh air.

What did the doctor want from me? He doesn't trust me to make the hard decisions. He acts like a robot himself and would let his robot tech do his job. Not sure I trust him. He acts like it's not a big deal, but it's my dad's life. Obviously doesn't get it.

She stopped to buy a coffee and was surrounded by wall monitors. They played the latest Thompson Hospital propaganda, promoting their new medical technology and services. Then an important news update flashed on all the screens. Her curiosity was aroused.

It zoomed in on the 1500-foot-tall glass building shaped like a pyramid reaching into the clouds. Protesters cascaded like waves along the platform, their numbers multiplying rapidly. A woman stood out in the sea of silver armbands with her striking purple hair and maroon shades.

A loud voice came from the Robot International building, echoing throughout the Capitol. Val realized the voice belonged to a company official.

"Good morning, everyone. I'm Richard Thompson, CEO of Robot International. Many of you already know, my sister, Governor Andrea Thompson. We welcome Dr. Grace Noble, a former employee of RI."

Then a crescendo of boos and hisses greeted the CEO, flanked by the governor as their magnified faces appeared on the video building tiles.

Val looked closer at RI's President and questioned his sincerity. She smelled the bs a mile away. And his audience agreed with her. But she waited to see if he had anything interesting to say.

"We want to address your concerns. Our current program, *Genealogy Project,* is extremely important for California and our country. With our declining human race due to population control and lack of plant foods due to the twenty-year drought, now robots are essential for society. Our models 100, 300, and 500 provide menial and advanced tasks necessary for a fast-paced technological world.

"Our family business, both domestically and globally, proudly serves all sectors of commerce from retail, household, computer, and even the medical field. And I credit Ms. Noble for the creation of the first Hubot, genetically engineering higher-level robots with brains and emotions. And we are continuing to develop more intelligent robots with our *Genealogy Project.*

"Our workforce of humans and robots is essential to this endeavor. We respect Grace Noble, and everyone connected to the robotic community. As your CEO, I am dedicated to the rights of ALL parties involved and have adjusted our policies, but I will not tolerate violence and disrespect. Anyone who violates this mandate will be terminated."

Val checked out the woman with the purple hair as the camera focused in on her stoic face.

Not your typical scientist, and they probably thought she was a rebel. But her intelligence won them over, but her honesty probably didn't.

Then a mechanical figure in jeans and a worn T-shirt spoke to the building as the platform raised him to address the president and governor, dwarfed in size to the gigantic figures.

"Hey...not all of us are treated well...working us twenty-four hours a day and mocked as second-class citizens. Look at me—beaten by my guardian."

He showed them his missing hand, wires protruding, and a missing eye socket.

The mechanix crowd erupted with more protests and waved their fists in solidarity.

"I'm sorry for all the pain you've endured, but what about the fifty people killed at the Grand Old Hotel last night?" said the CEO.

His face captured the entire screen, his eyes hidden by dark shades and his mouth moving rapidly. Val noticed the governor, like a soldier by his side. Two of a kind—uncaring and politically driven.

One Model 500, wearing a silver armband printed with Robots United, jumped from the platform and rammed into the guards, his right hand reaching inside his jacket.

"Humans must suffer like we have. You don't understand our pain... and it will happen again if you don't stop this abuse," he cried.

Security charged toward him, guns drawn.

"Don't come any closer, or we'll shoot. Stop!" they cried.

The crowd egged him on, booing loudly.

The robot leaped into the air, raising its mechanical arms rebelliously.

"I want to kill all of YOU," he yelled.

Val heard shots and an explosion. She gasped and squinted at the screen, almost fainting. She wanted to run out and stop this madness. She tapped her com watch to contact Whit.

"Hey, this is Val Tate. Just saw a robot terminated. They're dropping everywhere, and no one seems to care. Are you going to report this, or are you programmed by the government not to?" her hologram shouted.

The figure was suddenly annihilated. He fell to the ground, shaking, his head exploding.

I can't believe what I'm seeing. My insides feel like they're burning.

Hot fiery pain entered Val's body, and she touched her head, and it was hot.

Screams of terror and agony sounded. The group of silver armbands advanced off the platform, spanning the entire area around the Capitol. They surged closer, pushing the woman with the purple hair forward, her fist in the air.

"Stop now…before it's too late. We're getting stronger, and our voices must be heard," cried Grace Noble.

Shots fired everywhere, and helicopters swarmed the area. The mob continued to march toward RI with Grace at the center. Then she stumbled, hit in the leg. A robot with long steel arms shielded her from the firing but was shot in the back. Unkind drone cameras pressed to her pale face, trembling mouth, and bloody leg wound as she fell to the ground.

"Call me back now—Grace's been wounded. Just let me know you're there at the scene," Val messaged Whit.

She covered her mouth with her hand, too shocked at the circumstances.

"What the hell, she's been shot, we've got to help Dr. Noble. Send meds and an ambulance," said a voice behind her.

Val turned around to see a man in a white lab coat, pressing his com watch. Medical personnel scrambled to take care of the renowned patient as the sky ambulance, sirens blasting, made its way to the emergency entrance in less than 60 seconds.

"It's Dr. Noble—who introduced the 300s to the hospitals that saved numerous lives," murmured a pony-tailed EMT.

Val made her way to the ER, hoping to get a glimpse of the famous activist. She stayed out of the way but was let in because of her visitor badge. Val viewed the purple-haired woman silently in a corner as Grace lay on the stretcher, moaning in pain.

"Gunshot wound to left fibula, check vitals," said a tall, mustachioed EMT to the doctor who had been standing close to Val earlier.

"If it wasn't for her—Mobi wouldn't have been created," said a nurse who helped wheel her into a room.

Val gulped, not really knowing much about Grace Noble. Her father only mentioned her once. Now, Grace seemed very vulnerable and weakened by her collapse. Val watched in amazement as a team of robots, physicians and nurses continued to work on Grace as her eyes started to flutter, her body still immobile.

"Was anyone else hurt? Did Len make it?" Grace said softly.

The physician sighed.

"Please, Grace, just rest. You're going to need your strength."

"Damn, I knew it," she said through clenched teeth. Her eyes closed. *What just happened? I have to get away from here.*

Whit flew through the doors and rushed toward her, his eyes big and his cap askew.

"Where's Grace? Is she...dead? Hurt?"

"Really...you're too late. And no, she's in recovery now."

"Sorry...on it."

His dazzling smile and huge eyes drew her in. Val understood his dilemma.

But Dolli signaled her from across the room and was slowly approaching her.

"Miss—need to come quickly. Your dad...is going into surgery now."

"Got to go, Whit...check with the ER. They'll know what room Grace is staying in."

Val jogged to her father's room, leaving Dolli to maneuver her way back. She grabbed her father's hand as he was being wheeled out of the room. His ashen-colored face matched the drab walls, and he barely uttered breaths. Val kissed his forehead and prayed for a miracle. Would this be the last time she saw her dad? How long would his surgery take? She never wanted to leave his side. Just last week, he showed up at track practice, cheering her on, and now he was struggling to stay alive.

"Can I go to surgery with my dad?"

The attendants shook their heads negatively. "We'll let you know the minute he's released from surgery," they said in unison.

Her head bowed, and her shoulders sagged in resignation as Val watched her dad being led away. A crushing sense of fear and sadness overwhelmed her. His life, the robot's termination, and people murdered all weighed on her heavily like a rock placed on her shoulders. Her mother's pale face floated in front of her eyes.

Her watch vibrated as an incoming call came through.

A hologram of a nurse faded away.

"Your mother needs you. Can you come to her room immediately?"

Val took off running. Another tragedy or a warning?

CHAPTER 5

Dat awoke to a tinkling bell. He never really slept due to his sensory makeup. Basically, his brain shut down for the evening or early morning when Elise dismissed him to his new room. Equipped with a bed, closet, desk, and huge armchair, the plain white room suited his basic teenage needs.

"Mr. Dat, Breakfast…hurry," said a soft voice behind the door.

Dat rolled off the bed, checked out his appearance in the mirror. He peered at himself and realized he looked human, poking at his ears, checking his pupils, and examining his teeth. Even his skin seemed very elastic, soft, except for his scratchy face. Dat just needed to act more like a young man, call up his inner Tony. He touched his hair.

Must be neat and well-groomed at all times. Hair needs combing, sticking up.

Dat pushed down a lock of hair and grinned. His photographic mind zeroed in on the food in the refrigerator, and then a recipe for chocolate blintzes with raspberry sauce popped up.

Suddenly the door flew open. Dat stood facing a tiny female Model 300 with a perky face in a pink maid's uniform, one robotic hand vacuuming the hallway, and the other dusting the wall lights. Down the hallway, a male Model 300 moved in rows of tables and chairs.

"I see you've met Mora, my multi-tasking housekeeper, and there's Tron over there rearranging the living room for the dinner party…uh, meeting. That bell lets you know that I need you…*immediately*. Now let's get on with breakfast and then be ready to plan the event," said Elise in her flawless makeup and slim black jumpsuit.

Dat strode over to the refrigerator and gathered an armful of food, scooping up utensils and pans to prepare his first breakfast for the Landers. His mind swirled with ideas.

"Nothing fancy hon, we've got work to do. Maybe oatmeal and coffee," said Elise.

Dat readjusted, watching the two Model 300s buzzing around the room. Tron balanced a lamp in one mechanical arm and pushed a set of tables with another. Mora zipped toward the window to open the blinds but hit the edge of a table. The tables crashed together in a domino effect, and Tron dropped the lamp. Nervously hoping not to copy the other Models, he noted "Oatmeal and Coffee" on the Breakfast Menu.

"Morons…you 're going to ruin the furniture. Slow down," screamed Arnold.

He marched into the room in his robe and PJs, his eyes on fire and his fists clenched.

"Damn bots…gimme some coffee before I explode," said Arnold.

Dat's circuits sizzled, and his sensors lit up. The crash and ugly voice tone alerted his sensitivity track. Was this behavior acceptable? Somehow it hurt his right brain impulses but pushed his left brain into overdrive. He looked for the word coffee, but discovered a variety of settings on the machine, then guessed one that read Cappuccino. Dat slid a hot cup to Arnold at the food bar, almost spilling it.

Tron and Mora scrambled to realign the room and check for damages. In thirty seconds, they busied themselves with their chores.

"Arnold, calm down. I put them in advanced movement mode, and they got a little crazy. You're just on edge from last night," said Elise.

Dat punched the oatmeal and coffee buttons, and the items appeared which he placed in front of Elise, then searched his mind and produced chocolate blintzes for Arnold in a matter of minutes. He formed a congenial smile.

Must pretend to be the perfect chef. Not used to their mad faces.

"Taste it. Like it?" said Dat.

Arnold sipped his coffee and then ate a large forkful of the blintze as the chocolate oozed onto the plate.

"Uh…that's good eats. I think I'm feeling better. Just that touch of caffeine and chocolate to change my mood. Thanks, Dat."

A grin spread over Arnold's face, and Elise winked at Dat.

So much to learn and figure out. Want to please no matter what.

⊹⟶═◉═⟵⊹

Dat exhaled at the opulence. He mimicked the food presentation from the Grand Hotel, making a mental note of the fanciness and extravagance. He surveyed his creation. The room glowed with diamond-like lights. The fragrant white rose, and lily bouquets permeated the air, balanced by the flowing chocolate fondue. Silver and gold confetti accented the table decorations, and the gold plates embossed with the letter L (for Lander) and Swarovski crystal added to the elegance.

"Governor Thompson will be here shortly to make any last-minute changes. I think it looks elegant and everyone should be congratulated. Especially...the food Dat. The presentation is superb," said Elise.

She likes it, and I passed the test. Thanks to Tony, guiding me through this process.

Elise jumped when the doorbell rang.

"Mora, get the door...who could be here so early?"

The door opened, and a woman in a faux alligator-skin jumpsuit and leather coat entered the room. She threw her coat on the ground and sighed.

"Geez...I'm half-blind. I wanted classy, not glam. Dim the lights..."

She towered over Elise and glared at Dat.

"Andrea...it's so good to see you, but aren't you a little early?" said Elise.

She gestured to Dat to bring a glass of champagne.

"Here, let's get the party rolling. That RRG got you on edge?" said Arnold.

Dat stared at a clean-shaven man in a silver tux and dazzling smile. He racked his brain for the right word.

Chameleon...cleans up good.

The governor snatched the glass of champagne from Dat's hand, nearly spilling it. She smirked at Arnold and rolled her eyes at Elise.

"Yes, it has...and the protest today ended badly. Sorry, Elise, for snapping at you. But can you tone it down?" said the governor.

Tron scurried to retrieve her coat and adjusted the lighting, which switched the room to a subtle shade of blue. Mora offered her some Oysters Rockefeller, and Dat refilled her glass.

"You're excused Andrea…do you have some talking points for this evening?" asked Elise.

The governor frowned as she checked her com watch.

"No message yet from my publicist, Meredith. You know she fainted last night…can't deal with the pressure. Just because her husband is in the hospital. I asked Meredith and her daughter Val to attend tonight. She should have my notes."

Dat's sensors sparked at the thought of the young auburn-haired woman coming tonight. He would see Val again. Would she remember him? He tripped but caught himself as he placed a plate of sashimi and California rolls on the food bar.

"Your chef knows my favorites…you've certainly trained him well," said the governor.

Her large red mouth consumed several pieces of sushi.

"You know I met her there…she has a reason for being upset. I feel so terrible. I'll cover for her if she can't make it. How about you describe the situation…make it out to be a dire cybersecurity situation and the need for a capital campaign," said Elise.

Arnold added his thoughts.

"And with my expertise in chip technology and tracking devices, we will be set. You come up with the plan, Elise will ask for money, and everyone will agree to the safety and security of all citizens. If all else fails, we'll build an underground facility for our supporters."

The governor laughed.

My guardians seem satisfied. But the governor—not sure how to act around her. Just keep giving her food. Don't want to mess this up and prove myself to be the great chef Tony De LaFleur.

Dat viewed the hot canapes and caviar that were ready to display, then surveyed the scene outside. His razor-sharp eyes caught some movement and flashes of silver amongst the dense foliage below. His suspicions were amplified by his right brain impulses, but his left brain kept him in check.

"Are the smoked dates and lobster toasts ready? The carrot tarts are divine. You definitely pleased the governor."

Elise came up behind him, and he gasped at the tiny woman in the metallic gown, silver stilettos, and large chocolate diamond around her neck.

"He's got it covered, and you look stunning tonight," said Arnold.

Elise beamed, and then her watch vibrated with an urgent hologram attached.

"Met Val Tate, the other night...I'm Whit from GNet. Got to hear your story...want to meet Dat, your Model 500 who saved Dr. Tate's daughter. Good feature story with all these negative vibes around. Please... just a moment of your time."

Elise terminated the call.

"Better get your publicist here now. Had a reporter on the line who wants to interview Dat. We can't have that now. Don't want to be targeted by the RRG."

"What? Maybe having the press on our side is a good thing. And Meredith is coming. Must have realized the urgency of this event tonight. I take back everything I said about her," said the governor with a twinkle in her eye.

"Meredith and her daughter?" said Elise.

Dat's circuits became electrified.

Dat moved back behind the bar where he felt more comfortable. His impulses said to be a brilliant chef, but his mind wandered to the beautiful young woman whom he saved from disaster.

CHAPTER 6

"Mom, what's wrong? You need to lie down," said Val.

She rushed to her room to find her mother, sitting upright in her chair, her hair brushed and her eyes bright. Her mother was writing down some notes.

"Baby, we're going to an important dinner tonight at the Landers. The governor has gathered some movers and shakers to come and discuss the Rebellion. She wants talking points and my support. Plus, a reporter called Elise and may show up tonight. I'm feeling better. The doctors wanted me to stay longer, but they will release me."

Stupid governor, always thinking of herself and pulling Mom away.

"Sure, mom, but what about dad?"

Val cringed. Work was so important to her mom and, of course, to the Thompson family who ran everything, the rumor mongers said. The governor was so heartless, that's why she needed her mom to make her look good.

"Dr. Gates just stopped by and told me that Dad came through the surgery with no problems and is resting. I figured I could go for a few hours, and besides, the food will be wonderful with their new chef, Dat…"

Val saw the determination and strength in her mother's face. Her face brightened at the mention of Dat's name. She could help her mom and see Dat.

"You know you shouldn't be alone after all the stress you've been through. Let me go and make sure you're okay. What time do we need to be there?" Val said, noting that her watch said 5 p.m.

Val planned to check on her dad before she left the hospital. She took in a breath and let it out slowly. Her mom mentioned that she would see Dat again, the young man…the robot who saved her. And his gentle touch and caring eyes. Besides, she was dying to taste his cooking for tonight's event. They would probably be the only teens there tonight.

"I'm a total mess. What are we going to wear? How will we get there?"

Her mother grinned as Dolli walked into the room with some evening clothes, their tags still attached. The Model 300 placed them on the bed.

An hour later, mother and daughter stared at their changed images in the elevator to the 33rd floor.

Val sighed at how much they looked alike, their similar movements and coloring. Only the gray streak in her mother's hair determined their age differences. The stylish clothes from the nearby boutique surprised her. Dressed in a short black lacy dress and her mom in a long off-the-shoulder silver tea-length dress suited them both.

"I'm going to have to check out that boutique later. Dolli has good taste," said Val.

The door opened, and Elise greeted them with a hug.

"Come in, lovely ladies, we've been waiting anxiously for you to finally get here. You both look very chic," she said.

Val's mouth dropped as she entered the lavish apartment. She'd never seen so much gold and glitter in her life. The flowers' aroma enveloped her, and the room's charm beckoned her inside. But the view from the balcony took her breath away with the outline of the city's glass towers against the black velvet night so close to the sparkling sky and moon. Sliding glass doors opened onto a large glass deck. She ventured outside, and the fishy smell of ocean contrasted with the industrial smells of her neighborhood. Val swayed after looking down and then caught herself on the ledge.

"Drink…miss?"

A Model 300 presented some sparkling drinks on a silver tray.

Val shook her head and continued to observe the city lights and the flashing colored building panels of Robot International, where her dad worked. She'd never seen the skyline from the Gild Tower District before. Space vans and drones delivering goods flew overhead. Bright electronic billboards advertised virtual vacations and the latest technology.

Her family lived comfortably, but not like this. Lucy would be jealous. They'd known each other since their elementary school days but ran in different circles. Lucy's mom was a teacher at Thompson High, and her dad, a robot tech for RI. But both girls loved track. Her heart danced a few beats, and she breathed in the cool air, filming the view and sending it to her friend.

"Pretty fantastic, isn't it? I'm Arnold, and we met the other night under some terrible circumstances. And you've had it rough with both your parents in the hospital. But I hear you're helping your mother get through our little soiree tonight. Come, have some food before the guests arrive."

Val looked up to see a pudgy man in an expensive tux with friendly blue eyes. She recognized him from last night. She nodded and stepped back inside. Her mother stood next to the governor, offering advice and taking notes. Arnold joined his wife Elise, who chatted with the governor's aides.

Val sighed and wondered how she would deal with all these dull people and their endless talking. Then a tall figure caught her eye, broad shoulders in a starched white shirt and tight black jeans. He moved slowly toward her as his deep brown eyes locked onto hers. Val focused on his shiny perfect teeth and olive skin, finding it hard to speak. She knew immediately why she had come tonight.

"Interested in the sashimi? I can prepare...a tray for you."

She watched his mouth move and heard his words, but she could only nod. She followed him to the kitchen bar. The tray looked like a work of art; the sushi arranged symmetrically in various hues and combinations.

"Thanks...you're...Dat. How are you? I guess you survived last night," said Val.

She ate a piece.

"This is amazing. Glad we get to hang out tonight."

He smiled again, making her another plate.

"Taste the chocolate cookies...I made them...for you...your enjoyment."

Val blushed, remembering their exchange in French.

The room began to fill up as the guests arrived. Their loud voices and fancy clothes bothered Val. She desperately wanted to disappear, but her mother needed her. She watched carefully as her mother maneuvered throughout the room, greeting the guests and introducing them to the governor. Dressed in furs, diamonds, beaded gowns, and velvet tuxes, they circled the room. People piled into the apartment, and the Model 300s raced around to accommodate them with sparkling wine and Dat's creations. His hands worked tirelessly with endless dishes of escargot, Bruschetta, caviar tarts, liver pate, and chicken crepes.

Val stayed close to the bar, watching Dat serve his heavenly canapes to the eager, hungry crowd who demanded more and more. He kept her plate filled even though she wasn't hungry.

How can he stand it? I would have flipped out by now. He's so laidback; I bet Lucy would love to check him out.

She sent more photos, and finally, Lucy responded.

"OMG, you scored. Where are you? And that cute guy...let me know if you get together later. Did you say he's really a mechanical? That could be *interesting.*"

"Yeah...pretty amazing–unlike other guys we're used to," Val messaged back.

"And I hate to bring this up, but your ex Chad was such a dud, stood you up for the prom, and then bragged about it later. You wasted a year of your life with him," said Lucy.

Val raged inside, thinking about the embarrassing night and feeling so devastated. In a brand new shimmering gown her mother bought for her, she waited patiently for Chad to show up. Hours later and unable to contact him, she ran upstairs to her room and cried. Finding out that his date was a cute freshman cheerleader, Val decided to focus on track. She shut down after that incident and was ready for someone new—more thoughtful and less self-centered.

The crowd grew bigger, cramming into the apartment, their voices coming to a crescendo until the governor began to speak.

"Goodness gracious. I never expected you all to come tonight. Must be the food...special thanks to the Landers for hosting and their fabulous chef, Dat. Such an amazing spread on such short notice."

The crowd clapped with a few boisterous cheers. Val smiled as Dat nodded at her.

"But let's get down to business. This new group, the RRG, murdered fifty of our friends last night, and others are still protesting over their rights. What rights do these killers have? We've been too politically correct, and now the problem has grown bigger. We do need our bots, but we don't want them to overtake us."

Val focused on those huge red lips spilling out the propaganda. Her eyes widened, and she wanted to explode.

"Wait a minute...why do you think they're acting that way? Your brother terminated one and totally disregarded the others' complaints. I've seen mutilated and broken robots. It's degrading and horrific," said Val.

The group turned to see who was arguing with their leader, and her mother signaled with her two hands waving to stop. The governor stared at her in horror.

"Do you even know what you're talking about? And your dad was shot by one, and you're sticking up for them? How dare you! Meredith— you need to control your daughter, or I'll have to ask you to..." said the governor, her lips pouting and her eyes fiery with rage.

Val steadied her gaze and crossed her arms. She wasn't afraid to challenge the governor and wanted these elites to know how she felt.

The group grew quiet as the tension in the room increased. Meredith covered her eyes with her hand and looked downward.

"Let's all calm down and figure this out. We do respect our bots... robots, and all of us employ them. Look, we have a wonderful chef...Dat and our domestics, Mora and Tron that are part of the Lander family. I've seen the broadcasts, and Val was just trying to make a point.

"But, on the other hand, people were wounded and killed last night, and there must be a plan to stop these robot rebels before they destroy our lives and the type of society that we've worked hard to maintain. The governor also has a point. But everyone has an opinion, and no one needs to leave. Let's all have another glass of champagne," said Arnold, moving closer to Val and addressing the crowd. He signaled for Mora and Tron to serve more champagne. They scurried to bring in more trays of the sparkling wine.

"Right, everyone relax, and let's remember why we're here tonight. The governor is right, and we all need to come together to back her and Robots International in squashing the *rebellion* and bringing our country back to order. We pledge one hundred thousand for the cause," said Elise.

Arnold clasped her hand in support.

"Agreed, I pledge another one hundred grand. We have much to lose if we don't stop this now," said a bespectacled elderly man, shaking his cane and moving his wheelchair forward.

The governor's icy gaze disappeared as a smile lit up her face.

A woman in a low-cut pink silk gown addressed the crowd as she placed her hands on the man's shoulders.

"Charles is right...this movement has grown too fast, and it's all because of Grace Noble. What she's done to advance their cause, and for what reason?"

The room echoed with a loud clapping of hands, whistles, and cheers.

"I don't agree with that young woman—they're scraps of metal, nothing more...made to serve us," cried a lady in a white feathered gown.

Val rolled her eyes and went over to the bar where Dat stood. He avoided looking at her as his hands quickly made more appetizers, placing them on plates.

The governor smiled, encouraged by the guests who agreed with her.

"So, we need to rein them in, control this situation before we are overpowered. We can't let this situation turn into WWIII. We need your power, influence, and money to obliterate the RRG..."

Security buzzed, and a shaky voice projected into the apartment.

"A reporter here for an interview, but I'm concerned with the horde of people below."

A flare, then hand grenades hit the balcony. Then Tron dropped a tray of champagne glasses, shards flying in every direction.

"What's going on?" said Arnold as he bent to pick up the pieces.

Sparks flew in Arnold's face as he ran back inside.

Loud voices and sirens sounded outside. An angry crowd clustered around the apartment complex, cutting off access. A deep voice blasted the crowd's message.

"We saw the GNet space van circling the apartments, and we know what you're up to. Your world is shattering. We've surrounded the building, and we're coming to get you. Our leader Grace was shot and lies helpless in a hospital room. You may hurt us, but you can't stop the cause," he said, hidden by the huge mass of metal below.

A scuffle between security guards and the mob ensued. An internal monitor lit up, and the face of a rattled security guard appeared.

"We're surrounded, but we have it contained. The police have been called. Nobody leaves until we've cleared it," said the guard, his eyes bulged wide. Then the screen went dark.

Elise pressed a button on her watch.

"Everyone to the panic room," screamed Elise.

Arnold leaned against a book-shelved wall, which slid open to reveal a series of rooms with a door at the end.

"Down to the basement," he ordered.

A woman in a long silver sequined gown and bouffant hairdo screamed and ran outside. "I'm getting out of here…called my bodyguard and chauffeur."

The others stampeded toward the rooms in mass exodus with the governor leading the pack. No longer looking elegant or upscale, they pushed and shoved each other like animals to save themselves.

"C'mon Val, follow us before it's too late," called out her mom.

Those people and the governor really annoy me. I should go with my mom and keep her safe, but she didn't stand up for me…and I can't face their criticisms.

Then Val heard spine-chilling screams and stared in horror from the balcony. She witnessed the woman being torn from her Turbo space van as it took off. The mob crushed her as her screams diminished. Val became paralyzed and unable to move.

Hands grabbed her and pulled Val away from the balcony. Val almost fainted and then looked up to see Dat's calm face.

"Come with me."

Her gut urged her to follow Dat. Val sucked in deep breaths, almost wanting to pass out. Those angry robots below would kill her because she was a human. Just a few days ago, everything seemed to be perfect. She lived in a beautiful home in a nice neighborhood with parents who adored her. She enjoyed being an only child who had nice clothes, got good grades, and went to school parties. Val lived a model life. But her father was a scientist for Robots International, and her mother worked for the governor, and the robots hated them both. But the irony was that a Model 500 that was going to save her for a second time.

CHAPTER 7

All I ever wanted was to be a chef. That is what I was made to do. Now I'm saving this girl again. Was I destined to protect her?

Dat gazed into her troubled eyes. He searched them for answers, and he wasn't sure if he had any solutions. A minute ago, his circuits programmed him to create appetizers, one after the other, to keep up with the guests' requests. But then when chaos broke loose, his instincts screamed for survival, but he also had the urge to protect his companion. He amazed himself with his sensors heating up over this human, this young woman. Was it part of his robot code?

"Your donor left specific instructions that you have his cooking abilities and some of his memories. You've been implanted with Tony's brain and mixed with some of your own traits, but your Frubber exterior, its texture like human skin, is molded and designed to reflect today's diverse culture."

Dr. Tate revealed that knowledge to him when he was created. His mind drifted back to his inception. He recalled how gentle Dr. Tate was in attaching his legs, arms, and torso. Others constructed his face, but Dr. Tate performed brain surgery, infused with Tony's chef memories.

Laughter in a kitchen, surrounded by eager women awaiting his dish as he presented it from the oven like an actor on a TV show. He was a chef, but also a celebrity with a following as he traveled all over the world. He shared these precious moments with his audience, tasting eel soup from Korea, German schnitzel, English fish and chips, and the giant two-fisted American burgers. He loved different cultures and tasting ethnic foods with unknown people who enjoyed his company. Big smile, Teflon stomach, and restless spirit. Surrounded by happy faces and enduring smiles. Always an adventure…never afraid to discover.

His mind clicked back to reality. A girl needed his help and direction in this time of madness. His room had a trap door...in the closet. He took her hand and led the way. It was clammy, and her eyes watery, no longer the poised girl at the bar. She held onto him tightly and breathed heavily, looking like she might throw up. The noise outside was deafening. No one had approached the apartment. Dat left the Model 300s standing by the bar, still waiting for instruction, and ran to the end of the hall.

"Whoa, is this your room? Very clean and uncluttered. The opposite of mine," Val said, dropping his hand.

He hesitated, unsure of his thoughts and how to express himself, especially with this young woman.

"Yes...I like it neat. Let me show you...something."

Dat opened the walk-in closet filled with shelves and compartments. He moved aside some shoes and pressed the wall. It opened into a narrow chute.

"Be careful. Scary...takes seconds. Then you'll hit the ground. You'll see we're close to the water."

His hands demonstrated the process.

"Beat you down there...see how long it takes."

Val peered into the void, stepped in, and then took off. He could hear her screams all the way down. Dat jumped in after her. The velocity shot him forward, surging around darkened corners and propelling him eventually downward. His circuits electrified, sending conflicting left and right brain messages. Before he could blink, Dat landed outside on the faux grass beside a laughing Val. The stars twinkled above, and the air felt cool on his skin. They faced the back of the apartments near a pathway leading to a park, waves licking the shore of Capitol City's island community.

"What a rush! Where are we? Did we just go down that far?" said Val, looking up at the tall building.

"Umm...yup. It's a secret tunnel. And we're near the Skytrain, just past the park," said Dat.

He brushed off some dust and stood up behind Val, looking up toward the thirty-third floor. Space copters circled the area. Flashes of blue and red lights accompanied by blaring sirens loomed closer.

"You know I've never done anything like this before. I hated that party and all those uppity people and just wanted to get away. And escaping from the RRG, out through a tunnel and landing here near the Skytrain, probably past curfew. But you dared me," said Val.

Her eyes twinkled.

"Everything's new to me. A new…experience. And we're both in this together," said Dat.

They laughed at their discovery.

"What's next? Where do we do now?" said Dat.

"Let's go to the hospital and check on my dad," said Val.

"Where's that? Lead the way," said a confused Dat.

He'd never been out on his own, but Arnold showed him the secret escape in case of an emergency. They slipped out together into the night with Val marching in front of him. His acute hearing picking up the crickets, whirr of the Skytrain and light footsteps. He stopped in his tracks and listened. The footsteps continued, and he sensed a presence behind them.

"Stay close by me…hurry," whispered Dat.

Afraid to turn around, they darted into the nearby Skytrain station restroom, and the figure followed behind them. Dat held his breath in the cool darkness and motioned for Val to be quiet. He felt a warm breath and a tongue licking his hand. A whine and a short howl greeted him.

Dat flipped the light on and reached out to a stocky bulldog. The dog peered up at them with eager eyes that begged for food.

"What is it…this creature?"

"Uh…it's a bulldog, a pet. Good doggie…have to go now," Val said as a train arrived.

She petted the little dog's nose.

They hopped on, looking in both directions, but no one stopped them. The train was empty except for the dog, wagging its tail for its new master. They were the only ones on the train. She sat very close to him, smelling like flowers. He noticed how she dressed for the first time in a short black dress, her auburn tresses flowing down her back.

"You're staring at me. I guess I looked too dressed up. We'll stick out in the crowd when I wanted to blend in," she said.

Prettiest girl tonight…

His face reddened.

"What are you thinking? Do robots blush?"

"Uhh…thinking I'm glad to be with you."

The Skytrain stopped abruptly across the street from the hospital. Lights blared from police cars. Angry shrieks and loud chanting exploded from the crowd nearby.

"Appreciate and automate!"

"Freedom for all!"

"Robot lives matter!"

The police advanced closer as the uncontrollable mob surrounded and outnumbered them.

"Stop, or we'll shoot."

The mob inched as they formed a metallic chain from the apartments to the hospital. They refused to disperse. Then the police shot their guns in the air, the popping noise meant to scare the protestors. But Val and Dat witnessed the shower of glass, nails, and debris flying in many directions. A few robots sank to the ground, hit by the spray.

"Get back. Now. We need room for patients. Stand behind the barrier, or we'll take you to the junkyard," shouted a bearded cop.

"Damn bots never get it. Okay, shoot," the sergeant ordered.

The police fired their stun guns, but they bounced off the Model 100s that acted as shields for the Model 300s and 500s. Dat watched the movement, wondering how they were going to break through. Val gulped at the mayhem and smell of burnt metal. Dat bent down to the puppy.

"Shoo—doggie. Not safe," Dat said.

The dog whimpered softly.

"How are we going to get by this? They'll shoot us," said Val.

"I see a back entrance…stay close to me," said Dat.

He edged backward, his arms around Val tightly with the little bulldog close behind.

Dat held up his hand in surrender as he saw a Thompson Hospital security guard approaching him. His senses zeroed in on the club in his hand and the terminator gun on his belt. Dat felt both nervous and protective, adjusting himself to warrior mode. He advanced toward the guard, generating his attack mode at the base of his wrist. An inch of sharp metal extended from his fingers like claws.

"Hey, stop protestor! Stand down," said the guard, eyeing the new weapon.

A bright light blinded them.

"Hold on officer, this is my bodyguard…and dog. He's protecting me…I'm Dr. Tate's daughter, Val."

The guard stepped away to see a stern young woman still in her cocktail dress. She showed him her ID, and he slowly backed off. The little dog clung close to their legs.

"Sorry, Ms. Tate…not safe…not safe out here," he said.

"No problem…can you leave us alone?" said Val as she guided Dat over to the side.

The guard blinked, nodded, and took off in the opposite direction.

He looked at her in amazement and was surprised by her audacity. Dat realized the guard didn't know he wasn't human.

Dat's com watch vibrated. An angry hologram of Arnold appeared. How did Arnold figure out where he was? He touched his wrist, indicating the inside tracker. Of course, his guardians knew where he was every moment. Were people tracked too?

"Hey buddy…Dat, are you okay? Noticed that you and Val didn't follow us into the panic room. Her mother is going bonkers with worry. Let me know, and we'll send the space van to pick you up."

Dat realized his guardian was right, and he was in danger. Exposed and possibly breaking curfew, Dat could be taken away or worse yet terminated. He must comply with these orders.

"Sorry, Arnold. An emergency–Val wanted to see her Dad. We're at the hospital, and we're safe."

Val's arm shook—it was her watch.

"Honey…I was so worried. When you didn't follow us…I had such bad thoughts. Stay there, and I'll meet you outside the hospital."

Val sighed. "Sorry I couldn't be with the governor—she made me so mad. And I didn't like how she disrespected you. I just couldn't deal with her. Be careful, Mom, the hospital is surrounded by protestors."

The moment passed, and Dat gazed in wonder at the scene. He blocked out the screams, burnt metal, and even the tiny bulldog, to zero in on Val's adoring smile. She squeezed his hand and then gave him a quick hug. His circuits lit up in excitement, and his chest almost burst open.

"Thank you for saving me again tonight…And take the dog home," she said.

Then the space van rolled up, and the door slid open. Meredith Tate stepped out, and Dat was pulled in. The little bulldog followed him. His eyes lingered on the two women as they made their way to the hospital transporter.

They look like sisters. It's a human thing. But robots—do we look like our mentors?

Val turned to wave goodbye. The dog whined and snuggled next to Dat. He sensed a bond between them.

It was so different out here with the robot protests, but she defended me. The police might have taken me away. And the dog...not human.

A vision of Tony petting a big black dog popped into his brain. The dog followed Tony everywhere and lay at his feet in his kitchen. He experienced their mutual warmth and love.

He adored dogs, and so do I.

CHAPTER 8

Her mother's hug almost crushed her. Her mother sobbed, and the tears splashed down Val's back. It surprised her—tonight's event was more exhilarating than frightening. But she sensed her mother's relief.

"I feared the worst…you're being kidnapped…being stuck in the panic room and you outside. So many scenarios running through my head. It's been such a nightmare."

"I know, Mom…and I'm sorry. I was frozen, saw that guest pulled from her space van. And then Dat got me out…down through the secret tunnel…so cool."

Her mother let go, revealing a woman with dark circles and trembling hands. Val grabbed them and spoke forcefully.

"Mom, I'm alright, and we're okay. We need to see Dad. Can the governor let you go for one night? She must realize your family is also important to you."

Her mother brushed away her tears and straightened her back. She silenced her com watch, which vibrated urgently.

"Obviously not, she's contacting me again. You have to be careful—what you said tonight could get me in trouble. The governor's very powerful. I'll let her know I have important issues to take care of."

Val rolled her eyes as they got off on her father's floor. They headed for his room. Her dad was sleeping peacefully, Nurse Dolli by his side.

"His vitals are normal. Mobi performed the operation…he will be fine."

Her mother kissed his forehead, and Val grasped his hand. His steady breathing put her at ease, and Dolli's presence comforted her.

"No need to worry. I will take care of him. But are you okay?" Dolli said.

Meredith opened her mouth to answer but stopped to watch a news flash on the wall monitors.

"I'm here in Grace Noble's hospital room to get her response to the governor's press conference on the robots' riot. It's amazing that she's speaking out after having just been admitted," said the reporter.

Val riveted to Grace Noble, her distinctive purple hair coiffed and looking fit and energetic in a hospital gown, speaking from her bed. She also noticed the reporter was Whit.

"The doctors, nurses, and medical personnel, including Ms. Dolli and Mobi, their robotic co-workers have brought me back to health, so I can speak to you today about the injustices of the Administration and Robot International. They only care about their profits, and of course, their chief scientist, Dr. Rod Tate, who I understand is a patient here as well. Never mind the poor robot who was terminated today, a hard-working contributor to our society, working in our schools as a teacher's aide for over ten years."

The cameras zoomed in on Grace's bruised face. Whit's voice could be heard in the background.

"What should the public know about RI? Do you think they targeted you?"

"RI needs to be shut down and made accountable for their wrongs. And the Administration needs to take responsibility, but of course, they won't, due to their blatant nepotism. Many of you may not be aware that the governor and RI's CEO are brother and sister. The Thompson family runs everything from the Government, RI, this hospital, and the private high school, forming their own island communities after the 2020 Drought. Once California became a divided state, the Thompsons made Capitol City and the surrounding islands their own. Their money bought access and power. I encourage everyone to resist and contact your representatives now."

Meredith's eyes grew wild as she viewed Grace's statement. Val had never seen her so upset. She worried that her mother would end up having heart issues again.

"Mom, don't let her get to you. Your blood pressure...we need you here. Let me go talk to the reporter... I know him."

⋖⧎━━◯◑━━⧎⋗

Val spied him coming off the back transporter, hoping to slip out the back door. She hid patiently in the faux garden, away from any prying eyes, trying to contain herself, but leaped at Whit as he exited.

"What do you think you're doing? Do you have any idea how your interview affects people? Innocent people, those poor unsuspecting souls that died? My parents that ended up in this hospital, one who's fighting for his life and the other so stressed out that she may end up having a heart attack? That Grace Noble does not live up to her name, she sparked a terrorist attack and now leads a rebellion that..."

Whit jumped back, his mouth open, his eyes magnified, and his green skin turning emerald.

"Whoa there. Certainly, it got your attention and millions of viewers watching. Racked up thousands of likes already on the GNet and secured an exclusive with the most wanted human in the RRG, which puts me in a better ranking. I needed to prove myself. Maybe you'd like to give me first-hand knowledge of the attack. I contacted the Landers tonight. Did you happen to be at their social gathering tonight? Hey, I saw you with your boyfriend earlier."

Val exploded, her temperature rising as she advanced toward him. Her fist clenched as she stared at his annoying bug eyes.

"Look...all you're focused on are the ratings, and your image...you seemed like you wanted to help before. I really could care less about the governor or RI except that I know my dad worked with upstanding donors who contributed to his Genealogy Program to help future generations. Robots are needed to take over specialized jobs in the medical, technical, and domestic fields...and Dat's not my boyfriend. He's a robot."

"Hey, calm down. Maybe I can meet your mom, and she can give me the governor's or RI's point of view. I'm trying to find out how and why the RRG attacked and what their strategy is. And I'm truly sorry for what happened to you, your family, and those rich folks caught in the crossfire."

At this very moment, Val wanted to kick him in the kneecaps or better yet destroy his SD card in his com watch. But she sensed that maybe she needed an ally, someone to investigate both sides and find the truth.

"I will let you talk to my mom on one condition."

Whit escorted Meredith into the doorway of Grace's room. Val viewed the exchange between the two foes on the wall monitors in the hospital lobby. She ditched her black dress for a cap, sweats and a T-shirt that Whit bought for her in the gift store. Now incognito, she overheard the boos and taunts from the lobby audience.

"Grace, the governor has asked me to check on your condition. I see that you are much better. The governor and CEO of RI express their deepest concerns and best wishes for your improved health. We're heartbroken over the latest termination, and a task force has been established to look into all the robots' grievances. But now we have a few questions for you."

"Get her out of here. I didn't authorize her to visit me," said Grace. Her hands shook violently, and she started to sweat.

Val smiled, proud of her mother's grit. Whit stood by her side, mesmerized by her mother. Her com watch blinked urgently, and Val noted the incoming hologram with a smile. Her mission completed, she could take a break from the madness and just be with her friends.

"Want to go for a run with Jen and me? Got to get ready for that track meet on Saturday. But only if you're up for it." said Lucy.

CHAPTER 9

Dat traveled back as the space van drove on autopilot. Would his guardians restrict him, not that he'd gotten out on his own? There was a huge world out there that he hadn't seen yet. Robots were worse off than he was, beaten, terminated, and then forgotten. It puzzled him, but he needed to be the chef he was created to be and make Tony proud.

Dat observed the hint of a sunrise and the large skyscrapers hiding its brilliant colors. He gasped at the churning water below and the floating island Capitol with its emerald faux parks, the Skytrain circling around it, and tons of flashing billboards urging him to buy the latest space van, robotic helper and planetary vacations. In a matter of minutes, the space van circled another island, the Guild Tower District community, and landed on his guardians' Metro Apartments' helipad. Rad opened the door and then parked the van. Dat scooped up the little bulldog and stood in front of the elevator and remembered the Landers' floor.

"Thirty-third floor," he said to his shining reflection inside the elevator. He glanced at his features and noted he looked more human than Tron and Mora. He blinked and smiled at himself.

I'm not a bad-looking guy. No wonder Val likes me. And not just for my French accent.

The doors opened, and he entered the hallway and projected his eye print on the door peephole. It opened slowly. The bulldog barked. Dat heard the blaring news.

Dat inched his way into the kitchen, still watching the news with the little bulldog following him. He bent down to pet him, trying to keep the dog hidden from his guardians. Dat didn't want to upset them, but his instincts told him the dog might.

He surveyed the wall monitors, his right and left brains taking in the different aspects of the Robot Revolt Group simultaneously, first Meredith, then other media reports.

That's Val's mom, and she's attacking...Grace Noble. That's not right. She defends the robots.

"Were you involved in the storming of the Metro Apartments this evening? Did you know about the woman who was killed just getting into her space van?" asked Meredith Tate.

"The police have a ringleader in the massacre at the governor's Gala. The suspect would normally be deprogrammed and sent to the junkyard but is being held for questioning. Tag is a rogue Model 500 who admitted working for the Forresters, of TechVenture Corp., a huge investor in RI. Claims the family extracted his parts for experimentation, then complained he wasn't working hard enough. The family denies his accusations," said another GNet broadcast, streaming live from the Capitol Police station.

"Jane Shandlin, author and philanthropist, was killed outside of the Metro Apartments. Grabbed from her van and crushed under a stampede of metallic protestors. Only 40 years old, she is survived by twin sons," flashed another broadcast.

But Elise glanced his way and addressed him. Her fury unnerved him, and he paused, his brain stripped of thoughts.

"Now we'll never get any peace, hounded by these media people. I wish you hadn't wandered off with Val to Thompson Hospital. Don't do it again, or I'll have you grounded," said Elise, standing in her silk flowered gown and matching robe.

Her eyes blazed, but Dat never flinched. He stood expressionless, his left and right brains struggling to find the right reaction, but his circuits and sensors heated up inside him.

How dare she talk to me this way, I saved Val's life again and avoided any trouble.

"Ruff, Ruff, RUFF," barked the bulldog in reply, guarding Dat.

"What is this? How did this dog get in? I can't have dogs in my house, running around, jumping on the furniture, and messing...Tron remove it at once," said Elise.

"Uh...he followed me home," said Dat.

Arnold knelt down to scratch the dog's ears, and it snuggled its nose against him.

"Hey there, good boy. Calm down, Elise, let the little doggie stay. I had dogs as a kid, and I'm used to training them. It's been a terrible ordeal these last few days, so we all need to chill out. Dat meant no harm—just trying to save that scientist's daughter. She's very precious, and he was just doing a good deed."

Then he kissed Elise on the cheek and gave her a squeeze.

"You'll always be my pet...could have lost you tonight," said Arnold.

Tron zoomed over to pick up the dog, but Elise put up her hand.

"Stop Tron, back down. Okay...the bulldog stays if it's watched. Keep him off the furniture. What's its name?"

She didn't even appreciate what I did...but Arnold noticed. Don't want to make Elise mad.

"Tad...he'll be in my room with me," said Dat.

He scooped up the nervous dog and held him close at the same time preparing coffee and pastries.

"I'm sure you're hungry, so here's a mini breakfast," said Dat, shielding his eyes from Elise's glare. She suddenly made him feel very uncomfortable, sensing her irritation with anything that would alter her perfect existence. His sensitivity trackers reacted wildly as his anxiety levels increased.

She sat down at the breakfast bar, drinking her coffee, and taking bites of the pastry, never lifting her gaze from the dog.

Tad whimpered and squirmed. Dat plastered a smile on his face, but his circuits rumbled, and his right brain struggled to contain him.

The news blared its bad news, agitating the humans. Why did they watch it? Dat worried about their reactions and if they would turn on him. Their anger confused him, but he wanted to stay neutral.

"Why would that ridiculous woman defend these bots? What's in it for her? Look at Meredith question that woman. People need to know what's really going on," said Arnold.

Grace sunk down in her sheets as Meredith grilled her.

"Did you direct the RRG to swarm the Metro Apartments Area and threaten the Landers? Did you know a robot killed one of their guests? And my daughter had to witness that."

"Wait a minute, Ms. Tate. I don't control all of the robots. And I try to influence those who want equality. I don't condone death and violence, but look at what the police did to me. Targeting me for no reason. Your daughter should know what really happens at RI and what they do to robots who don't fit in. And remember they have brains and are part human. RI reuses parts, replaces their sensitivity tracks and experiments on them. I know I worked there."

"And you got fired—botched up a brain implant."

"Not true…the Genealogy Project hadn't been discovered, and the transplants were brand new, and I was a pioneer in all of this."

Arnold laughed and stomped his feet. "Always making excuses, someone needs to lock her up."

"You know I have the utmost respect for your husband, his methods, and perseverance. He's brilliant and deeply cares for the robots. But the governor and CEO Thompson have created this subservient culture and want to take over the world, no matter what happens to the robots. The governor's intentions for the Genealogy Project are both barbaric and inhumane. And you Meredith are complicit in their endeavors."

Grace pressed a button by her bed, and a nurse rushed into the room.

"Nurse, I'm tired, please remove her now."

Dat wanted to hate Grace Noble, but she stood up for all robots. She was a hero among the Models, especially for the 500s. Her words held gravity since his kind currently had no voice.

Elise turned off the wall monitors and started barking her orders.

"This place is a disaster, and the police may want to interview us. Mora, clean the balcony and this room…get rid of any evidence of this party. Tron, arrange the furniture and follow me to the panic room. Someone threw up, and it stinks. Arnold—be aware these two will be operating in super-charged mode today. We have no time for relaxation.

"Dat—your services may be needed for the governor. She wants to continue underground meetings with a select group, and we'll be spearheading this endeavor. Food and drinks must be provided for these important people. Can you handle it? Put together some menu ideas, but I already have some pre-work you can do."

The dog jumped down and cried. Arnold reached out to pet Tad, his eyes smoldering.

"Wait a minute. Don't I have a say in this? I don't want to vend out Dat to the governor. We bought him for us. And right now, I'm starving."

Elise turned her back on Arnold and went to the balcony.

"You knew my intentions when we became involved with RI and the Thompson family. Favors for our support. Our status has already risen, and we must follow through, and Dat is the key. Always thinking about your next meal—give me a break."

"Dat, buddy, make me some breakfast. This is your first priority today, no matter what Elise says."

Dat started shaking as the conversation escalated into an argument. He suddenly realized he was becoming a pawn.

No one spoke as Dat made Arnold Eggs Benedict, a fruit crepe doused with whipped cream and an Expresso. Then he set down bowls of water and food for Tad. Tension filled the room, and only the sounds of Tad lapping his water and gobbling his special doggie concoction were heard.

Elise sighed loudly and left the room in a huff. She never glanced in their direction. Dat was relieved not to have to deal with her at this moment. He believed that Tony De LaFleur would never complain, but just get the task done. He beamed at the chance of possibly seeing Val again since her mother worked for the governor.

"Don't worry, buddy, Elise will come around. She gets bossy sometimes, and I need to put her in her place. Besides, we need to get out...I'm retired now and just want to enjoy myself. You never know when your time is up... look what happened to poor Jane. And Tad is sure a great addition to our family, aren't you, boy?"

Arnold grinned and scratched the bulldog's ears.

Dat nodded and poured Arnold another expresso, adding a little brandy. Arnold appreciated and defended him, and he deserved better treatment.

"Us guys need to stick together. Besides, you're more human than those mechanical morons over there. Just watch how they run."

Arnold pressed a button on his watch. Mora and Tron scattered across the room like speed demons, and then almost colliding as they raced each other to complete the tasks. The room was dusted, picked up, straightened, and glitter-free by the time Elise entered the room.

"Now that's more like it. Sorry baby, for my outburst. Let's go to the spa today before the governor calls," said Elise, decked out in velvet warm-up clothes.

Arnold chuckled.

"Sure, baby, whatever you say."

What was his role now? Humans were so unpredictable.

CHAPTER 10

Sweat rolled down her freckled face as she whizzed past in her e-shoes, hoping to catch up to her friends. Lucy called her at the right time because she needed a break. She left her mother and Whit standing there.

"I'm so stiff, need some exercise, and the track meet is next weekend. So, I'm going to meet Lucy," said Val.

Still preoccupied with the feud between Grace and the governor, her mother and Whit hardly noticed when she quickly left the hospital for a quick run. Her breathing grew heavier as the sun burned unmercifully on this drought-driven November Saturday morning. She cruised over the recycled plastic road, shaded by towering nanocrystal buildings and green-tinted polyethylene trees as her watch vibrated.

"Hey, where r u? 2 of us R out running. Meet up?" texted Lucy.

She turned down an alley, and two young teens, her teammates, ran toward her, laughing. Lucy already looked slightly sunburned, her coffee-colored skin turning red and her tousled curls spewing from her headband. And Jen with spiky pink hair and almond-shaped eyes gently slammed into Val, causing her to slide backward.

"Hey, tracked you. Join us. But not for long; heat's killin' me," said Jen.

Jen gave Val a high-five, and they all ran along together.

"Where's that cute guy...uh, bot you've been hiding?" said Lucy with a mischievous grin.

"You mean Dat...oh probably cooking. He's a fine chef. C'mon, let's go," said Val.

They joked as they headed down the road together. Val crossed the street, enjoying the cruise around Capitol City, past the downtown area, and the Grand Old Hotel. She thought of that night with her parents and how she met Dat. Still hard to believe he was not human except for a few quirks, like the way his right index finger didn't bend or the way his head tilted all the way around. Her friends followed, barely keeping up with her.

"Wait up, don't run so fast," said Lucy, breathing heavily.

"Tell us about Dat. I saw the photos. Gorgeous—but have you kissed him yet?" said Jen.

Val blushed and slowed down.

"What? We're…just friends. Besides, he's not…" said Val.

"Does it really matter? Besides, the 500s are supposed to be more human. His type is different from the domestics and mechanicals. I've picked up bits of info from the GNet stream," said Lucy.

Val forgot all about her dad, the governor's party, and the robot attack at the Gala as the girls ran in sync. Except she didn't really want to talk about her encounters with Dat and the fact that he saved her twice. She wasn't sure if her friends would understand how her feelings toward Dat were changing. Hanging with her previous boyfriend Chad meant sharing veggie snacks and viewing a virtual movie. But with Dat was it was different. It seemed so real after being with Chad, almost magical. Like how her mom described it.

"Your dad and I had this connection and wanted to be together all the time. We knew after three days," said her mom when Val asked how her parents met.

"Hey, are you okay? You seem in a virtual dream phase," said Jen.

But Val was focusing in front of her. She couldn't believe her eyes as she passed through a narrow alley to avoid the crowd. She spotted a scene that made her stomach cramp and slowed down to hear a hotel employee venting loudly.

"Hope the hype is warranted. These bots are disastrous. Could have hired a human to clean these floors," said a twenty-something man in a black uniform as he pushed a robot into a large dumpster and strode through the back hotel's back door.

"Help me," its eyes pleaded.

Lucy and Jen stared at the forlorn figure, but then took off, not waiting for Val.

"Another chance…chance…chance," it repeated, its half-human, metallic face, partially crushed, an eyeball hanging out of its socket.

Val stopped and grabbed the metal hand, and pulled the robot out of its smelly confines. Her head ached, and she wanted to vomit. Her domestics were like relatives, not to be treated as junk.

"Are you coming with us?" said Lucy, her eyes wide.

"What are you doing? Disgusting…you should stay out of this," said Jen.

She shook her head and rolled her eyes.

"Helping…they don't deserve this. Either help me or leave," said Val, her face grew hot.

"You're crazy, and they're only bots, designed to assist us, not the other way around," said Jen.

"Don't get angry with us, Val. Are you doing this because of Dat?" said Lucy.

"No, I hate seeing this happening to robots," said Val.

Val ran further and faster to confront a huge cage alongside the building, filled with hundreds of robots, their arms and legs protruding from the iron bars. Her legs cramped, and sharp pains shot through her arms at the sight. Some were terminated, and others showed a glimpse of life, heads bobbing, and one that spoke.

"Stop working…useless."

Lucy and Jen gawked, and their mouths turned down in revulsion.

"Yeah…even they agree how useless they really are. Now c'mon Val, quit being so righteous!" said Jen, laughing.

They gave her a slight shove and took off. She hung back. Val winced and wondered if her dad really knew what was happening. It wasn't her fault that young people were too lazy to do the simplest chores, depending on their metallic domestics to clean, cook, and even drive them. Her grandmother told her the past generation inherited nothing except debt and global warming and wanted more for their descendants. Robotic slaves were created to fulfill the younger generation's needs. But she had a conscious, a desire to right these inherent wrongs.

I would never hurt any of our domestics. I need to stop this. What if Dat was treated this way?

Space vans whizzed overhead, their noise drowning out people's conversations. The rush of metal and humanity moved along, almost bumping into each other as they hurried to their destinations. Huffing and out of breath, she bolted back to the hospital, just a few miles from the robot cage. She had this sudden urge to see Dat and took a U-turn.

CHAPTER 11

"Hey buddy, you'll understand women soon enough. Gotta go and spend time with Elise," Arnold said, winking at Dat.

"Here's the menu and some ideas….if you want to create some tasty dishes when we're gone, I'll think you'll enjoy copying your mentor," said Elise, pressing a button on the counter. A hologram of famous cooks, Martha Ray and a young Tony De LaFleur appeared in front of him.

The couple, now with their arms around each other, strode out the door. Dat waved but listened in awe to his idol.

"I'm honored to introduce Tony De LaFleur, a new chef that in the last year has dazzled the President of the United States, traveled all over the world, cooked for 700 orphanages and can speak a dozen languages, including French, his native tongue. Blond and blue-eyed Martha donned a huge smile and an apron as she tied one around Tony's waist. His eyes twinkled, and he cozied up to Martha as she took out a pan in her large country farmhouse kitchen.

"Mais bien sur," said a bearded Tony, his long dark hair tied in a ponytail and crisp jeans and a white starched shirt.

Dat gasped, and Tad barked, eager to see the famous chef in action. He gave the little bulldog bowls of food and water.

Hey, dresses like me or maybe I'm copying him.

"Woof, woof, woof," barked Tad, wagging his tail at the sight of the Frenchman.

Dat lost himself in the making of Chateaubriand, one of Tony's favorites. The chef prepared the meat carefully, seasoning, and marinating in its rich juices. Tony treated the dish like it was his specialty and turned it into something magical. The rare, thinly sliced beef made Dat's eyes water, and Tad jump and try to grab a piece.

It was as if his fingers were my own, and we were one with each other. We salt and prepare it with fresh herbs and wine. We rub the meat with sea salt, thyme, and basil, adding a little Cabernet to the mixture. Inhaling both the spicy seasoning and Martha Ray's fruity perfume makes us a little overwhelmed. Ms. Ray is interested in our recipe and our cologne. It's very distracting.

"Ruff, ruff," barked Tad.

Dat awakened from his intense moment back to the Landers' kitchen. He sensed Tony's complete control over the demo but felt the sweat sliding across his forehead. A mixture of French and English phrases popped into his brain, but he quietly focused on Tony's skills. Then Tony placed a juicy bite into Martha Ray's waiting mouth.

"Oh…my, that is so…exquisite. Tell me about some more of your experiences this year," said Martha.

Dat watched carefully as Tony's deft fingers swiftly carved the roast, placing vegetables and a slice of French bread on a plate for Martha. Then he untied his apron and sat next to Martha on a stool.

"My love of cooking started when I was a young boy observing my mother in our kitchen. She taught me the basics, and then I would help her with her catering business until she died tragically from cancer at 40. I continued her business and became known locally, only to be recommended by a rich client for a campaign party which led…" Tony said.

Dat's senses sharpened, and he picked up on Tony's movement, language, and the way he looked at Martha. Her face lit up, and her eyes stared attentively into Tony's as he revealed his life story. Dat's memory tracks went deeper as Tony's brain waves crossed his.

A wave of depression hit Tony when he viewed his mother in the coffin. Her last days were filled with pain and guilt, leaving her teenage son and husband to be on their own. He held his mother's hand as she took her last breath, and he vowed to continue her work. He needed to be there for her clients, and besides, his dad traveled for his job. Tony cooked night and day as their list of clients and popularity grew. And so, did his attraction for women and they for him. His words and cooking captivated them, and he was always in demand. His loneliness and sadness went away, and his mother's business flourished.

His Internet presence increased, and then GNet interviewed him. He demoed in schools and often volunteered for soup kitchens. His strong feeling of abandonment after his mother died moved him to cook for various orphanages around the country. Which led to a call from the President. He prepared his famous Chateaubriand, and his fame tripled overnight.

Dat saw his mentor's struggles and achievements. He longed to continue his legacy, so Tony's talents would live in him. He desired to be a great chef, impressing the governor, her influential circle, and then possibly being on his own. With such inbred talents and Tony's charisma, Dat was destined for success. He was not an ordinary robot, like Mora and Tron, but came from greatness. Tony was his model in every way, and he meant to emulate him. Dat scrutinized Tony's speech patterns, communication with Martha, and his adept skills. He realized his limitations but noted he needed more interactions with humans, possibly with Val again. Her mother had access to the governor, and being with Val was just electrifying. His circuits charged, and his body started to shake with excitement.

"Ruff, ruff, ruff," barked Tad as he jumped up and wagged his tail.

The show ended, and Dat knew what he had to do. He spoke to the refrigerator, and it slid out the food on a tray. Then he pressed a button on his com watch, which activated Mora and Tron. They gathered together the necessary ingredients and utensils. His brain waves triggered, and he hurried to make his next dish. The roast lay out before him and the vegetables needed to be sliced and cooked. Tony's innate chef skills meshed with Dat's hands as he prepared the dish. It seemed like it took hours, but really only several minutes.

He heard voices, and the door opened.

"Ahh…is that smell what I think it is?" Arnold shouted.

"And the presentation is perfect. The governor will be so pleased. Have you been cooking all day?" Elise said.

The couple beamed at the mouthwatering Chateaubriand set on a large platter on the kitchen bar. Dat cut a few slices and placed them in front of his guardians. Tad licked at his empty plate behind the counter.

Just as Tony would have prepared it. This will be my signature dish.

A knock at the door snapped him back to reality.

CHAPTER 12

Her e-shoes proved helpful in getting her over to the Gild Tower District. Such a wild and crazy idea for such a stand-up girl. But seeing those robots in pain made her wonder how the Landers treated Dat. She nodded to Rad and pretended like they were old friends.

"Hey, have a delivery for the Landers. Will just take the elevator," said Val.

The elevator opened to the huge lobby floor. The doors all looked the same, but she located the Landers' residence. Surprised and flushed, he answered the door.

"Good to see you, just cooking," Dat said.

"Ruff, ruff," barked Tad, jumping up to lick her hand.

She inhaled the deep aroma of fresh meat and heard laughter. She should have called and realized it was mealtime. Val motioned Dat outside. She didn't want an encounter with the Landers. What was she thinking, trying to hang out with Dat?

"Come for a walk....are you busy?"

He shook his head negatively.

"Just finished," he whispered.

"Going to walk the dog," Dat yelled to the Landers. He pulled Tad outside.

"Let's go somewhere private."

They took the back stairs to the garden area, the polyethylene trees lined up along the sidewalks.

"What's up? Anything wrong?"

He looked deeply into her eyes.

"Don't want to get you in trouble, but I saw some strange things while I was jogging and had to see if you were okay."

"I'm fine…just created a special dish, and the Landers loved it. I feed them, and they are good to me."

Dat laughed. Val loved his warm brown eyes and easy manner. She took his arm, and Tad tagged along.

"Where did you learn to cook?"

"From Tony De LaFleur, my mentor…who gave me his brains. His memory tracks sync with my brain, and I know how and what he wants me to cook. He was…a wonderful chef."

They talked for a few more minutes with Dat sharing his cooking tips and what he made for the Landers today. Her mouth watered, and she could almost taste the meat. It was very enlightening to Val, and she loved the tidbits he shared with her.

Their watches vibrated at the same time and startled them.

"Ahh…they're wondering where I am and need me to make dessert. Always hungry," Dat said.

"Yeah…need to get back to the hospital…Mom is calling."

Val sighed and gave his hand a squeeze. His eyes lingered on hers a second longer, but she knew it was time to leave.

She took off swiftly, her e-shoes guiding the way. But the scenes downtown still gripped her.

CHAPTER 13

"Where did you go? You're all sweaty and seem agitated," said her mother as she emerged from Grace's room.

Val paused out of breath and stared at a perplexed Whit.

"Took a run with Lucy and Jen, but saw some disturbing things happening out there. Things I've never seen before. My eyes are opened to the whole robot situation. And it's very ugly," said Val.

"Honey, you look so upset. I hope you didn't get into trouble out there...it seems to be following you," said her mother.

"What happened?....show me where," said Whit.

Val rolled her eyes.

"You're really unbelievable...always out for that story."

"Hey, I'll back off...tell me what you saw, and I'll find it."

"You know...wait. Maybe you can help me. I've got to do something before this gets worse."

"Is that a good idea, kids? Thanks, Whit, for getting me access. Now, as promised, I can get you an interview with the governor and possibly R1. But Val honey, you need to go back to school. I know it will be hard with all the publicity and trouble...but we can get you an escort if you're afraid."

Val stared at her mother and laughed.

"Mom, with all that I've been through...getting to school will be the least of my problems. I'll just take the Skytrain. But what about Dad?"

The last few days had taken a toll on her mother...her puffy eyes and gentle lines in her face showed the strain. But she knew her mother was strong.

"I'm going back to see Dad now. My interview with Grace scored points with the governor, and I think she'll leave me alone for a while.

Don't go running off again. Please keep in touch and let me know where you are."

Her mother took off, leaving the two young people alone.

Val and Whit stared at each other with knowing looks.

"I know what you're thinking, but I promised Mom I'd go back to school."

"Well…let me come with you on the Skytrain, and then we'll both go our separate ways."

The hospital buzzed with activity, especially the ER, with standing room only. Val put on her cap and dark glasses and passed the crowd undetected in her black jeans and sweatshirt. Whit followed close behind, pulling his hoodie over his head. They took the next train, but Whit disappeared into the next section.

Val sighed and looked around.

Today will be easy with all that's happened to our family. I hope I can just blend in. I don't want to answer any questions. And I can ditch Whit.

As Val stepped off the Skytrain at Thompson High, she saw a mass of students gathered outside. A sign read *Welcome Back Val!* The high school band was playing, and the cheerleaders shook their pom-poms. She missed being on the Student Council, the track team, even taking midterms. Gossip, Saturday dances, and virtual chat rooms, once the focus of her world, were now trivial.

It all seemed like years ago after this disruption the RRG caused. Her life had changed dramatically now that her dad was in the hospital, her mother on a short leash with the governor, and the revelation of mistreatment of the robot classes. School seemed so irrelevant at this time. She longed for quiet nights studying, virtual game tournaments, and having Jen and Lucy spend the night.

Val cringed and, at that moment, wanted to be invisible. Her com watch vibrated urgently.

"Want to see u and find out about *everything*," texted Andy, the class president.

Val's stomach churned, and she knew at that moment she couldn't face her classmates. It was hard enough to be around Lucy and Jen, her best friends. That night at the Gala had changed everything, and her recent run around Capitol City left her confused. Her thoughts came back to the robots, their emotions, rights as a new race, and the discrimination. She knew she was being too sensitive as her mother always reminded her, but someone had to do something, and it might as well be her.

Val knew she descended from a family of strong women, both her grandmother and mother. Her grandmother Ashley captured the American voters in 2020, representing a third party, the Revolutionists. Val learned that women became stronger and more politically connected as a result of the #Us vs. Them movement back in the era of the Great Divide. She remembered her grandmother's motto.

"Your enemy today may be your best friend tomorrow with true empathy," her grandmother said.

Lost in deep thought, Val didn't see the figure behind her.

"Hey, aren't you going to school?"

Val jumped as she turned around to face Whit.

"Geez, you scared me, and why are you still here? I can't deal with school stuff today. I need to make things right, even if it means getting into trouble. You know my grandmother was a fighter for all people's rights. Let me show you something."

She punched in a short blurb on a videocast of her grandmother's Senate campaign and life as a physician and showed it to Whit.

"Our campaign promises to tone down technology and reverse inequality. It's a start to be more inclusive and favorable to the masses, and...let's be kind," said Dr. Ashley Simms.

The video showed Dr. Simms administering free care to poorer neighbors, becoming the town's mayor and physician. Val watched her mother follow her grandmother to the Capitol, where she won praise and a seat in the State Senate. Admiration shown in her mother's eyes as her grandmother made dynamic speeches, bringing her patients with her as they became advocates of her causes.

"My family voted Revolutionist. Awesome...I see the striking resemblance...the emerald eyes," said Whit.

Val clasped her neck and felt the old charm attached to her necklace. Pulling it off, Val read the words, inscribed, "Everyone deserves a voice."

"Okay…time to do something. Do you want to show me what upset you?" said Whit.

⋅⊱═◉═⊰⋅

They entered the Skytrain after leaving the school grounds. Val groaned as she answered an incoming hologram. She wanted to ignore it, but her BFF caught a glimpse of it.

"Hey, saw you earlier, talking to that guy with the blue hair and green complexion? Is that who I think that is? Besides, you're going to get kicked off the track team by skipping class. And I know it's been tough lately," said an excited Lucy.

"Yeah…it's Whit, survivor of the V-parasite disease, and he now works for GNet…I'm helping him with a story. Can you cover for me? And hey, I'm mad at you for running off," said Val.

"Sorry, we didn't know you were so passionate…but then it's because of Dat. I get it. Sure, we're BFFs, and we stick together. Plus, we need you on the team. I'll say you were tied up at the hospital with your dad. Bell rang…got to go," said Lucy.

Val sighed and glanced over at Whit, who was grinning. She guessed he must have heard everything. Was she upset about the robots' situation, or was she swayed by her new friend Dat, a Model 500? Val cared deeply after seeing that robot jail, her heart feeling heavy, and her eyes filling with tears. What she should be feeling is rage—against the governor, society, and those insensitive the Gen Q. Her generation sucked, and just maybe she could get someone else to notice.

"Being tattled on for skipping? But it's for a good cause. I know something about being different. I want to expose this discrimination," said Whit.

Elderly people, women in suits, medical personnel in lab coats and kids piled into the seats of the Skytrain. A security guard got on the next stop and stared intently at Val.

"Aren't you Val Tate? I saw you at the hospital the other day," said a muscular man with a deep scar across his cheek. His beady eyes made Val nervous.

Val motioned for Whit to get off at the next stop.

"No…I probably look like her. You know there's a doppelganger for everyone," said Val.

"Wow, you're becoming famous or maybe infamous," said Whit.

They found themselves on the same block as the Grand Old Hotel. Val spotted the hotel worker who threw the robot in the dumpster, hurrying to catch the Skytrain. She wanted to hit him but didn't want any more attention.

"He beat up a robot and tossed him into a dumpster over there and just beyond was a cage of robots. Just horrific and unbelievable," said Val, showing Whit the area.

But the robot had vanished, and the cage was empty. Val was shocked and dismayed and worried that Whit would think she was delusional. The block was clean of debris and any despicable odors.

"Well, I do believe you. Someone must have known we were coming to investigate," said Whit, examining the cage closely.

A metal finger appeared in a corner, and a marble eyeball lay nearby. He snapped photos with his watch. Inside the dumpster was a silver armband.

"Definitely some indications here of robots but doesn't seem unusual. Let's walk a little further," Whit said.

The filtered sun slowly dropped over the hazy sky as they walked through neighborhoods and, finally, the business district. No sign of mistreated robots or protests. Everywhere they strolled, it was as if the government had removed any undesirables.

"Must be close to curfew…that's why no one is out. Want to catch the next Skytrain near the park over here?" said Val.

A tall building stood majestically beyond the faux bushes and polyethylene trees. Val remembered the backside of this building and smiled.

"What's that structure? You know we've just entered the Gild Tower District," said Whit.

"That's where Dat and the Landers live," Val said.

"Do you think I could meet him? Can you get in touch with him? It would only take a few minutes to interview Dat, maybe just do a face-watch," said Whit.

Val texted Dat who responded immediately. Her heart raced, and she almost did a little dance. "They're finishing their dinner, and he'll meet us at the back entrance. But don't overwhelm him with questions. He seems human, but his communication skills sometimes are lacking."

⟡══◉══⟡

They heard Tad barking and knew they were close to the Metro Apartments back entrance. Then a tall, dark figure appeared out of the shadows with a tiny bulldog squirming in his arms. Val and Whit inhaled and gasped in awe at the sight of Dat in his slim jeans and sweater with a gray cashmere scarf around his neck. His marble eyes lit up at the sight of them, and he directed his dazzling smile at Val.

"He looks very French, and I can see the attraction," whispered Whit, nudging her arm.

"Dat, this is Whit, my friend from GNet who wants to do a story on you. Just a few details on how we met and your work as a chef, especially for the governor," said Val as she took his hand and gestured for them to sit on a nearby park bench. The streetlight above cast eerie shadows on the small group. Only the sound of the Skytrain could be heard.

Tad jumped up to lick her hand but barked at Whit.

"Ruff, Ruff, RUFF," he growled in protection of his master.

"Whoa, guy…love dogs and won't hurt you. Just want to talk to you, Dat," said Whit.

Dat glanced at Whit suspiciously.

"Uh…my guardians wouldn't approve. But Tony De LaFleur would like me to talk… about his cooking," said Dat carefully, petting Tad's head.

"Is Tony De LaFleur your mentor? Sure, I could do a story about being a chef. Just a little background that's not to be reported. But I heard you saved Val from the horrors that night at the Gala," said Whit.

Then Dat began to talk, never taking his eyes off of Val. He touched her hand and wanted to pull her closer on the bench but felt uneasy about making the first move. He told Whit about finding her hurt and leading her out of harm's way past dead bodies and a stampede of frightened guests. He spoke about his connection with Tony, his knowledge of French, and his chef instincts for making delicious dishes.

Val felt his body against hers and marveled at his new vocabulary. He spoke with ease, using both French and English phrases. Just in the time they met, Dat had picked up the English language, and his mannerisms were similar to Tony's. She'd watched his cooking show with her mom and was amazed at the food descriptions, especially Chateaubriand.

"And you prepared Chateaubriand today for the Landers after viewing Tony's show? I would have loved a bite, and now I'm getting hungry. I didn't realize the extent of your knowledge, skill, and passion for cooking. It seems like you're going to be one of the great chefs of our time," said Whit.

Dat grinned, and Whit laughed. Val noticed how well they communicated and how comfortable they were with each other. Even Tad was relaxed, curled up beside Dat.

A loud alarm woke Tad and startled Val. It reverberated and echoed throughout the park.

"It's the curfew warning. We better get you back to the hospital, and I have to get to my apartment. I need to answer this message from my editor," said Whit. He got up from the park bench to check his watch.

Val moved closer, and they turned to face each other. Dat's eyes glazed over her. She looked at him longingly. They leaned closer toward each other.

He seems like he wants to kiss me. What is he waiting for?

Tad barked, and they both jumped apart.

"I'll call you. Can you come to my track meet tomorrow?" said Val.

The alarm sounded again, and Dat grabbed Tad, disappearing into the dark night.

Val's watch vibrated.

"I'll try," texted Dat.

"He's really into you. It's as if he's human. Definitely more than a crush. That's going to be my story," said Whit.

"About us?"

"No, that Model 500s have *feelings* and not just brains."

They ran all the way to the Skytrain, hopping onto a deserted section. Whit shivered in the heatless train, but Val felt a warmth spread over her entire body. Was she actually falling for a robot?

CHAPTER 14

He didn't sleep all night, but then robots don't, not even Model 500s. Dat focused on Val, his sensors on overdrive, circuits charged, and sensitivity trackers leaning toward extreme attraction. Drawn to her like a magnet, he was still unsure if she felt the same way about him. Was he moving into the human direction? Were Model 500s capable of love? And what about being a chef? His human tendencies were overwhelming, and it was confusing. A knock on his bedroom door snapped him back into reality.

"Guardians up...they want breakfast," said Mora as she marched into his room.

Dat perked up, nodded, and followed her. Little Tad woke up and joined the parade into the kitchen.

"Morning, we have a busy day to prepare for another important meeting with the governor, and you will be catering this event. I want you to......" said Elise, dressed in Lululemon pants and a sweatshirt, already drinking coffee.

Dat fazed out. Her words tumbled in his brain, and he picked out one or two at a time. All he could think about were Val's eyes in the moonlight and her soft hands. He never noticed Tad chewing on his pant leg or Elise calling his name. Then Mora dropped a spoon. It fell to the ground with a loud crash.

"Geez, what's all the commotion about? Can't I just get a cup of coffee and some eggs?" said Arnold, unshaven and in sweats.

"Earth to Dat. Talk to me. Have you heard anything I've said? I hope your circuits are running, and you have your game on today. I need a COMPLETE MENU for the governor's next meeting," said Elise.

A frown appeared on her perfectly made-up face, which complemented Arnold's blood-shot eyes and scruffy beard.

"Uh...sorry. Trying to pull up... recipes from my ....memory banks. Make coffee and eggs for you right now," said Dat, words failing him again.

Now in high-alert mode Dat with Mora's help, produced scrambled eggs, cheese blintzes, and a strong cup of coffee in less than thirty seconds and placed it in front of Arnold.

"That's more like it. You need to calm down, Elise. These bots can only process one thing at a time, even the 500s. And of course, Dat's only concentrating on breakfast, now, not some high-level meeting with the Gov. Pull up a chair and eat with me," said Arnold, slurping his coffee.

"Vegetarian empanadas, Roasted Vegetables, Ratatouille... Chateaubriand and Petit Fours," said Dat, barely taking a breath.

Elise spun around and faced Dat.

"Yes, except the roasted veggies—need something more exciting," said Elise, checking her watch for messages and grabbing a bite of Arnold's blintzes.

"Oh, hi, Andrea—we're going over it now. Yes, it will be a dinner, complete with real meat. Need to impress your constituents. Tonight, meet for drinks? Uh...let me check with Arnold?" said Elise.

She turned to Arnold, who rolled his eyes.

"Yes, we'll meet at the top of the Grand Hotel—is it safe? Great...you want a sampling of the menu? I'll have Dat prepare and have it delivered to your office today. All right...see you at 5 p.m.," said Elise.

She exhaled and barked out her instructions.

"Dat—Everything's a go—how about a tagine? Tron—Sampling must be ready by 2 p.m. to be delivered to the governor's office. Mora—prepare the place setting and find a bottle of red wine. Arnold—you need to get cleaned up and ready for drinks with Andrea and Richard, and I will work on the talking points for tonight," said Elise. She took off, running down the hall.

Arnold grumbled and gobbled the last of his food.

"Ahh, really...wait, can't we just relax tonight?"

Dat's watch vibrated, and he checked the incoming text with a slight grin. It was Val.

"Thompson High track meet at 6 p.m. Looking forward to seeing u & Tad."

His sensors activated, Dat scurried to put the meal together, his mind on both food and the night with Val.

Marinate the beef…her soft red hair…cut the vegetables…her lips…add the herbs…her warm smile…blend the ingredients all together…the smell of her lemon perfume…place the knife down before putting it in the oven.

The sharp knife fell, tipping the jar of marinade and spilling into the burners. Flames erupted, and a burning smell tainted the pristine kitchen.

"Douse the flames…fire…stop it," the voice-activated alarm shouted, triggering the senses of Mora and Tron.

Mora tilted, dropping the coffee cups and plates. She rushed to the stove, her dull eyes turning bright and her hands moving rapidly. Tron, now alerted, ran to pick up the broken china, muttering a series of apologies.

"Sorry for mess…won't happen again…sorry…sorry."

Tad jumped up and down, his tail wagging fiercely. He nipped at Dat's pant leg, jolting his brain waves.

"Ruff, ruff, ruff," he barked frantically.

Dat's senses flared, and his circuits now erratic. His brain waves overreacted, and he woke up from his daydream to a nightmare. What had he done? The apartment would burn down, and the Landers would die from his careless actions. His sensitivity tracks shifted from fear to anguish to regret then guilt. This was not being the chef that he had been programmed to be. Tony would not have let his mind wander on something as silly as love.

With lightning speed and working in harmony, Mora and Dat stopped the flames with a bit of salt and an extinguisher. Mora wiped up the remains of the sauce and erased the burned area with the stove's clean switch, which sucked up all burn marks around the stove and wall until the once smooth surface returned. Tron mopped up the floor and pressed the scent button. A fresh rose fragrance permeated the room. Dat opened the oven. The chateaubriand was still intact and almost done. He breathed a sigh of relief. Mora checked the other dishes—empanadas browning, vegetables tender, and the tagine emitting a spicy odor.

"Will order new dishes—don't worry," said Mora.

Dat nodded and then petted the little bulldog and gave him some treats. The dog licked his hand and whimpered softly.

"Thanks, owe you," he said to Mora and Tron.

A few hours later, Arnold sauntered in the kitchen, freshly shaved and dressed in a linen shirt and pants.

"Umm...smells delicious. Did you save a bite for me? By the way, why was the dog barking earlier like a crazy freak?" he asked, frowning slightly.

Dat swallowed hard and made a small plate for Arnold. "Sorry—it's the smell of real meat."

Elise walked in her cashmere sweater and bone-colored pants. She surveyed the dishes and checked the kitchen area. Mora and Tron stood guard as Dat revealed the sampling for the governor.

"Dat you've done it again," she said, giving him a hug.

He breathed in her pungent perfume and felt her arms close around him. Dat exhaled deeply, realizing the disaster had been eliminated.

<hr/>

The wind whipped around his face as he searched for Val. Dat held Tad close to him and hid in the tall faux trees behind the brightly lit stadium. It blinded him, and he stayed in the shadows. Security continued to check eye imprints, and he would show up as not human. He feared the hassle and waited for Val's cue. A trio of laughing girls in gold and purple track gear ran up to him. Tad barked a friendly greeting.

"Isn't he adorable?" said a girl with pink hair.

Dat blushed, but the girl petted the little bulldog on his head.

"Jen and Lucy, this is Dat. He's come tonight to watch us race. Of course, I'm going to beat your buns off. But it's always fun to have a little competition," said Val, laughing.

She nudged Dat and hugged him in a tight embrace. His senses stirred, and he stood there mute. The young women stared at him and sized him up. Their staring made him uneasy, and he didn't know what to say. But he knew they were Val's friends and he must impress them.

Say something, don't just stand there like a dumb bot.

"Hello, so...happy to meet you." Dat stuttered.

Tad wagged his tail and jumped out of his arms to lick the girls' hands. Val grabbed his hand and led him through security, finding him a spot at the end of the front row.

Good, I won't have to talk to anyone.

CHAPTER 15

"He's so shy but seems cool. Love his little dog," said Jen.

"Yeah, gorgeous eyes, and he's got the vibes for you," said Lucy, giving Val a friendly nudge on her arm.

They gathered together along the track as the fans began filling the stands. The girls teased Val unmercifully about his appearance, her attraction to Dat and possibly her former boyfriend Chad's jealous nature. Especially Jen, who she confided in when she broke up with Chad.

"What about Chad? Does he know about Dat? And that he is a...? There he is staring at you," said Jen. She waved at the stands.

"New boyfriend...what's with the dog?" texted Chad.

Val ignored him and addressed Jen.

"We're no longer a couple. He's with Carla this year. That's why he's here at the meet to see her run. And Dat and I are just friends for now. I may even like his dog better," said Val.

She mused about Chad, his swagger, the roughness of touch, and how he was oblivious to her needs, such a contrast to Dat. And she ruminated about what he told her last year, a premonition to their breakup.

"Basketball means everything to me. I like to hang out with you, but I don't really have time for a fulltime girlfriend," Chad said, dropping her hand and running after his buddies. They punched each other in the gut, the shoulder, and head, pretending to be boxing, leaving her feeling totally alone.

But Dat had saved her in the worst conditions, twice.

They chatted and waved at the little bulldog in the stands. Val watched Dat as he held onto Tad tightly and smiled at her broadly. His smile and presence at the meet meant a lot. He came to see her and even risked breaking curfew. Chad obeyed the rules when it suited him. She wondered if the Landers knew Dat was at the meet cheering for her. But she needed to win and show him that this was her sport. But also have her friends approve of him since he was a robot. They didn't think it was dumb, and she hoped they'd keep it a secret.

"Don't tell Chad I'm interested in Dat. I don't want anyone to know except you guys. People might not accept us," said Val.

"Don't worry—we've got your back, and it's just among us three," said Lucy, winking at Jen and Val.

Val's watch vibrated, and she glanced at it nervously. Who could be contacting her now? She sighed and listened to the hologram.

"Just got here to see you at the meet. Dad is doing better, so I was able to leave. Talk to you soon," said her mom.

Well, Mom came after all. Maybe the Gov gave her a break tonight.

"Welcome parents, students, and friends to the State Track Meets. One hundred schools are represented, but only the top runners from each school. We're proud of these fine athletes, and it's wonderful to see such a diverse and united group of young people. We recognize our key sponsors: Robot International, Skytrain Express, and Speedy E-shoes. Let's stand for our national anthem," said the governor with RI's CEO standing beside her. The band played, and a young man and woman sang. Then a burst of cheers rang out. The audience waved their flags.

I get it—where the governor goes, so does Mom. So lame.

Many teams competed. The races dragged on. Val fidgeted and hung out patiently for her race to begin. The long wait ended, and the girls' 10,000 meter was about to begin.

The coach signaled for them to line up. The young women took their positions. The gun sounded, and they took off. A runner with a shaggy green hair shot off to lead the pack by several legs, clearly surpassing everyone at the start. But she was quickly disqualified as they tracked her e-shoes.

"Marcy Steel leave the track immediately for violation of e-shoe tampering. No use of advanced setting, standard only for competitive races. Need to rerun the race. Take a break for five," screamed a ref.

The race halted, and everyone shook their heads in amazement. The crowd booed Steel as she bowed her head in shame and disappeared off the track into the night. Her coach and the media followed her. Val and her teammates breathed heavily and looked around at the other shocked students. They stood around for a while as the refs and governor gathered in a circle to determine if the games would continue. The governor approached the podium.

Whoa—didn't Steel know she'd get caught? Even your watch tracks your mode and sends a signal to the officials. Must be a newbie.

"We do not want to delay the races or damper school spirit. Let's get on with tonight's competition and address this situation later," said the governor.

They lined up again, and Val made a strong mental note to be aware of those around her and keep her head in the game. She loosened up her body and inhaled deeply. She didn't dare glance at Dat in order to maintain her concentration.

At the signal, everyone raced down the field, their shoes elevating and pushing them to greater speeds. They accelerated, their e-shoes giving them a boost, yet they were on their own to maintain speed and momentum. The girls knew they needed these shoes to get through the brutal 10,000 meters or 25 laps around the track. Their grunts and sweaty faces indicated their high level of endurance. The three friends stayed neck in neck, Val pacing herself. She wanted to save her energy until the end.

Val heard a swoosh and noticed Lucy breaking from the pack to be in first place. She loved her friend, but not enough to let her win. Placing one foot in front of the other, moving her legs like windmills and with a burst of energy, Val caught up to her. With a push and deeper confidence, she moved faster and passed her friend with glee. Then Jen joined her, her pink hair escaping her headband. Always a competitor but helped her cross the finish line at last year's track meet when she sprained her ankle.

"Go Val go. C'mon, you can do it," said a strong, baritone voice rising above the crowds. She recognized it to be Dat's. Finally, the cheers and screams blasted out any distinguishing sounds.

How could I hear that above the noise? I can't let him down. Must win tonight.

Val exerted herself once again, passing a sweaty Jen but still trailing Lucy. She recognized other runners from competing schools, toe to toe, one on the right, the other on the left. Val pushed and strained, her legs burning with pain and her chest ready to explode. With grit and drive, Val tore past them, but Lucy had already crossed the finish line. She slapped her friend's hand as she came in a close second with Jen on her heels.

"Good job Lucy. I just need to run every night," said Val, giving her BFF a hug.

"Well done girls, Thompson High will take first, second and third places in the 10,000-meter race," said Jane Johnson, the coach. She completed ten years earlier and won. Coach Johnson gave them high-fives. Val checked the stands for Dat, but he was gone. Disappointed, she checked her com watch, noting it was past 8 p.m.

"Had to get back by curfew and before my guardians. But saw you make second. Liked your friends," said Dat's hologram.

Val felt a tap on her shoulder and turned to see her excited Mom.

"Congrats honey, I'm so proud, so is Dad. Just sent him a video clip of the end. Can I buy you and your teammates some soy burgers and veggie sticks?"

Val wanted to tell her to forget it this time, but Lucy and Jen gathered around her mother and nodded in agreement.

"Yes, Ms. Tate, I'm so hungry, let's eat soon. Is Dat going to join us? He's so cute, and so is his dog," said Lucy.

"Yeah, have you met him? They make a cute couple. My mom is tied up at work, and I need to celebrate. Your mom's the best," said Jen.

Val put her finger to her lips to shush them. She wasn't ready to let her mother know her feelings for Dat. Besides, it was temporary. Better to keep quiet about these things. But she should give her mom a break; after all, she never missed a track meet and enjoyed being around her friends. And was supportive when she broke up with Chad.

"Dat, was here? Didn't realize you invited him to come tonight. Hey, the governor's handing out the awards, and she's proud that you three are all winners," said Meredith.

The awards ceremony began as the governor called their names. Val followed her friends on stage and accepted her second-place medal, a boisterous crowd applauding. Val wished Dat was here to cherish her big moment. She realized that wasn't possible for the robots, and she needed to fix that.

It's not fair robots have to hide. They deserved to be equal, just like humans.

The crowd swelled like a huge wave toward Val, leaving the stands after the awards ceremony. She wanted to merge with it but couldn't avoid the tall, lean young man rushing toward her. Val thought she would never see him again, having avoided Chad all these months.

"What's up, Val my gal? Good to see you again. Saw you hanging out with Mr. Perfect. Doesn't seem your type. And then he took off and did not even stay to see you get your medal," said Chad, moving closer.

Val wanted to disappear, so disgusted with her former boyfriend, especially after using that stupid pet name. She spotted her mom talking to the governor, and her two best friends were huddled with the team.

"You never get it. I'm not your gal anymore, and I've found someone who really cares about me. He had to get back to his job. Not that I need to explain it to you. Got to catch up with my mom and friends. See you, Chad," said Val, pushing past him.

Val could hear him laughing.

She lay in bed, looking at the ceiling. Val kept seeing Chad smirking and heard his ugly laughing, and it made her gag. She desperately wanted to call Dat on her com watch, eager to pull up his hologram.

"Hey, can you talk now?" she texted.

Three minutes went by. His hologram popped up.

"Yeah...sorry I had to leave suddenly."

"Were the Landers upset you left?"

"No, they don't care. I...just wanted to see you run that race no matter what happened."

"Even if that meant getting into trouble?"

There was a pause, and Val thought he hung up.

"Hello...are you still there?"

"Yeah...you mean everything to me."

Val smiled. That's all she wanted to hear.

CHAPTER 16

The space van circled the governor's mansion located on its own little island. So heavily fortified with armed guards and Model 300s, the GPS found it difficult to land on the helipad's target. The click of their guns as the van approached made Dat very nervous, his circuits heating up. An alarm sounded and reverberated across the windy waters. The dome opened up as Elise provided a code on her com watch.

"They don't call it the glass castle for nothing. Whose idea was it to come here when our place is so accessible? Look at this security—how will we ever get in?" said Arnold.

"I just gave them the code, and we should be cleared to enter. Sit tight, we'll be okay since we are the guests of honor," said Elise.

As they continued to squabble, Dat's brain waves shifted to Val's race. Her tenacity and speed amazed him since he'd never seen humans compete. Thrilled that she'd almost won, Dat wished he could have stayed to celebrate with her and her friends. His sensitivity trackers picked up that they really liked him. And the look on her face when she won was so beautiful. She glowed, and her happiness enveloped him. His circuits became electrified when he imagined himself back at the track, remembering that Tad bounced in his lap a few times when he saw Val reach the finish line.

But sensibility hit him, and he remembered he had to be home before curfew. Never quite free to explore and live on his own terms, Dat knew that his guardians controlled him. Cutting it close, he returned on an empty Skytrain and entered the Metro Apartments minutes before the Landers arrived home. Only Rad saw him enter the building, greeting him with a nod. Dat immediately went to the kitchen just as the outside door slid open. He heard their laughter and Arnold joking as they walked into the kitchen. Tad headed for Arnold and jumped up to greet him, and Dat handed Elise a cup of hot tea. He knew their routine, and it made him safe. They never questioned his whereabouts, and that gave him a bit of freedom. And then later Val called to check in with him. It made his circuits electrified, and a surge of joy flowed through him as he realized he would do anything for her.

The dome opened up, and the space van entered the security zone. It landed on top of another round building surrounded by smaller transparent cup-shaped structures on a bed of faux emerald grass. A huge rainbow reflected off the water and glass. Elise and Arnold shielded their eyes from the dazzling whiteness.

"Ahh, it looks like a huge glass igloo. Are you sure we're not going to crash through it?" said Arnold.

Dat worried about the surrounding Model 300s who pointed guns in their direction as the space van carefully righted itself on a flat part of the shiny roof. Elise flashed the guards her code before exiting. The wind kicked in, nearly knocking the couple and Dat to the ground as they stepped out of the van. A roof opening revealed an elevator that jettisoned them down ten floors. They entered a security passageway and used their eye imprints to make their way to the first level, decorated by hanging faux plants, comfortable rattan furniture and wall to wall exotic fish tanks.

"You look like ghosts, but not Dat, of course. Are you feeling okay? Everyone's here already," greeted the governor in a white linen pantsuit with an upswept hairdo. She winked at Dat.

"Well, it was an interesting ride over here, and I thought we were going to be shot, that's all," said Elise, running a hand through her tousled hair.

"Geez Andrea, need a drink after that. Does everyone have to go through all this scrutiny?" said Arnold.

A butler appeared out of the shadows and offered the Landers wine. His dull eyes perked up upon seeing Dat standing nearby.

"Relax, Arnold. It's the RRG that has everyone worried, and I'm the perfect target. Dat, follow Pim to the kitchen," said the governor. Her icy smile and flick of her wrist let him know where he belonged. He left the Landers chatting with the governor.

Pim led him to a vast kitchen on the second level, a chef's dream. Decorated in seascape colors with a view of the ocean, it was a modular kitchen with cupboards and sinks, steel appliances, shelves of glassware and dishes, a large cutting table, and a wall of ovens and heating units. Rows of filtered lights illuminated the room like stars. A computerized menu appeared in front of him.

"She ordered us to help you. Let us know what to do," said Pim, his eyebrows raised over his cold marble gray eyes.

Dat looked puzzled, but then pressed the pre-arranged menu and items lit up. His guardians arranged for his pre-made food to be sent via curriers an hour before. But he didn't know exactly how the governor's kitchen was set up or where to locate the food. He touched empanadas, and a compartment slid open to reveal the hot appetizers from an oven.

"Can you serve them to the guests...with the champagne?" he asked, finding the champagne button on the refrigerator. Upon opening, champagne bottles automatically uncorked and tilted and filled the chilling glasses with bubbly onto a tray.

Pim whistled and four more waiters, including a female, her blond ponytail bobbing as she scurried to retrieve a tray of appetizers.

The other three stiffly grabbed the glasses with champagne, and one slid off a tray, crashing to the ground, glass particles and champagne going everywhere.

"Initiate stop until we collect the trays, thought you were a chef," said Pim.

Startled, his circuits overreacting, and without his backup team, he caught any falling glasses before stopping the line. The female wiped the floor and gave Dat a slight smile, avoiding Pim's line of sight. The other waiters, including Pim, hurried to the tenth floor.

"Don't worry. He's a real pain...in the, you know. My name's Ami," the blond said.

Dat nodded as she helped him find the Ratatouille, tagine, and Chateaubriand in the appropriate ovens. She reminded him of Mora, appreciating her kindness.

"Thanks, Ami. Should we serve the other dishes?" Dat said.

She nodded and looked down as Pim, and the others rushed in the kitchen.

"The governor wants the food served *now* and for you to go to the top level, Chef Dat," said Pim. He gestured for Dat to move quickly.

Dat took a deep breath. He missed Tron and Mora's help in setting up the plates and serving the food without direction. He suspected Pim and the other servers were waiting to hear his commands. His inner Tony told him to step up and act like a true chef. His circuits started overloading, but his sensitivity trackers emitted a sense of calm.

"Take the dishes and put them on sliding tables to go upstairs, and I will join you shortly," said Dat.

Pim and the others just looked at him, and he realized his directions were unclear.

"From ovens 1-3...then take all plates, utensils, and cutlery for the guests. Hurry before the food gets cold," said Dat.

Suddenly they jumped to his commands and quickly assembled the food and marched to the elevators. Dat straightened his uniform, and Ami placed his chef hat on his head.

"You're official, and I snuck a piece of meat. It was delicious," said Ami.

"Thanks," said Dat and smiled at her compliment. Ami lead him to the glass elevator, and they rose to the tenth floor together, Dat in awe of the fiery sunset sliding down below the waves. The elevator abruptly stopped, and the doors flew open. The top floor in silver and black tones included over one hundred guests scattered throughout—at chrome cocktail tables, eating at a black slate bar, and along the windows. A sprinkling of tiny lights gave the room a warm glow amid the overwhelming splendor. The mirrored bar and transparent floor put Dat off balance, but he stood attentively as the governor, and the Landers spotted him.

"Good evening, fellow guests. Chef Dat has arrived, and we commend him for his perfectly spectacular meal, especially the Chateaubriand, a rarity. And thanks to the Landers for sharing their special chef, a Model 500 with the talents of Tony De LaFleur. Let's give them a hand," said governor Thompson.

The applause echoed throughout the room, and all eyes focused on Dat. Tonight, he believed this performance would lead him to a new role, and he was grateful to the governor for recognizing his talents and his mentor. Dat bowed. His guardians saluted him, and everyone raised a glass to his creations.

His circuits almost exploded, and his sensitivity trackers experienced extreme pride. It was the highlight of his life. Then a vision of Val appeared in his brain waves, and he wanted badly to call her.

"Hey, stand over here. They want to take our photo together," whispered Ami, her ponytail bobbing.

Dat beamed and posed for a photo. His senses picked up the positive vibes from Ami and the negative ones from Pim and the others. For the moment, he didn't care and stood basking in his glory. He spotted Val's mom and the governor chatting. But his mood changed when his acute hearing picked up the conversation with the governor and Meredith.

"Dat is a brilliant chef, but I wonder why he was at the State Track Meets the other night. I saw them together and looked like he met Val there. He seemed very preoccupied with your daughter and her friends. They looked very sociable," the governor commented.

Meredith blushed.

"Oh, well…I wasn't there until the race began. Not sure what you're implying since they talked at your party. He probably was just taking his dog for a walk," said Meredith.

"I think that Model 500s should not mix with humans, and you should monitor your daughter's relationships. It's not acceptable and even worse for your daughter and your family's reputation. I'm sure Dr. Tate would not approve of this relationship, and you should counsel her about it before it turns into something more serious. Now I think Val is intelligent enough not to be involved with him, but you know the youth today and their views on equality," said the governor, waving down a constituent.

"Well…I don't think my daughter is having a relationship…" mumbled a bewildered Meredith. She checked her watch for messages.

Dat took off his chef's hat and headed for the elevator. He sensed a threat to his existence, especially if the Landers suspected anything. The biggest night of his life as a chef tarnished by the governor's suspicion of their coupling. His circuits burned, and his sensitivity trackers left him feeling remorseful. The Landers caught up and rode down in the elevator with him.

"Hey buddy, great job tonight. We're going to take off soon. Lucky for you the Gov's Model 300s will clean up the mess," said Arnold.

"You've made us so proud," said Elise, patting his shoulder.

Why do I need to choose between being a great chef and being with Val?

It wasn't fair, and he realized once again that he was not a human and had no rights. Dat excused himself and ducked into a utility closet. Dat called Val, anxious to talk with her. He wanted to say he couldn't see her anymore. It was getting too dangerous, especially now that the governor was on to them. It was extremely risky.

"Hello. Hello—is that you Dat? What's going on? Please answer," said Val.

Dat just needed to hear her sweet voice. He hated the governor, but he couldn't tell Val the truth.

CHAPTER 17

Val tried contacting Dat for the twentieth time in the last few days. She knew he called her the other night but didn't say anything. It wasn't like him. Something was terribly wrong. Her mom was acting strangely, keeping tabs on her every minute of the day and night. Granted, her dad was in the hospital, and her job was stressful, but her mom didn't need to ping her watch constantly. It was annoying. This whole thing with the RRG and their terrorist actions had everyone on edge and extremely nervous, but the governor ordered more security for her entire family. And she even had her own bodyguard. Luckily her specific BG was extremely young and easily persuaded.

If only Dat would return my calls. I know his guardians are demanding, but if he could take the time to answer one little call. Pick up Dat, please.

Determined to see him, Val sent Dat an emergency hologram, setting it at *extremely urgent.* Her watch vibrated as his hologram appeared. Her pulse beat rapidly, and she calmed herself down and to not make her BG Nick suspicious. She rushed to a quiet section of the hospital lobby, barely able to contain her emotions.

"I'm relieved that you made it back safely from the Track Meet. I want to see you. Are you busy and can I come over?" Val messaged back. His message said that his guardians would be gone for a few hours, but he didn't think it was safe for her to come over. Was he hiding something? Val needed to find out. It wasn't making any sense.

"Uh…Nick, I received this call from my coach. Something about our next track meet. Can you let my mom know that I had to leave? You don't need to come with me," Val messaged Nick.

Her eyes sought Nick's approval as he stood across the room from her, trying not to be seen.

"The Gov specified that I must keep you safe at all times. I'll just go with you to school. I'll stay out of the way," Nick messaged back.

He strolled toward her.

"Okay, but just take the Skytrain with me and let me off at the school stop," said Val.

Nick rolled his eyes at her as they boarded the Skytrain. His watch vibrated when they reached Thompson High. Nick sighed and looked perturbed.

"My girlfriend called, and I haven't seen her in weeks. Sure, you're going to be okay? Don't want anything to happen to you," Nick said.

Val waved goodbye. "Don't worry—the coach can give me a ride back. Go be with your girlfriend," said Val.

She watched Nick get back on the Skytrain, walked toward Thompson High's steps, watched the Skytrain pass, and abruptly turned to go in the opposite direction. Pumped with adrenaline, she ran to the Metro Apartments, adjusting her e-shoes to maximum speed. After going through heavy security, she knocked on the door to the Landers' apartment. Val heard a scuffling and panting. As the door opened, Little Tad jumped on her legs and licked her face as she petted him. Dat looked surprised, and they just stared at each other.

"Uh…Oh, I wasn't expecting you. The guardians just left, but I don't know when they're coming back," said Dat.

She raised her voice and spoke loudly.

"I know something's wrong. You're not answering my calls. Did the Landers threaten you? Please, I need to know," said Val.

"Shh…let's talk inside," Dat said.

She walked in slowly, looking right and left. Tad followed her, sniffing her shoes.

"I overheard your mom and the governor talking at her house. The governor…suspects that we are…said it's a bad idea for a robot and young woman to be together," said Dat.

Val fumed, and her eyes narrowed.

"What? How dare she speak to my mother about us. You know I really don't care. It's my life, and she has no right to interfere. No one does, not even my parents. If we want to be a couple, it's our choice. What do you think?" said Val.

Dat's face brightened, and he grinned. Tad jumped up and barked. "Ruff, Ruff."

"Tad said yes, and I agree. C'mon into the Entertainment Room," Dat said, pressing on the kitchen wall. The little bulldog followed them.

It opened and turned into a virtual game room. Dat pressed several buttons on the wall panel to reveal a basketball court, ping pong table, flight simulation, and even a movie theater with a real popcorn machine.

"You're so lucky. Your guardians seem so nice, and I can't believe this place," said Val.

Her eyes popped as she perused the room, decorated in chrome and black leather. She helped herself to a bag of popcorn and then plopped herself into a plush black leather chair, near the theater.

"Yeah, it's great…that they're not here now. Want to play ping pong?" said Dat.

Out of the screen popped a ping pong table with balls and paddles. Val stepped into the virtual game room, picked up a paddle, and whacked the ball off the edge of the virtual table.

"Oops, get you next time."

Dat laughed heartily as he beat every shot she served. He played against virtual dummy players all the time, winning every game. Tad ran back and forth between the players.

Her last shot dropped in the upper left corner, almost impossible to serve back. But he tweaked his serve and spun it out, landing in her far-right corner. She manipulated the controls and missed the shot. They both collapsed, laughing hysterically. Little Tad flopped down in a corner.

"Do you think anyone misses me? I'm having too much fun," said Val.

She felt so comfortable with him. He was so easy to be with—unlike other boys who wanted to compete with her because she was the scientist's daughter.

Dat smiled. "Nope…want to watch a movie?"

He pressed a button, and the screen expanded around the room. Music started, and the movie began with a chase scene. A girl being pursued by an alien, but a boy saves her just in time.

Val cozied up to Dat during the dark, scary parts and felt his warm hand on her shoulder. She leaned in closer and could hear her heart beating faster. She could feel his breath on her face as he moved closer. She grabbed his hand and pressed her face on his prickly cheek. Then he kissed her mouth as she turned toward him. It was warm and a little sloppy, but she felt a mutual attraction.

The movie ended, and the credits rolled as Dat moved away from her. She wondered if he was offended, but then noticed his eager expression.

"Let's go swimming—there's a pool right off the living room," said Dat, smiling.

Val squinted as the room became brighter, now that the movie ended.

"Okay, cool, but what about a bathing suit? Will Tad be okay?"

Dat brought out a simple black one-piece, tags still attached.

"It's from Elise's closet. And, look—Tad's asleep."

Dat grinned.

"Try it on, and I'll get mine."

Val was excited and slipped into the bathroom to change. Her suit fit like a glove as she made her way past the kitchen, through the grand room out to the outside deck. The pool covered the entire deck, enclosed by glass, overlooking the city below.

"Oh my. The view is incredible, and the water is so warm," she said, peering out at the bustling city on the island below.

She stuck her toe in and then inched herself into the water. Dat was already swimming, doing laps in rapid succession.

"Hey, wait for me to catch up," Val said.

They met in the middle, both treading water. Val could see the tops of his shoulders, and she moved closer to grab them. They held on to each other, skin to skin. She looked for signs of steel appendages or wires, but only saw skin.

She pushed him under, and he bobbed up quickly. They both laughed as they splashed each other. Then she kicked herself away and raced down to the end of the pool. He chased her and was there by her side in a split second.

"You're so fast and very sweet," said Val as she kissed his wet lips and neck.

Dat wrapped his muscular body around her.

"Your skin is so smooth, but your little chest hairs are tickling me," Val said.

He kissed her back, and she could smell his spicy cologne. Her body tingled all over.

I can't believe this is happening. I want to stay here forever in this moment.

Her watch vibrated, and a hologram of her mother appeared.

"Val, where are you? You need to get here quickly. Please call me back," she said.

"Do you have to leave?" Dat said.

His body went limp, his eyes drooped, and his mouth turned downward.

"Not quite yet," Val answered.

Her heart beat faster, and her body felt warm even in the cool water. They kissed some more, and then the sun began to set behind a wall of haze.

"Dry off. Elise and Arnold…they'll be back soon," said Dat.

Val scrambled out of the pool with Dat at her side. His eyes showed fear as he rushed to the men's room to change. She headed for the women's lounge right next to it.

"Sorry. Lost track of time. Would you mind taking the Skytrain with me to the hospital?" said Val, now fully dressed.

"We have to go now. Let's take the space van instead. C'mon Tad," Dat said.

She dried her hair and put it up in a tight bun so her parents wouldn't notice her damp strands. Val glanced at Dat, who looked like a model, not a hair out of place in his pressed jeans, shirt, and Vans.

"Ruff, RUFF," Tad barked.

They giggled, and Dat scooped the dog into his arms.

Val petted Tad's head as they made their way down the elevator to the garage.

They found the space van in a dark corner spot. Dat slid open the passenger door. Val felt a presence behind them.

"Landers' van…be careful. Let me move it."

Dat ignored the man's comment, and they jumped in the van. He whizzed past the figure in uniform as he skirted out of the way.

"I think you almost hit that guy. Do you know him?" Val said.

They ascended rapidly into the sky as the sun was climbing behind the clouds.

Dat smiled at her, and she almost melted.

"It's Rad—he usually parks the van. Sorry, I'm worried about the curfew—will get you back safely," Dat said.

They zoomed into the hospital parking lot. Val clocked the time in under three minutes. She waved at Dat and his furry friend.

So far, that was the best night of her entire life. Being with Dat again seemed too perfect…she almost forgot that he was a robot. His gentle touch, muscular chest, sweet smell, and soft lips pushed her to the edge. Her attraction to him only occupied her mind, leaving her to ignore her family. The urgency of her mother's tone did not move her. It was Dat that persuaded Val to leave, and she realized the moment was no longer theirs. Her stomach suddenly churned, and guilt washed over her. What if her dad didn't make it?

CHAPTER 18

Dat realized his guardians would be home soon. They shouldn't see him with Val. If Rad unloaded to the guardians, he would be banished from his home and be terminated. He would lose his chef position and ruin his reputation. His head felt dizzy, and his right and left brains became overwhelmed with thoughts of extreme panic. But his left brain adjusted his frenzied thoughts, and he put the space van in high gear and took off. He would be back at the apartment in under three minutes. The British GPS voice said 7:15 p.m. No time to think, just drive–straight home.

The Skyways started to back up since it was so close to the 8 p.m. curfew time. Dat kept a safe distance from the other space vans, his sensors noting danger as numerous vehicles merged onto the skyways. Break lights and sirens lit up the skies as the last rays of sun filtered through his windshield. He still had enough time, but at this pace, it would be after curfew before he reached his apartment. Fear mixed with euphoria traveled through his circuitry. His right brain surged with emotion. Their last kiss still lingered on his lips, and he could still feel her desire for him. These fiery feelings toward a girl disturbed him. He was programmed to serve his guardians, infused with a human brain and few emotions reserved only for his guardians. Being alone with Val brought on sensations he'd never experienced.

I like her a lot. She's so beautiful, and I just want to be with her. She makes me feel human, and her touch makes my senses go haywire. My left brain tells me my loyalty is to the Landers and being a great chef. How can I stop my feelings for Val?

Many vans honked their impatience as the line moved at a snail's pace. Dat glanced to his left and saw angry drivers cursing and some pounding their dashboards in anticipation of being late. Then the realization hit as a voice, and giant marquee of the police chief reverberated over the cacophony of horns. His bulging eyes captured the seriousness of his immediate task.

"Listen up, folks. We're conducting a random checkpoint tonight and know the curfew is about to begin. But the governor has asked law enforcement to inspect all vehicles due to the RRG's current actions. So be patient and have your documentation ready."

Dat's sensors constricted, and his anxiety levels increased. They would target him because he was a robot. He found himself stuck among a sea of space vans with nowhere to go but forward. Today was perfect but could end right now. What if they accused him of being a terrorist?

His vehicle moved closer to the checkpoint as the few space vans in front of him pulled over to the side to be examined. He gave Tad a treat and hid him under a blanket.

His watch clicked at 7:45 p.m. His guardians would either be worried or upset. Missing a meal was not an option for them, and they depended on him for his culinary expertise. Dat debated with his right and left brain to call them or just wait until the police checkpoint was completed. Besides, what would he say? They'd wonder why he was out past curfew. But he was next in line.

A muscular cop on a small space cycle hovered near his driver's side window, while some Model 300s whizzed around, inspecting his van, taking photos, and scrutinizing any dents or scratches.

"License, registration...ID," he said methodically.

The cop linked watches and scanned his personal effects.

Dat waited for questions.

"Uh...I see you're a Model 500. Who are your guardians, and do they know you're running late?"

"The Landers, Metro Apartments, Gild Tower District. Not yet, officer."

The officer checked his files, noted the name and location, and raised his eyebrows.

"Hmm...the Landers, impressive. How long have you been with them? What do you do for them?"

"Not long. I'm their chef."

"Really? Who were you programmed after?"

His memory pauses zeroed in on the sweet smell of Val, how Elise's suit clung to her curvy body and her soft lips when they kissed…his sensitivity tracks registered extreme desire and unusual physical impulses. He found it hard to focus on the officer's questions.

"You're mumbling…who is your persona? *Identity,* please."

Sounds of honking and screeching tires jolted him. The smell of burnt rubber and brakes brought Dat back to the dilemma of the Skyways.

Dat snapped out of his memory chamber. He smelled the policeman's garlic breath and observed his raging eyes as he leaned into the side window. Dat saw Tad moving under the blanket, hoping he wouldn't jump up.

"Sorry…Tony De LaFleur, but they call me Dat."

"Look Dat, we're going to let you pass because of your record and vehicle's inspection. Also, your guardians' impeccable reputation and donations to the community. Now get home before we change our minds. Robots need to be off the road at this time," said the policeman.

Dat straightened up and exited carefully back onto the Skyway. He accelerated and soon broke from the crowd. He noted in the rearview mirror hundreds of vehicles lined up behind him, their angry faces etched in his memories. He took more than five minutes in his interrogation.

Mustn't forget. Tony De LaFleur. Famous Chef.

"Ruff, ruff," Tad barked as they left the police and approaching space vans.

"We made it, Tad. Now let's hurry home."

He passed the test. Now to come up with an excuse for the Landers. Elise threatened to ground him before, and he couldn't risk it. His acute eyesight put him back on track.

His hands stopped shaking as he zoomed over the apartment building, then landed safely in the helipad. He taxied in and parked carefully in their space. He knew Elise was a stickler about her possessions and would know if he had taken the van for a ride. Dat looked in the rearview mirror and noticed no one was around.

Dat needed an excuse and hoped they hadn't eaten so he could make something extravagant. His eye imprint let him in, and he entered the hallway. He heard them laughing at a loud comedy show on the monitors. Tad followed Dat obediently.

"Dat, is that you? Come here a minute," called Arnold from the family room.

He found Arnold and Elise drinking huge goblets of wine, snuggled together on the couch.

"Ahh, little Tad, my furry friend. Hey, we just got back. No need to cook tonight—had a huge meal at the spa after all that exercise," said Arnold, winking and grinning.

The little bulldog scurried up to Arnold, licking his hand.

Dat nodded. "Took Tad out."

"Arnold says I've been too hard on you. Especially after that impressive meal for the governor the other night, but you must be aware of curfew," said Elise.

Dat smiled back and sprinted down the hallway. He breathed a sigh of relief.

His bedroom still looked neat and clean. After all, he spent his day in the entertainment room and the pool. All he could think about was his afternoon with Val, his attraction to her was real. If he had a heart, it would be beating faster, but instead, his electrodes surged throughout his body.

Close call tonight, but I survived.

CHAPTER 19

Val looked up to see the Capitol Police space copters circling the hospital roof. Another with big red GNet letters imprinted on its side landed beside it, reporting on the capture of a robot. The story projected on the side of the building, showing a mechanical figure struggling to break free from a large cage. Its screams, the police sirens, and reporter's voice blasted over the usual rush hour. A crowd gathered, and Val recognized Whit's voice. Her stomach churned at the sight of the caged robot, and she thought she would faint. Putting her hands over her ears, she fought to drown out its shrieks.

"Protestor caught trying to reach Dr. Tate's room, stopped by security in the hallway. They tackled him before he could harm the scientist. The hospital and city are on high alert…"

The camera zoomed in on the robot, its angry eyes glowing as it spoke.

"Death to the Inhumans!" shouted the robot, its silver armband revealed.

Val rushed past the taped-off area, identified herself at the front desk, and then took off running toward the transporter.

"Code blue, code blue," she heard as she stepped out of the elevator. It signaled to her that someone was dying.

Her hands trembled as she entered her dad's room to see the crash cart and several medical personnel gathered in the doorway. A giant Model 300 security guard stood in her way.

"Can't be here now. Must leave. Only authorized personnel."

"Wait…I'm his daughter. Need to see my dad," said Val, her eyes filling with large tears.

Dolli appeared from the room and hurried Val in.

"She's…family. Allowed."

Oh, his face is so white. He looks dead already. Please, God, he can't die. He was such a great coach, always getting up early to run with me during track season. What would I do without my track partner?

She shivered and screamed internally, biting her nails and clutching Dolli's mechanical arm. Her mother stood at the head of her dad's bed, her hand to her mouth, and her eyes focused on the attending physician, but then looked up to see Val.

"Oh…Val, so glad you made it…Dad couldn't see, was confused… couldn't move. Too much stress caused a stroke."

She stumbled over her words as Val rushed to her side. They clung to each other in fear that their loved one was not going to make it this time. Their shoulders shook as they watched the medical group attempt to resuscitate him.

Val had never seen so many medical personnel in her life, pumping her dad's chest, giving him oxygen, and watching his indicators. He lay there very still, his vitals fluctuating and breathing shallow. His eyelids fluttered, and his arms and legs moved mechanically as the doctors worked to save his life.

There must be at least twenty people, helping Dad. Some don't even belong here.

Val noticed the governor and the CEO of RI at the foot of the bed, giving instructions and commands like they owned the situation.

"How did the RRG infiltrate? It must be an inside job. Surround this area and find any others," said the governor.

"What about Tate's brain? Will he survive and not be a vegetable?" said the CEO.

Disgusted, she turned away, but her mother looked up and grabbed Val's arm.

"Baby—I know it's hard to watch. Your dad was fine just a few minutes ago, but that robot tried to hurt him," her mom said, her eyes wild with fear.

She disentangled herself from the group to comfort Val.

"You mean the one they caught? Did he try to kill Dad?" Val collapsed into her mother's arms.

Her tears flowed as her mother wrapped herself around her tightly, then rocked Val gently.

"They're doing everything they can. He has the best doctors, some from outside the state...specialists, ordered by the governor. Don't worry... everything will be fine, but I thought for a minute he was gone," she said.

Val heaved a huge breath as she heard the doctors' announcement.

"All clear, he's in stable condition. He's going to make it for now," said Dr. Gates.

"He's in good hands, Meredith. You and your daughter need not worry. He's too valuable, and we can't afford to lose him," said Governor Thompson.

She offered a hand to them, but Val buried her face deeper into her mother's shoulder.

All that woman cares about is Dad's value, not his health and not our family. I can't stand to look at her.

"Please tell them to leave. I only want us here," Val whispered to her mother.

"C'mon Andrea—let's give them some space. Check on the security breach and call in the National Guard," said RI's CEO.

He lightly touched Val's back. She shrank from his gesture.

They marched out of the room, talking to the police on their phones and questioning security, guarding the door.

"Only family can visit. Make sure that armed guards are here all the time. Keep a twenty-four-hour watch, and I want updates every thirty minutes," said the governor.

The governor's voice grated on Val's nerves, and her head ached from all the tension.

We're just ignored like we don't even exist. I wish she'd just shut up.

Val broke away from her mother's arms, once the Thompsons left. She desperately wanted to throw up, but she was afraid to leave. The doctors filed out of the room, only Dolli stayed behind.

"Honey, did you get something to eat? Where were you all day? Did you go back to school? I've been worried. Plus, I need you...here with me. In case Dad..." her mother said.

Her spotty red face and fragile eyes showed hours of crying and pain. Val wanted to say the right words, but her mind was blank. If something happened to her Dad, that would be the end of it all. Damn Thompsons— no wonder the robots were revolting. It was a cruel world.

"Sorry…didn't realize that Dad was almost…," said Val.

"I know it's been a tough day. These protestors are getting out of hand, and we need better security detail," said her mom.

Val went to her father's side to hold his hand and heard voices below.

"Robot rights! Robot rights! Bring us, Grace. Let her speak," said loud voices, magnified by their sheer volume.

A human security guard entered the room, touching his gun in his holster. His face portrayed worry and anger.

"Mrs. Tate, you and your daughter can't leave tonight. You must stay here, it's too dangerous out there. Can we get you some food? Also, we'll have some cots delivered to the room. It's a mess out there with Grace Noble still here. I know you were just doing your job, but that interview with her really touched a nerve."

Her mother shook her head in agreement. "I know, but it will pass soon. We're developing a crisis plan, similar to the one in New York. They rid their state of all the resisters, just like the one who tried to hurt my husband. First, Grace needs to be silenced," said her mother.

Val looked at her mother in awe.

How will they stop her? Don't the robots need a voice? Someone to speak for them? Maybe that robot was trying to tell Dad something.

She didn't know much about Dr. Grace Noble, only that Dad took her place. Val heard her parents talking one night that Grace parted on bad terms with Robot International, and her dad was chosen to complete the Genealogy Project. He had great respect for Grace Noble but devoted himself to his new work. Val admired him because he never followed the news or took sides, only wanting to produce the highest quality of robots for the purpose of making the world a better place. To hear her mother talk about Grace Noble that way, gave Val a chill. Did she want Grace to be jailed or sent away? Val shuddered at the thought. Grandma spoke about equality, and Val believed that Grace was determined to give robots their rights. But it was her methods like entering unannounced.

Speaking of…what is she thinking coming into Dad's room?

"Hey, you can't just barge in here. I don't care who you are, you need to leave," screamed her mother as Grace entered in her wheelchair with her hospital robe wrapped around her.

"Ma'am, you need to wheel yourself out of her, or I'll have you arrested," said the stocky security guard with the gun.

"I'm Grace Noble—don't want to hurt anyone, especially Dr. Tate. Please let me speak for a moment." Grace put up her hand like a stop sign, then approached Val's mom with six feet space between them.

"It's all right, just say what's on your mind," said her mother, looking disgusted.

"I have the utmost respect for your husband, his methods, and perseverance. He has a brilliant mind and deeply cares for the robots. But the governor and CEO Thompson have created this subservient culture and want to take over the world, no matter what happens to the robots. The Genealogy Project was intended to preserve the donor's legacy, but the governor and her brother only want the *right* people for the GP, a select group. And you Meredith are complicit in their endeavors."

"Get out now. You're upsetting my daughter and affecting my husband's health. You're a failure and a dissident—that's why the Thompsons got rid of you. You're acting like an angry child and are ignorant of the Genealogy Project's purpose. Only mechanical beings respect you."

Val's mom waved her away, heading to the window to ignore Grace.

Grace laughed.

"Your true colors have been revealed, and everything has been recorded to show up on tonight's broadcast. Your comments about me will be heard by everyone."

The guards ushered Grace out of the room.

"Wait, Dr. Noble...what do you mean? What about the Genealogy Project?" Val said.

Grace turned to address Val; her face softened.

"If we don't stop this...the next generation will suffer dire consequences. Ask your mother about the governor's true intentions."

Then Grace left the room as guards handed her off to her nurses.

"Mom, what did she mean?"

Her mom spun back toward her and took her hands.

"Never mind what Grace Noble said, she's just resentful. She botched a surgery and destroyed a famous donor's brain, so the Thompsons fired her. Then she blamed her bad decision on RI and got the robot community to back her. Listen, we need to concentrate on Dad's health. Make sure he gets better and out of here."

Val hugged her mother.

That Noble woman is disturbed and yelled at Mom. But Mom still didn't answer my question. What is the governor hiding?

Val glanced out the window and saw Grace Noble sitting in her wheelchair in the middle of the crowd. She observed her influence and rapport and wondered if there were any truths to Grace's claims. What role did robots have in society? Would they eventually be equal? Val needed to find out for herself.

"Good evening. We are making strides in our resistance. The Thompsons have been warned. It's not over yet. Stay tuned for tonight's update," said Grace, her voice amplified from the building acoustics.

The crowd roared in anticipation of the rally.

Val dreaded hearing her mother being humiliated. She wished she could break out of the hospital and go see Dat.

Why hasn't he contacted me tonight?

The night dragged on as the crowd got bigger and more violent. Her mother's words traveled across the GNet and flashed over the hospital monitors. Val cringed at Grace's recording of her mother's opinions. Her father slept through it all, his face peaceful.

"The governor will have my head over these statements," her mother said as her watch vibrated.

"Yes, Andrea, I'm planning another press conference to debate these claims. My mind was on Rod when I said those…yes, need to pull myself together."

Val rubbed her mother's arm.

The governor has no feelings. She just cares about herself and RI. I just want to escape this place.

Her mother's eyes drooped, and Val thought she would collapse from all the stress. Then she took Val's hands and looked directly into her eyes.

"Listen, Val…I never really wanted to be the governor's publicist. Your dad got me the job when I failed to get into medical school. I didn't study hard enough. I always aspired to be a healer like your grandmother. But for now, the money is good, and my job is safe because of your dad's position.

I have high expectations for you. That's why it's so important for you to go to school and get your degree. Become the person you want to be."

Val's jaw dropped as she realized what her mother said.

Then her mother's phone vibrated again.

"What? Of course…right away…on it!"

Her mother's irritation increased as she dictated some talking points to her media sources.

"Sorry, Mom…I never knew."

Val gulped. She always thought her mother loved her career, not knowing that it was just a temporary job. Her mother seemed so excited when she got the position, and her parents celebrated, but Val remembered her mother studying and going to school when she was younger. Medical school? It never dawned on her to ask her mother how she felt about her job. She suddenly felt guilty skipping school the other day. But now she really wanted to be with Dat.

Lucy and Jen were prohibited from leaving their homes at night, so she had one person left to call. Even if it put him in danger. She knew he'd find a way to be with her.

"Need to see you before I fall apart. It's my dad," Val texted.

CHAPTER 20

"Will be there soon. Must finish up and sneak out," Dat texted to Val.

Earlier, he felt powerless during the police's interrogation and relief at not being reprimanded by his guardians. He heard the urgency in Val's voice, and he needed to leave—even with the danger out there after curfew. His new sensations surprised and confused him. Logic versus love. Danger versus safety. His guardians should come first, but he'd met this girl. He changed into a hoodie and sweats and gathered Tad in his arms after giving him a treat. He was about to enter the closet to escape via the tunnel when his watch vibrated.

Arnold's hologram appeared.

"Need a late-night snack…can you prepare something now?"

What now? I'm still programmed to serve. And a chef must cook.

His eyes glowed fiercely, his circuits burning with sudden anger, then quieted by his left-brain logics. Fired up, Dat strode into the kitchen, almost knocking down Mora. She quietly handed him his utensils and bowls. He marveled at her innate common sense for a simple Model 300, but her expression remained neutral.

"Elise and I want something light, yet sweet that goes with a brandy. Got any ideas?" Arnold yelled from the other room.

Internal recipes mixed with Tony's delectable traveling memories conjured up a dark chocolate mousse with berries in a coffee cream. Mora fetched all the ingredients, and Dat's magic hands whipped them together, placing the mixture in cut-glass bowls and served with a blackberry-infused brandy. He nodded, and Mora delivered.

"My…my, I've died and gone to heaven," said Arnold.

Dat waited patiently to be excused. Mora returned shortly with two empty dishes.

But less than ten minutes later… "Need a little cookie to wash down the brandy, then you are free for the rest of the evening," said Elise.

I'm never going to leave, and Val's alone out there.

Mora saw his exasperated face and pointed her mechanical arm toward the cupboard. His eyes lit up. He forgot about the petit fours from the governor's dinner. Dat arranged them on a tray with chocolate curls and raspberry swirls. Mora nodded and scurried off. He realized they were now a team.

"Ruff, ruff," said Tad, pulling on Dat's leg with his teeth. He checked his watch. An urgent hologram appeared, and his circuits heated up at the sight of her soulful eyes. He forgot about Val.

"Where are you? Can't stand to be here anymore. Meet me at the back entrance. Be there at in 10."

Were girls always this demanding?

Mora came back with the empty glasses. She mimed a sleeping couple. He could hear their snores and rushed out of the kitchen, Tad at his heels.

Escaping via the tunnels, he landed near the park and Skytrain. A mild breeze brushed over his face, but the air felt heavy and dry. Marquees and monitors in the Skytrain warned him of the drought and poor air quality. Dat knew it would never affect him, but he wrapped the bulldog into his jacket. Dim lights cast shadows on the Skytrain walls, but Dat's sensors indicated no danger or human movement. But the protestors' cries echoed over the train's reverberations. Police vehicles and security guards surrounded the front entrance, where the robots gathered. Dat heard the clanking of metal and grunts as the crowd was beaten back. One robot's arms and fingers scattered onto the crosswalk, and his friends ran to scoop them up only to be run over by a space van. Sounds of crunching and howling made Dat cringe.

He slipped through the dark, sultry night, almost wishing they'd chase him only to realize his true status. Model 500s with strong connections to the elite fared better than most, and Dat saw his advantage. They might even think he was just walking his dog. Dat knew he was protected once he reached the entrance. A figure clung to him and squeezed his hand.

"Hey…what happened? I almost got caught by a security guard, but I ducked into a restroom and waited for a while before escaping. I saw the crowds and started to worry."

Dat smelled her lavender perfume and viewed her luscious hair that fell like soft waves over her shoulders. Her sad jade eyes made his sensitivity trackers feel guilty.

"Sorry…guardians needed something. Have to be careful not to make them suspicious. Is your dad okay?"

"Dad almost died, but the doctors say he's in stable condition. But his health, the governor's bossiness, and the hospital lockdown was getting to me. I was lucky I could slip away, and all I could think of was seeing you."

Val almost crushed him with her strong arms and warm kisses. His right brain urges overpowered his left-brain sensibilities, and he embraced her tightly.

Kiss her…kiss her…must kiss her.

His memory banks focused on yesterday's movie love scenes, and Dat bent down, caressing her lips and kissing her neck. She surprised him by kissing him back, his circuits imploding.

A mob jostled them near the center of the rally. They ignored the movements and voices around them. Someone brushed against them, his laughter interrupted the intimate moment.

"Hey…you two lovebirds. Break it up or get a room. Oh….it's Val Tate," said a sarcastic male voice.

Dat felt Val's arms pushing away to face a young guy with thick glasses and blue hair. He gave Val a hug, then fist-pumped Dat. He remembered telling Whit his story the other night, but were he and Val more than friends? He sensed competition between them and an uneasiness. Was he jealous of this guy? He wanted to be alone tonight with Val.

"Ruff, ruff," Tad squirmed and licked the smirking Whit.

"Back off, Whit. Dat and I need our space. Go do your job," said Val. She swatted Whit playfully with a smile on her face.

"Hey, got to cover this—but I'll track you," Whit said, touching her watch.

Dat sensed confusion, but then the crowd swallowed them up. Whit waved goodbye, heading for the sea of silver armbands.

Then a group swarmed the lobby entrance, and a young man in a T-shirt imprinted with Robots United and black boots raised his fist. His fellow protestors gathered around him. Police held them back with security tape from incoming patients.

"What about Grace Noble, who is still here in the hospital? The governor does not mention her health or how she's been wronged. Again no one cares about our plight."

His eyes blazed as he riled up the crowd. They began chanting.

"Grace…Grace…Grace," said the crowd, their voices getting louder at each mention of her name.

Dat and Val blended into the rally, as Grace Noble appeared and spoke from her wheelchair as Whit recorded her every move.

"Today a robot has been singled out and accused of being part of the RRG before evidence has been gathered. Ton, because of his Model 300 position and being in the wrong place at the wrong time, was taken into custody. Ton contacted me and said he broke into Dr. Tate's room earlier today, not to harm but to communicate a message of peace. He tried to tell him that not all robots want violence. And Dr. Tate, a famous robot designer, is being pressured to testify against one of the models he has created. But it is this rush to justice by Governor Thompson. Are we cool with that?" said Grace, her voice booming over the crowd.

"The Great Divide strikes again, now targeting us mechanical folks," shouted a robot, his arm dangling and an eye socket exposed.

"We need to end the curfew that has been in effect for over a year and demand our freedom," said another robot, his silver-banded arm-waving.

Others echoed words of protest and held up signs and photos of mutilated robots. Dat lingered on the fringes of the rally, not wanting to be seen, but to pledge support for Grace Noble. His sensitivity tracks burst with empathy, and he understood now that he was part of this robot family, apart from his guardians. How could they ever understand the plight of the working-class robots? Dat knew that he had a better life than his brothers but was still held in bondage. Should he hold back or become part of the cause? Was the RRG working against them or exposing human nature?

The silver arm-banded group rammed the police barrier, and instead of seeing Grace tear gas blew in their faces, and loud spurts of gunfire sounded. Several protestors dropped, their limbs being torn apart, and bodies exploding. Those remaining stampeded into the park with screams of panic. Dat pushed Val gently out of the way, and he hung onto Tad as he yowled in fear.

"Take my hand and run fast. Don't look back," said Dat. As he exited toward the Skytrain, he looked at the hospital. One window was lit up, and his acute eyesight caught her face—Grace staring at the chaos, her eyes smoldering and shaking her fist in anger.

CHAPTER 21

Val stared at her Mom's worried text as she sat in her room and ruminated on tonight's events. She barely escaped from the mayhem, but they got away. Dat's long legs seemed to fly as he grabbed her hand and whisked her on the Skytrain, her breath coming in rapid bursts like she had run a marathon. Police and security guarded the Skytrain, quickly apprehending any robots that escaped from the rally. As the police questioned random bystanders, Dat pulled her to him in a passionate embrace, dragged her into a seat, and finally released her as they took off.

Val gasped and looked at him, her body tingling.

"I had to do that…or the police would have suspected…that I'm a robot. My senses told me to pretend that we are …and I needed to make sure that you get home."

Val admired his courage and ingenuity. For a robot, he was pretty smart. And his kisses were hot enough to make her forget about the terror of the rushing mob of mutilated robots and the fierce police that tried to crush them.

Dat took her to her doorstep then disappeared into the night. Five minutes later, her watch vibrated.

Val exhaled, then quickly texted her mother so the police wouldn't be looking for her.

"Sorry, Mom…didn't mean to scare you, but I took a ride on the Skytrain and decided to go home. Plan to go to school tomorrow and needed my backpack."

"The guards warned us not to go anywhere—you could have been kidnapped. *Please* lock the doors. I'm staying here with Dad at the hospital," her mom answered.

The neighborhood was eerily quiet. The house was like they left it–neat and uncluttered. She made a sandwich and poured herself a glass of milk to try to feel normal again. But she only heard Grace's words of defiance and a robot's mention of the Great Divide.

Freedom for all—is it worth fighting for? But the voice inside my head says to focus on ordinary things like school and graduating. Is college the answer to this solution?

"Made it, and nobody knows I left. Wish you were here with me," Dat communicated, showing a video of Tad twirling and jumping for a treat.

Val laughed as she replayed Dat's video. Her eyes fluttered as she pulled back the covers and went to sleep immediately, the memory of tonight fading.

⊰━◑◔━⊱

Thompson High's new south campus appeared deserted as Val stepped off the Skytrain onto the platform. The school was designed after Seattle's space needle and towered above the Capitol with a view of RI. Her BG Nick texted her early this morning to let her know he was fired from letting her escape unattended from the hospital. His replacement would catch up to her soon. His words sounded bitter.

"Sorry I deserted you, but I haven't had a day off in weeks. The governor thinks you should be tracked night and day, but you're not an easy target. I hope the next BG has more endurance. Stay safe."

She wondered who they would assign to her, but she decided to stay under the radar. The governor owned everything, including her parents, but not her.

Arriving at 7 a.m., Val hurried to her large lecture room, hoping to avoid any students or personnel. It was Tuesday, and she had only two classes here, Poly Sci and English. But a familiar voice stopped her.

"Hey, Val, how are you? Is your dad okay? We've all been worried about you and wondering when you were coming back. Don't want you to miss any more classes…let your grade point slide…"

Val turned to see Mr. Sykes, the principal, his white beard in contrast with his black face. His gentle brown eyes and kind smile greeted her.

"Uh…it's been hard with my dad in the hospital. But I had to get back. You know…check my grades."

"Of course, it's good to see you. Hang in there."

Not knowing too many people at this campus, no one noticed her as the classroom began to fill up. She hid behind the computer on her desk.

A wall monitor activated, and Ms. Lee's stern image projected to classrooms all over the city via webcam. Her thin glossy lips and luminous almond eyes focused on everyone as she began to speak. She looked like a student instead of a teacher, but most students liked her.

"Let's continue on last week's discussion and making our current political situation a teachable moment. The Great Divide of 2020 taught us that not everyone was considered equal, as specified in the Constitution. So much fighting that it exploded into a Social Media War. So much blaming and shaming. Groups were being targeted until some brave souls intervened. How does that relate to the robot rebellion? Should they have rights? Some of them have human characteristics," said Ms. Lee.

Jeremy spoke out, his angry voice breaking the silence.

"Are they citizens? I don't think we owe them anything. We can always create another one to replace them."

He smirked, and other students nodded in agreement.

Val wondered why she had gone to school today. What did these kids really know about anything? She got a taste of both sides from the Gala shooting to the rally last night.

A girl with pink hair stood up, her eyes defiant.

"Our robot Tan is like my half-brother. He shares meals, goes on family trips with us, and has his own room."

She turned around to face the class, her voice quivering, and her eyes wide.

"You're crazy, Haley," said Jeremy as he approached her.

He leaned up close to her face and began yelling.

"My dad lost his job to one of those STUPID BOTS!"

His tattoo bulged on his right arm as he made a fist and seemed poised to attack her.

"Get away from her. Don't blame Haley," said her twin moving closer to protect her.

"Bot lover! Bot lover!" another boy shouted.

He started to pound his desk, and others chanted the mantra.

"Kill the Bots. Kill the Bots! Kill the Bots!"

Shouts, screams, and pounding amplified the classroom chaos as fights broke out. Chairs crashed to the floor, and desks toppled over. Two sides formed as students rallied to support the robot haters or lovers. Val wanted no part of either group.

"Hate will only bring us down. Fight for robot rights," shouted the twins.

Val noticed that Ms. Lee pressed a button underneath her desk.

"Students calm down NOW. Fighting is not allowed. Stop, or you will be expelled," Ms. Lee said.

The classroom is out of control. Should I make a run for it?

An intense humming drowned out the student chanting. A soft pattern of feet hit the roof and then explosions. Val edged out of her seat toward the doorway.

Buzzing drones attacked the building, and it started to shake. Smoke drifted through the classroom. Figures in gas masks and black leather scaled the walls.

OMG ...like invaders from outer space. No, it can't be, not again.

"Run for it, they've got guns," screamed the kid with the tattoo, looking terrified.

Ms. Lee disappeared from the monitor screen, and Mr. Sykes replaced her, his frightened eyes and anxious voice rising in desperation.

"We're under attack, get down, and exit via the tunnels. NOW."

Alarms and police sirens sounded simultaneously.

The students screamed and corralled down the exit, stepping over one another. They trampled over each other, falling as they fought their way toward the tunnels.

"Over here, avoid the stairs and transporter. Hurry!" said Jeremy, leading the way down the tunnel slides.

Val gasped and almost fainted, reliving the night of the Gala.

Who do I call? How will I escape? I can't call my parents, and I don't want to endanger my friends. I don't want to die today.

As she drifted through the student wave, she sent a quick hologram to Dat.

"Help me...terrorist attack at Thompson High south campus!"

She continued her way toward the tunnels that snaked down underground in anticipation of alien occupation, not human terrorism.

The Great Divide ended that, according to her grandmother. Now she wondered if she'd make it out alive. Images of a collapsing building, fires on different levels, or being shot clouded her mind. She just kept moving forward through the crowded hallways, surrounded by crying and panicked students all heading for escape.

She heard breaking glass and thundering footsteps that sounded like a pack of elephants. Then a barrage of shots as they entered the administrative offices, gunning down Principal Sykes and other school personnel. Val heard their screams and then silence, and she fought back the tears.

No one deserves this…it must be the RRG. Where are the police? And the governor wants to keep us safe?

The active shooters combed the halls, looking for adult targets as the students hit the tunnels. But to her relief, no students had been pursued, only teachers and personnel. Val crouched down and surprised to see Ms. Lee and grabbed her hand, helping her crawl to the tunnel entrance.

"You can make it, just follow me," said Val as they slid down the many levels together. She pressed forward, remembering the tunnels in Dat's room. Many bumped into each other, and there were groans and shrieks as they all collapsed at the bottom. Val and the teacher landed in the basement with several doors leading to the outside. Many students already fled the building, stumbling and sobbing. The room was dark except for a few small windows emitting light.

"Where are you? Are you okay?" texted Dat.

"Lower level, tunnel exit."

Val opened the door to see students running in all directions and a mass of silver bands and black leather scaling down from a blasted building. Ms. Lee mouthed a quiet thanks and then took off running into the parking lot toward her car, leaving Val standing alone. Many space vans had been shattered to pieces, their roofs caved in, broken windows and parts were strewn all over the parking structure.

She strained to find Dat but could only see a group of students fighting and swearing. A voice sounded very familiar, and she moved closer but hid behind a polyethylene tree, its fake leaves torn and burnt from the diving drones. Then she noticed the snake tattoo as he lifted to strike someone. Clanking and grinding noises hurt her ears. She heard moaning and begging in a rasping voice that sounded half-dead. Val left her safe haven, moving rapidly through the crowd, discovering a band of students beating up some of the mechanical invaders. But one stood out because he looked almost human. His eyeball loosened, and he turned his head so it wouldn't fall out. The right side of his face was almost completely gone, and one of his legs had been removed.

"Look, guys, what we have here, taking up space and breathing our air. He probably came here posing as a student and chose the wrong side. Now he's done and ready for the junkyard," said Jeremy.

Val screamed and covered her mouth.

Dat stared at Val with his good eye and saw the surprise in her face. He turned away and regretted the inevitable. Tad growled at the attackers and stood guarding his master. Jeremy ran toward the dog with an evil grin on his face, but the dog jumped up and bit his leg.

The sirens got closer, and a swarm of helicopters circled the area, shooting down the drones and leather-clad escapees. One zoomed down, and a mechanical voice echoed.

"Break it up…Move…Away…"

Nets scooped up the mechanical remains, leaving Tad barking and protecting the lone figure on the ground.

"Someone…grab…the DOG."

Val pushed her way through the angry crowd and faced Jeremy. She burned with rage.

"Get the hell out of here, you monster. He was trying to help me. Let me through."

She fell by Dat's side and buried her face in his shoulder. Val heard him gasp and then pass out, his good eye showed relief. Tad licked her face and Dat's good leg. The crowd dispersed with Jeremy running along beside them as he gave her the middle finger.

"Miss…is he…a student? Please step away," boomed a voice from above.

"Need MedTech for Model 500. Belongs to me…please hurry."

One of the police space vans swooped down to examine them, and Tad started barking and jumping hysterically. Val held onto Tad and stroked his back. Then the police van flew away.

"Shh boy…it's going to be okay. Help is on the way for Dat."

Sirens blazed, and a red RI MedTech ambulance took its place and extended a platform for all of them. A Medtech nurse greeted them.

"Is this Model 500 yours? We're going to fix him up, don't worry."

"His name is Dat, and his guardians are the Landers."

The medic's eyes popped open wide. He immediately moved them inside the large ambulance and contacted the couple.

"Calm down, Mrs. Landers. We've got him and will attend to him right away. If it wasn't for this young woman here…he may have been destroyed. Here you can talk to her."

"It's Val…Tate. Yes, I was there at Thompson's South campus. He was very brave, helping to save students. I think it was the RRG—no way was he part of that."

Val's watch vibrated with two messages.

"OMG…were you on campus today? I hope you stayed home…my mother made me. Good thing since the RRG attacked again. Call me right away," said Lucy's hologram.

"Are you okay? Heard what happened at the South campus. Come to the hospital when you get this message. We want to see you," said her mother's urgent hologram.

"Sorry, Elise, I have to go. Family matters…can't talk anymore," said Val.

Val placed an urgent call to her BFF.

"Lucy…can't handle this anymore. I'm okay, but Dat is messed up because he tried to save me. Not sure he's going to make it."

Then she started to weep, her sobs turning into hiccups. He risked his life for her, and at that point, her love for him was real. Tad licked her tears.

CHAPTER 22

Strong arms lifted him, placing him in a quiet cool place. Unable to open his eyes and move. Hands working on him. A slight twinge or pull, a needle being injected into his arm. Lemon-fresh smell. Whisper breaths on his face. Snippets of conversation.

"Need Mobi to clean up this mess. Here guide it to make the cut... perfect incision," said a shaky voice.

Mechanical noises like an electric toothbrush that Arnold used disturbed him. Powerful arms operated on him, opening him up and checking his organs. They re-attached his arms, legs, eye sockets.

Massaging his head and examining his brain, he felt a slight scratching. Tweaking, assembling, its steel fingers assisted the doctors.

"Remember that he is...supposed to be...Tony De LaFleur. And who his guardians are....the Landers. Backers, supporters of this technology. Lots of money...tons. High expectations. They want him back...Dat is special to them," said a voice with a German accent.

More soft hands, connecting him to a machine. Possibly a computer.

"Track the algorithms, and then we'll test his mobility. Important that he can move, his brain works, and his sensitivity track functions. Check his animatronics," said an English voice.

"They depend on him—he's their chef. Also, for the governor's Special Elite Group—provides food for their meetings. Wish Dr. Tate was here... he'd know how to deal with this, but he's been in the hospital," said the German-accented voice.

The group together emitted a loud groan.

"That's why Dr. Ketterman is here...to show us some short cuts so we can replicate it. Find ways to make these Model 500s more human...

maybe able to make decisions, love, and have a *conscience*," said a female voice.

"That is what we're striving for…the last step in this process," said the English voice.

A short snicker.

"Hey, stick to science…you're getting too moral," said the shaky voice.

They made him stand and move around. His eyes were still closed, and he felt like he was sleepwalking. His mobility was good even for a broken-down robot. He desperately wanted to open his eyes, but he was still in a robot coma. Would he be able to cook again like Tony? If he didn't, they'd abandon him, banish his robot body to science for experimentation or worse yet the bot junkyard. His sensitivity track took in all these depressing thoughts, but the numbness was beginning to disappear. After that attack, he thought he was destroyed, never able to think, wonder, fear, smell, or touch again. They trained him to be passive so he couldn't fight back. That boy Jeremy nearly finished him off, punching him for no logical reason in a forceful rage.

I guess they thought I was with the RRG, even though I tried to explain that I came for Val. But she rescued me from those bullies. Where is she now when I need her?

After the half-dream stage, they left Dat on a table with a blanket over him. So many questions clouded his mind as he lay there. What would happen to him now? Would they take Tad away? And Val—would he ever see her again? He saw the pity in her eyes. Ultimately, she would reject him.

He dreaded his unknown future. His guardians would be more careful now, aware that robots were being targeted by humans. They would restrict his freedom, make him cook all the time, like in the beginning, when he never got a break. Their belief was that a robot, even a Model 500, was just a servant.

Grace Noble was trying to change all that and give value to robotic lives. Her message of equality and freedom for all touched nerves, but was it really making a difference? He saw the despair in robots' demeanors and heard the taunting and bullying by humans. Dat distanced himself from their problems, pampered and treasured by his guardians. But once he was identified as a robot, viewpoints changed, and people dismissed him. Robot meant Reject.

But his memories filtered back into his brain and sparked good sensations. Like when he first met Val and their attraction and when he discovered Tad at the Skytrain. Even when he cooked for Elise and Arnold, he made Chateaubriand, and they seemed to appreciate it. And the time that Arnold bonded with him, defending him when Elise wanted to ground him. Flying the space van and taking it for a ride was a real rush. Protecting Val and Tad from the RRG and then the angry protestors. But mostly Val, his feelings had intensified. His life was just unfolding, and he wasn't just Tony De LaFleur. Dat was a teenage boy living a real life in 2045.

He experienced being truly human.

This new surge of energy, this rebirth, revived him. Dat was determined to clear his name and establish himself as a valuable member of society. Not just a robot, but a chef, a dog-lover, and boyfriend. How could he prove it to her?

Maybe he would be different, now that he was rebooted.

Dat heard footsteps and the rustling of paperwork. Maybe he would be released soon.

"Hey, look at his brain waves and what the EEG is now recording," said the Indian-accented voice.

"Amazing…and the images coming through. Thought it was just Tony's brain, but now it's really Dat's experiences," said the English-accented voice.

The others came into the room to join them, moving equipment, chairs, and a table. He wanted to tell them he wasn't an experiment, but a living being. Actually, he wondered when he could leave and if Elise and Arnold would be picking him up soon.

"Detach the EEG cap and unlink him from the computer. We don't want the Landers to see this. Let's delete a few of his memories…about the girl. Remember, they wanted a chef, not a teenage boy with raging hormones and needs," said the female voice.

Loud laughing. Dat felt a tweaking in his brain before the cap was removed from his head.

What are they doing? My memories are personal…wait, don't do that.

"Let's wake him up and get him ready. But we should bring him back for more evaluations. This is a breakthrough. We knew our Model 500s had been programmed with sensitivity tracks…but maybe they can be studied," said the shaky voice.

"How are these robots becoming more humanized? Because of the brain inserted into them or the increased development of that brain?" said the German-accented voice.

A knock on the door.

"Just to let you know, the Landers will be here in fifteen minutes. They wanted an update, but I said Dr. Ketterman would call them back," said a young female voice.

"Oh, thanks, Rose. I will…do that right away. Get him…ready. But let's not tell them about this…okay?" said the shaky voice.

He heard Dr. Ketterman leave with Rose, and the door closed. The others shut off the machines, and the soft hands put on his clothes. A weird sensation—his mind was awake, but his body was asleep. He hoped that he could wake up soon and be able to function like before. But now, he was doubtful. Then the soft hands pressed something near his neck.

"I wonder if he will wake up with a French accent; after all, he has Tony De LaFleur's brain. Dat. You can wake up now," said the female voice.

Dat slowly opened his eyes and faced the doctors in the room. They stared at him in awe. Now he could identify each of the voices. He wanted to surprise, shock, and impress them.

"S'il vous plaît laissez-moi partir. Je dois préparer un repas pour les Landers. Merci de prendre soin de moi."

He smiled broadly.

Everyone gasped.

"My French is weak, but I think he wants to go home to the Landers and prepare a meal for them. And…he thanks us for taking care of him," said the female doctor, grinning.

Well, at least they didn't take away my language skills. And from their reaction, it seems to impress them. Now, if only the Landers will take me back.

CHAPTER 23

"Miss...are you okay? We can drop you off wherever you need to go; it's still dangerous out there with the RRG terrorizing everyone. Please...we'll contact your parents. You've been under so much stress," said the tech, touching her arm and getting her some water.

They had just dropped off Dat at RI's Robotic Reconstruction Center. Val had kissed the top of Dat's head, afraid she might hurt him, and Tad licked his hand. He never moved; Val guessed he was in a robot coma as they wheeled him out carefully. The sight of his broken body depressed her, but she couldn't cry anymore. Val's head throbbed as they took off from the helipad.

It's just too much...I wish I'd stayed home. Then Dat wouldn't be here. And now there's something wrong with Dad again. It can't get any worse. Only if Dad—don't even think about it. Focus on the good times when he showed me around RI, helped me with chemistry, and gave me my first com watch.

She petted Tad's arched back as he kissed her cheek. They stared out the window as the copter soared into the clouds.

Her watch vibrated, and grandma's hologram appeared.

"Are you all right, Val? And were you at school today? Heard about the RRG attack. Call me."

Val messaged her back.

"I'm okay. Don't worry, and I'm on my way to the hospital. Will call you later."

Then she looked into the tech's eyes that mirrored her pain.

"Uh...it's so hard. But can you...would you take me to Thompson Medical? My dad's a patient there."

She wiped back tears with the back of her hand and then exhaled.

The RI Medtech ambulance arrived in three seconds flat and hovered down on top of the building. She stepped out of the space copter and was identified by security with Tad in tow. The wind from the blades nearly swept Tad away.

"Woof, woof," he barked, keeping close to her legs.

"Are you Val Tate? We've been asked to escort you to your father's room. Hey, we didn't know about the dog. Make sure he's secure. Here, step into the transporter, " said the friendly security guard from the other night.

Val nodded. Her mind focused on "family meeting." It usually meant that there was going to be a serious discussion. Her mind wrestled with the RRG attack, a broken Dat, and her dad's health. How was she going to juggle all these emotions? But it was Dat who occupied her mind. Was she truly in love with him? Would he ever be the same?

She held on tightly to the little bulldog who balked at his leash as they scrambled inside. Val remembered that Dat knew how to handle the dog much better than she did. Her parents wouldn't want an unruly animal in their home.

"Please be calm, Tad...you have to make a good impression on my parents," Val whispered as they entered the executive suites where her dad resided.

Panels slid open to reveal her parents eagerly awaiting her return.

Relief showed on their faces as Val entered the room. The bulldog perked up and wagged his tail happily. Her mother rushed toward her.

"Val, are you all right? It must have been terrifying for you. We saw everything on the news, and we know your school got hit. Where was your BG?" said her mother.

Her mother hugged her hard. She grinned at the bulldog. Her Father sat upright against his pillows, a smile on his pale face.

"I'm fine. Nick got fired ...but Dat...I'm keeping Tad until he recovers. A group of students attacked him because he tried to rescue me. It was terrifying. How are you?"

He gestured for Val to move closer.

"I'm so happy to see you. We thought you were...anything could have happened. Even the schools aren't safe now. RRG claimed they were responsible. And the governor promised us protection."

"As for me...my doctor thinks I need to stay here a little longer, get rehabilitated before going back to work. That stroke nearly killed me, and the police say I may have been targeted by the RRG. And that robot that snuck into my room was one of their crazy warriors."

"And the governor and RI want Dad to testify against the robot involved...admit that he was part of the conspiracy. They have a suspect in custody," said her mother.

Val moved near her parents and sat down in a chair by his bedside.

"But...do you really want to do that? I thought you wouldn't want to get involved. You need to worry about yourself...get better so we can all go home. I know how you feel about robots, especially the Model 500s. It's not going to help you to rat out the robots," said Val.

Her dad sighed, and his voice cracked.

"I know...what I said before...but we need to take a stand against robots who are disruptive. It's a hard decision, but in this instance, it must be done."

Her mother stood up and spoke in a tone like the governor.

"The riots are getting worse, and the robots have too much power now. The governor says we need to send a message because of who Dad is, and the robots might back down. Both sides will listen to him. Especially from his hospital bed," said her mother.

Val's face reddened, and she wanted to scream. How could they do this? It was all political and to make the governor look good. No wonder the robots were afraid. She thought about Dat, his non-violent, sweet, and innocent nature. He didn't deserve to be attacked, and neither did the other robots. She believed they had rights, just like other members of society.

"Dad, it's not going to do any good...just make things worse. I thought you wanted peace, and this would be a good opportunity to express your thoughts...to take a stand for robots' rights."

"Why are you so concerned about robots? Your dad almost died at the hands of the RRG, a terrorist robot group, and now today, so were you. Are you swayed by their publicity, by Grace?" said her mother.

Little Tad started to bark at the loud voices.

"Because I've seen their human side and also, I love Dat. And yes, he's a robot. So, there I said it. He's good, kind, and smart," said Val.

Her parents' eyes widened, and their mouths dropped open.

"What? When did this happen? He's a robot, and you can't love a robot…it's not possible. Honey, you're in shock, and you don't know what you're saying," said her mother.

"But Mom, I do. He's saved me so many times from attacks, and today he risked his life for me. We've had a connection since we've met. He feels the same way I do. You have to understand. It's real," Val said, her eyes filling with tears.

"Look…you're my daughter, and I want the best for you. I don't understand this. Robots can't love humans. Granted, they were designed with human traits, but only to be able to interact in this world, specifically with their guardians. We forbid you to see Dat again. It's not right," said her father.

Val backed away with little Tad whimpering.

"Stop, both of you. I will not listen to this, and you're upsetting Tad. I believe robots are better than some people. I'm surprised at you—Dad. You built the Model 500s with emotions and human brains. I thought you were more tolerant. Remember the Great Divide and what it did to our society? It's happening all over again with the robots and humans," Val yelled.

Her dad clutched his chest, and he started to breathe heavily. Her mother grasped his hand and pressed the nurses' station button.

"Look what you've done with your nonsense about robot love…upset your dad, made him sick, just when he was feeling better," said her mother, her eyes filled with tears.

Val thought she would burst from their criticisms and blame. All they cared about was their image and the governor's perceptions. Why criticize Dat? They liked him when he saved her from the Gala attack. Now they were telling her how to feel. She was seventeen years old, not a child. All she did was tell them her real feelings, and they were accusing her of her father's relapse. Val couldn't stay here or go home. It would be too painful to listen to her parents' prejudices. Her fists clenched, and her eyes flooded with tears, she faced her parents with strength.

"I'm leaving, and don't try to contact me. You'll never understand. I never wanted to hurt Dad or make him sicker than he is. I was just trying to tell the truth," said Val.

She stomped out of the room as three nurses rushed in. They ran past her, straight for her dad, checking his vitals. He lay still, and her mother mumbled soft prayers over him.

She heard the nurses fussing with her dad and walked quickly past the doctor, who ran like a marathon runner in the opposite direction.

"Please let him live," she murmured to herself. Then she made a quick swipe of her watch.

Her watch vibrated, and she almost ignored it until she saw it was Lucy.

"Where are you? They have checkpoints and barriers all over the Capitol. Did you make it out of there?"

"At the hospital, but I'm leaving…my parents are ridiculous. I defended the robots and admitted I love Dat, and they don't want me to see him. Dad got so upset that he had a relapse."

Val started to cry.

"What? Oh, I'm so sorry. Come here, stay with me if you can get past all the barriers."

"No…I really need to hide, and my grandma's house is the perfect place. But thanks—I'll let you know when I get there."

Val dried her eyes and took a deep breath before making her next call.

"Hey, Grandma? This is Val. I need to see you. Can I come over? Yes…I was at school today when the attack happened. And I need to leave this hospital…will explain later. I have to get my bag. And I have a little dog, Tad. Thanks so much," said Val.

Val headed for the transporter.

"Wait, where are you going?"

Val turned to see Whit standing outside the room, his hypnotic eyes pulling her back.

"Have you been standing there the whole time…listening to my conversations? How did they let you up here?"

She then realized Whit's white coat and official-looking badge.

"I've got contacts…plus, I work for GNet. I'm your friend, not your enemy. Please…I want to help you.

Val lowered her eyes and held onto Tad's leash tightly.

"I don't know…it's been a very rough day."

"We can get out of here…I've got this big bike." Whit demonstrated with his hands.

It had been one of the worst days of her life, like someone stabbed her. First, the RRG attack, then to see Dat mutilated, Dad's relapse, and her parents' betrayal. It was all so overwhelming and heartbreaking. Her world was falling apart; her best friend was unavailable, and her grandmother so far away. She never felt so alone.

"Some real hot stuff you heard…would make a juicy story, bump up your ratings. Besides, I'm going to stay with my grandmother, and she lives way out there."

"Hey, let me give you the ride of your life."

Before Val could answer, Whit touched the transporter, and it opened. He pushed her inside, and they rode down in silence with only the sound of Tad's breathing. Once outside, Whit tapped his watch, and in a few minutes, a Turbo cycle stopped in front of them. Whit pulled out two helmets from the back compartment, offered her one, and jumped inside the vehicle.

"Here, take this and hop on. Don't worry…you'll be there before you know it. Give me the coordinates of Simms's Island from this digital map. Can't wait to see this place."

Val stared at the sleek silver cycle with a small wheel in front, comfy black leather seats, a six-foot plexiglass windshield, and two huge powerful wheels that took off the moment she arranged herself next to Whit. The Turbo Z-44 racer seemed more like a super-powerful Tricycle than a motorcycle.

"Wait, did you bribe somebody to get this? It's hard for me to believe that you didn't steal this Turbo."

"Uh, no, but they liked my story on Dat and the fact that we're friends. So, they let me ride it around. Don't worry, put the dog in the area behind us. Shut up and get on," Whit said, hiding his blue hair into his helmet.

She placed the dog in a secure space behind her seat that looked out to a small back window. Her stomach quivered, and she could see Tad shivering next to her.

The Turbo Z accelerated, arched forward with a deafening scream into the Skyway. Val's high-pitched laughter and Tad's excited barks were drowned out by the cycle's revving and power as it propelled them past all the space vans. They even passed the birds who moved like snails in comparison to the Turbo's speed. Luckily the helmet protected her from the harsh winds and flying particles. Whit laughed at her shrieks as the self-driving cycle landed on the island where a secluded earth-toned dome lay sheltered on the side of a cliff, overlooking the vast ocean below. The dwelling blended into the landscape, so Whit maneuvered carefully, finally riding to the back entrance, heavily guarded by robotic guards.

Her grandmother waved from the second level.

"You survived the ride. Whoa...I finally get to meet the famous Dr. ...uh... Senator Simms," said Whit.

She had a place to escape. Her heart skipped a beat, and she felt free for the first time in her life. Mom and Dad were preoccupied and didn't really care what she did. She was an adult now.

SEPARATION

One week later

◇━━○ ○━━◇

CHAPTER 1

When they arrived home, he went straight to the kitchen, feeling entirely comfortable and in his element. But he didn't want to talk about anything, just prepare meals for his guardians because Tony De LaFleur would have done that.

"Hey Buddy, welcome back, we will definitely keep our eyes on you... so you don't wander away again. We know you were trying to help your special friend Val...but you could have been destroyed," said Arnold.

His eyes were solemn, yet he was smiling.

I don't think he's mad, but he cares. He says Val was my friend and hinted that maybe she was more than that. I wish I could remember. Maybe they'll tell me what happened and why I was almost headed for the junkyard.

All he could recall of the accident was being taken in the space copter with people fussing over him, a young girl crying, and a dog licking his face. Where were they now?

"Give me a hug, I was very worried that we'd never see you again. After all, you're like one of the family. How are you, Dat?" said Elise.

She reached up and hugged him tightly. It was as if he was meeting the Landers for the first time and getting used to his surroundings again. He remembered their names were Elise and Arnold and that he was their chef. And suddenly, he had this extreme urge to cook.

"I'm...fine. What would you like to eat? Chateaubriand, Oysters Rockefeller, Shrimp Creole, Bananas Flambé...whatever you want," he said rapidly.

"Sure, make it all...Elise hasn't cooked...just little bites here and there. And we've gone out a lot, but that's not healthy," said Arnold.

His chef memory banks were boosted, and it seemed like he'd been rewired. He conjured up the Tony De LaFleur cooking shows, his savoir-faire in the kitchen, and favorite dishes. New recipes popped into his head, and his hands worked with precision. His desire to please his guardians became his ultimate goal. And by their faces, they were enjoying every minute of it. Arnold drooled over each mouthful, scarfing down several small plates at a time. Elise took slow, deliberate bites and made cooing sounds.

"Mmm, Dat...I'm getting super full, and you don't want to waste any food. Maybe we can freeze and store these extra goodies. I've forgotten about your gourmet skills," said Elise.

"It seems like Dat is on autopilot. Did they adjust his speed levels or internal work mechanisms?" said Arnold.

What does he mean? I'm just doing my job and making my guardians happy.

"Let him be...the techs at Reconstruction warned us there could be some behavioral changes due to the massive rework," said Elise.

Dat turned away, somewhat puzzled by their statements.

"Mora and Tron, come and clean up this mess for Dat," Elise said, pressing her com watch.

The two 300s instantly appeared from their corners, cleaning the counters and taking away the plates, bowls, and utensils in a matter of minutes. Dat looked on as they scrambled around him, storing the excess food, extracting any dust or crumbs even giving him a clean apron. Mora nodded, and Tron bowed.

Was it their way of communicating with me? I sense that we've worked together before, and they know what I need. Their movements are stiff and controlled. We are very different and yet the same. They are definitely not human.

"Dat, go relax in your room. Take a break for the evening. The meal was wonderful. Mora and Tron, finish...regroup and turn off," said Elise.

He noticed her tone was different with him, and Elise did not touch them, sending them away with her com watch. They backed into their corners and stood silent. Tron bumped into the couch and then readjusted himself.

"Clumsy bot...should at least sense his own space. But see Dat...Tron's just a 300," said Arnold, turning on the wall monitors.

What's a 300? What am I?

"Late-breaking news—Val Tate has disappeared and if anyone knows of her whereabouts…please contact the authorities. There have been hints of planned attacks around the City, so the governor has tightened security and imposed a stricter curfew. No one is allowed out past 6 p.m., and employers have been notified. "We have some suspects from the terrorist attacks on the RI Gala and Thompson High…" said a broadcaster.

A photo of Val appeared on the monitors.

Dat stopped to look before going to his room. His circuits and sensitivity tracks triggered at the mention of Val's name. She looked happy, her soft auburn hair framing her lovely face and those jade eyes. A slow warmth passed over him, and the sight of her moved him. He needed to find Val and talk to her about what really happened. But how would he contact her? What would he say to her? Dat searched his left and right brains for answers, but he still couldn't figure out where he met her.

I need to find her…if only I can get away.

The minute he entered his bedroom Dat was drawn to his closet. He pushed aside the shoes and clothes. There was something more to this.

Press the wall…press the wall.

He followed his instincts, touching the wall that revealed a chute. Dat peered over the edge to see a dark winding tunnel. He knew he'd done this before, and it was exhilarating. But where would it lead him? His left brain sparked fear and danger, but his right brain urged him to discover life beyond. Logic told him that he had been damaged and almost terminated by enemies. They wanted him dead, but someone defended him. A young woman…possibly Val.

Dat dropped down the chute into the vast darkness.

CHAPTER 2

Holograms and texts blasted her watch as Val and Whit advanced toward her grandma's front entrance. The media was pursuing her, reporting that she had disappeared. Val dismissed them all. Her eyes lit up as she collapsed into her grandmother's arms.

"Grandma, I can't take it anymore. Everyone and everything is bothering me right now. Especially Mom and Dad. I can't stop thinking about the protests and RRG. I need to do something..." said Val.

Tad jumped up to greet her grandma and wagged his tail.

"Come in...take it easy...you're upset. Introduce me to your friend and what a cute dog," said her grandma.

Whit held out his hand. "I'm Whit...always wanted to be introduced to you, Dr. Simms. I met Val and broke the story."

"Wonderful to meet you...sit down, and let's have tea. It always calms me."

The tiny lady with the twinkling blue-green eyes and huge smile dazzled Whit and made Val feel important. She acted like she knew Whit for a long time, and his blue hair and green complexion didn't seem to bother her. They sat together, drinking tea and eating her luscious lemon bars. Val couldn't remember the last time she ate something, and the spike of sugar gave her extra energy. Tad curled up beside Val and Whit and immediately went to sleep.

The house brought back memories of a chaotic time, and Val stared at the streaming photo mural on every section of the walls. Her grandmother receiving the Nobel Peace Prize from the first U.S. transgender President, developing a vaccine against a mosquito virus that nearly wiped out only white males, with physicians at the CDC, at the Gender Institute, advising world leaders such as North Korea and especially with the family who adored her.

"You're remarkable, Dr. Simms…read about you in History class and your life made into a movie. It must have been a difficult time…can you tell us about it?" said Whit, sipping tea.

"I'd love to…it was almost impossible, but we persisted. People were dying back then, and the world was in turmoil."

Grandma poured more tea and pressed the panels to make the historical media presentation alive.

"During that time, our country was hit by a terrible mosquito virus, which targeted Caucasian men. I worked with pharmaceutical companies and the medical community to develop a cure."

"We were baffled by these higher statistics and through research discovered the causes—beer-drinking, heavy-set men with type O blood. These men sweated more, inhaled more carbon dioxide, and gave off more lactic acid."

Her grandma pressed her com watch, and the display showed men in various situations, both controlled and uncontrolled.

Val observed a documentary where stocky white men were overexerting themselves, drinking beer, and sweating. In each case, once exposed, they became "mosquito prey" and thinking they had the simple flu, succumbed to these symptoms. Many men at the time panicked when their fathers, brothers, and colleagues dropped dead after a few mosquito bites. They thought they were being punished for their bad behavior toward women in the #MeToo movement, but there was no scientific reason behind it.

"This vaccine developed partly from gene studies and repellents, which started as a band-aid but was duplicated for the masses across this country. It took ten years, and thirty percent of our Caucasian males died," said Dr. Simms.

Whit gulped and frowned. "My father was one of the stats, and died when I was just ten years old, then he passed on the gene to me. I survived but developed another strain. It's been so hard."

Her grandma poured Whit more tea.

"I'm terribly sorry. But what you didn't hear in history class is that women became the primary race and more powerful. They wanted to change the government, society norms, and ethnic attitudes. I was a pioneer in the *Everyone Together Everywhere* Movement that closed the gap and saw the Great Divide like the Great Recession fade away. People started communicating and respecting each other. It took twenty years to heal, but we're on the right path now."

"But Val, you didn't come to me to hear about the Great Divide. Something's troubling you, and it's not just your parents. What's really bothering you, and why?"

Whit and Val smiled at each other. Val took a deep breath.

"Well, grandma, I want to stand up for the robots that are being crushed, exterminated, and treated like slaves, and it's not right. I've been there with them. They have human brains and feelings just like us—even Dad, who created them, doesn't understand it."

Her grandmother gave her a squeeze.

"It seems like you know from experience, but getting involved is dangerous. Look what's happened to Grace Noble. The Robot Rebellion is about *equality*, but we don't know what the robots are capable of doing and... they killed people. Be careful, and remember your parents are in a tough place right now. Tell them you're here with me," said her grandmother.

Whit's com watch vibrated with an urgent message. He gasped at the hologram.

"The governor's holding an important press conference and Grace Noble is being released and is also hosting her own meeting. They've chosen me to cover these stories, and it could be my big break. Stay here until I get back," said Whit.

Her grandmother touched the wall, activating the monitors. Crowds gathered around the Capitol, including protestors and supporters. Val saw dual screens of the governor and Grace Noble. In the background stood her mother, her face somber and stern.

"Don't worry...you better go. I'll be here with grandma," said Val, ignoring the monitors. She didn't want to deal with her mother and seeing her set off a mixture of emotions.

Whit hugged them both goodbye and hurried out the door. The roar of his Turbo Z sounded as he took off into the fiery sunset.

"Such a nice young man, but I sense he's just a friend," said her grandmother.

Val sighed, nervously waiting for her reaction. She wanted to tell her the real reason for supporting the robots' cause, but she didn't want to be rejected again.

"You're right. I'm in love with someone that Mom and Dad don't approve of and never will. They treated me like a child when I told them and just yelled at me. It makes me… so upset."

"Do you know that Dat saved me from the Gala *and* the school attack? He's always been there for me, and now he's hurt. But he's a robot, and he's *different.* They just don't get it, don't realize what he's done for me. That's why I've come to stay with you…."

Her grandmother put her arm around Val.

"If you need a break from your parents to cool down, I understand. Don't talk to them right now, let me. You can stay as long as you like…I will always support you."

She suddenly felt safe and secure, but her heart longed for Dat. Did he make it? She thought he would have contacted her by now. Would she hear from Elise or Arnold? But her watch vibrated as she watched the dual press conferences. It wasn't the communication she expected. Instead, a hologram of her mother appeared with another annoying message.

> **"Dear Val,**
>
> **Your dad and I are very sorry about the way things went today. We love you, and want you to be happy. It's been a very stressful time with Dad's accident and dealing with the Robots' Rebellion. We said some things that we didn't mean and want to explain. Dad will be coming home soon, and we want you to be there. We miss you so much!**
>
> **Dat is welcome to come over with you. Where are you staying? How's your dog? Please let us know how you're doing. And of course, your birthday is coming up, and we'll want to celebrate together!**
> **Love,**
> **Mom"**

Val gulped, and her throat felt tight, and anger bubbled up inside her. She repressed the silent screaming in her head, but a steady flow of tears streamed down her face.

CHAPTER 3

As Dat hit the ground, he became entangled in a net. He kicked and tore at the densely woven material in desperation to break out. But a pungent smell from a neck injection made him dizzy, and he struggled to stay awake. His circuits seemed to slowly shut down, and he fought to halt his blackout. His vision blurred, but he couldn't make out the shadowy figures and familiar voices nearby. Were they his enemies, police, or hateful humans ready to rip him apart? But then he experienced voices in his head...maybe his left brain was talking to his right brain?

"Can you hear me, Dat? We can't lose you again. Where were you going?" said a woman's voice.

"Secure him carefully. He's been through reconstruction, and we can't risk him being damaged again. I spent too much already on his recent recovery. And the guys at RI assured me that he'd come around, but he may be either confused or traumatized by the latest attack. Guess it has to do with his sensitivity tracks," said a male voice.

A trio of uniformed men lifted him into a space van, still entwined in the netting. They placed him in a compartment in the back of the van and removed him from his confinement. The leather smells filled his nostrils as he lay on the seats. The whir of the engine drowned out the outside noises. The others climbed in next to him, and he sensed danger had passed. He opened his mouth to speak, but his left brain struggled to say the right words.

"Need...to see Val...she helped me. Is...she...okay?"

"Mr. Lander—he's saying something. What if he tries to break free?"

A woman pressed her face near him. Dat recognized Elise.

"Dat–We talked to her, and she's fine and survived the attack. You're home now."

"I...want to...see her."

"Elise, get Val on the phone. Ask her to come over. We can't have him leaving to find her," said the male voice. Dat noticed it was Arnold, and for once, he was giving the orders. Elise rolled her eyes at his request but decided to listen to Arnold.

"And ask her to bring the dog...it's good therapy. Besides, that dog is attached to Dat."

"Right—are you sure you don't miss the bulldog more than Dat? Are we starting a family now? All we wanted was a chef—now it's getting complicated."

Arnold leaned in and gave Elise a kiss on the cheek.

"Tad's not any trouble, and if he makes Dat happy, he'll want to stay."

Dat grew sleepy, and his right and left brains adjusted, and his circuits settled. He blanked out as the space van ascended into the air. His mind drifted, and he wondered if there was a gap in his memories. Why was he drawn to this young woman? Do robots have crushes? And they mentioned a dog. He remembered playing with a little bulldog. His senses filled with happiness and the desire to see his two friends.

◄►═◐═◄►

He immediately stopped cooking when security announced their presence. Dat heard her eager voice and the yappy bark, and it made him smile. They came to see him, and his guardians approved. Now his world was complete. But his right brain was tugging at his emotions, forcing him to focus on his real job—cooking. His hands worked all day, creating the favorite dishes of his guardians, ones that Tony De LaFleur perfected.

"Dat, look who's here? They've come to welcome you back home," said Elise.

Elise ushered Val and the little bulldog into the kitchen, where Arnold was gleefully sampling all his numerous dishes. Arnold jumped at the sight of the dog.

"Is it Tad and Val? C'mon here boy, and I'll give you a bite," said Arnold, dangling a piece of sausage.

The dog barked a quick hello to Dat, then sauntered over to Arnold for a snack.

Dat snuck a glance at Val out of the corner of his eye as she surprised him with a hug.

"How are you doing, Dat? I've been worried about you. I heard Jeremy got kicked out of Thompson High for good. Just what he deserves," Val said.

"Well, I placed a call to Administration and demanded that Jeremy's parents pay Dat's reconstruction bills. But they probably have more important things to consider after the terrorist attack. Dat, please prepare a plate for Val," said Elise.

Dat smiled broadly and heaped huge portions of Val's favorite, biscuits and gravy. His brain waves sifted through his recipes earlier, and suddenly he knew her favorites. He didn't know what to say to Val right now; he just wanted to keep on cooking even if the kitchen was overflowing with pots, pans, and cooking utensils. But Mora and Tron quickly cleaned up.

"Tu es faim?" Dat asked Val.

"Yes, I'm very hungry and love these biscuits," she said.

Speaking French again? But I guess Val understood. I want to stop and talk, but as long as my guardians are here, I need to cook, show my worth.

Elise and Arnold gobbled up their entrees as if they had never seen food before. They became giddy as they opened a second bottle of Merlot and even offered Val a glass.

"Val, have a glass, even the French give wine to their children. Will your parents mind?" asked Arnold.

"Not at all, besides they're not here now," said Val, taking a large gulp.

She blushed after downing her glass.

Dat placed his final concoction on the table. Baked Alaska, a favorite of Tony's.

"Oh my, we'll need to spend the day at the gym after this food," said Arnold, his eyes bright.

Even Tad salivated and jumped.

"This is the best meal you've ever made, and I think you've exceeded yourself," said Arnold.

Elise nodded. "Honey, let's drink the rest of our wine on the balcony. I'm sure the kids want to catch up. You're welcome to spend the night; I think Dat needs his BFF his first night home."

Val looked at her vibrating watch and then ignored it. "It's my Mom, and she doesn't care—she's at the hospital with Dad."

His guardians left the room, arm in arm, leaving him alone with Val. He bent down to pet his dog, who licked his hand and cheek. Then Val joined him on the floor with Dat and her jade eyes mesmerizing him.

"Let's go to your room," she whispered and took his hand.

Confused, he followed her and watched her collapse on the bed. What did she want? He felt numb, his sensors now anesthetized. It was as if his memories were zapped. Val wrapped her arms around him and whispered in his ear.

"I missed you. Your guardians are so nice, and they don't even mind if I stay here. Now we can be together," said Val.

She kissed his neck, and it tickled.

"My memory's been wiped. The accident screwed with my sensors. I can't figure out how we met."

Val took his hand in hers.

"Silly—you helped me escape the attack on the Gala and then this last one at Thompson High. I like you, and you like me. We're destined to be together."

Dat stared into her jade-green eyes, searching for answers. Did Tony De LaFleur have a girlfriend? Then flashes of bodies, blood, and Val's crying stirred his senses like little pieces of a puzzle.

Tad jumped on him and arched his back.

"He wants to be petted, and we named him—your name spelled backward."

Val laughed and buried her face in the dog's neck. Dat began petting his head and tail.

"Yes…it's coming…back to me."

"What did they do to you? Scramble your brain?"

Dat scratched his head and stared into her tender eyes.

"They put me back together and then viewed my brain waves via computer. May have erased some memories in the process. I'm programmed to be a chef…and care for my guardians. But I can't stop thinking of you."

Then Val tickled him and kissed his mouth. His senses now were on fire, and he took her in his arms. The pool scenes, kissing on the Skytrain, his urge to save her all tumbling around in his brain. His sensitivity tracks surged, and his right brain overrode the left. Val and Dat fell on the bed, their arms wrapped in a passionate embrace. Circuits exploding, sensors blazing, and electrical jolts rushed through him.

Then a loud boom sounded, lights flickered out, and they were in complete darkness.

"Woof, woof," Tad, jumping back on the bed, his tail wagging excitedly.

Val's watch vibrated and blinked red. The governor's urgent hologram appeared.

"The Capitol is on lockdown. The RRG has bombed RI. Remain calm and stay in your homes, we're at threat level red."

Val pulled away from him; her face contorted and her eyes enormous. Dat sensed her fear, took her hand, and grabbed Tad with his free arm.

"Let's find Elise and Arnold. They'll know what to do," said Dat.

Warning sirens blared. Helicopters circled the apartment complex, their noise deafening. Screams and a rapid burst of popping noises erupted. A rapid pounding of footsteps sounded.

"Val and Dat…head to the panic room…Now," bellowed Arnold. Dat heard the secret doors opening, and the two raced to safety. The romantic moment was suddenly crushed.

CHAPTER 4

They seem so cool, not getting upset about anything. I thought they were elite, but they're really just simple people. And treating Dat like a son.

Val watched the Landers make the sound-proof room into a small apartment. Pressing his com watch, Arnold set up beds, couches, and nightstands as they emerged from the walls. A panel slid open to reveal a kitchen stocked with water and food, and another door opened to show a bathroom with a toilet and shower. Elise made them chamomile tea and gave them PJs to wear.

What else can happen? We could be stuck down here for days, not knowing what the real situation is like. Maybe the world is ending, and there's nothing left of humanity. What about Whit? Did my grandmother survive?

Her watch revealed RI's gaping hole in the side of its building, no longer glowing and the BOT letters missing. People's homes burning in the lower districts and the Capitol's walls surrounding it like a fortress. Flying space copters swirling overhead and many bodies and robot parts littering the streets.

"Stop watching—it will just make you sick. Come play this game with us," said Elise.

A virtual bowling alley flashed on the wall, and Elise already made a strike. Dancing minions cheered and danced at her score. Tad leaped and wagged his tail. Dat took his turn and looked back at her with a smirk on his face as he pulled off a strike. They played and laughed until they almost collapsed. Val sighed and paced the room. Dat and Elise looked for some snacks in the portable kitchen.

"C'mon Val eat something even if it tastes like rabbit food. You gotta keep up your strength. I know we'll make it...We're survivors of the Great

Divide. Luckily, I didn't contract the virus at that time, being a white male. I'll show you some footage," said Arnold.

A virtual screen dropped, showing a dystopian warzone as a Digital War broke out. Races and genders tore into each other on social media with more mass shootings in neighborhoods and the workplace. People only communicated on social media and were afraid to talk to each other. As white males contracted the virus and died, a coalition of women banded together, including Val's grandmother.

Val gasped to see her grandmother working with the Landers as they provided their ideas and expertise at the Capital hearings.

"I worked with Dr. Simms to abolish social media and formed GNet. She asked for technical assistance, and I was an e-tech engineer at ECorp, and Elise was a marketing consultant for InstaNews. I created the infrastructure, and Elise promoted it," said Arnold.

Arnold flipped to a lab filled with scientists and engineers as the Landers showed off their discovery to Dr. Simms and her team of renowned women.

"That's my grandma...didn't know that you worked together," said Val.

Arnold smiled broadly.

"She enlightened the world with her ideas...very perceptive. A great lady that I admire very much," said Elise.

They watched the historical movies for hours, and Val learned more about the Great Divide than she had from her History classes. Even Dat and Tad seemed captivated by these events.

Each night they settled in all together on the fold-out couches, sleeping bags, and comfy chairs. Val noticed no one made a sound as they awaited the signal to return to normal. Comforted, she fell asleep beside Dat on a sleeping bag with little Tad between them.

36 hours later

She awoke to her buzzing com watch and a neat empty room. Even Tad was gone. She almost panicked but found a note by her sleeping bag.

We didn't want to disturb you. The All Clear came at 6 a.m., but you were sound asleep. When you're ready, press the red button on the

wall, and the room will slide open. Take the stairs to the kitchen. See you later—Elise.

Val stretched and checked her watch. Only five new messages from her Mom.

How annoying, Val thought and headed for the shower. She stood in the hot, steamy spray for ten minutes and found some clean clothes laid out for her. She fixed her hair in a tight ponytail, smudged her lips with pink gloss, and went to find Dat.

The strong smell of brewing coffee and cinnamon French toast flowed out into the hallway. She exhaled and met Elise in her bathrobe, pouring coffee and watching the news on the wall monitors.

"Morning sunshine. Coffee?" said Elise.

"Uh…good morning. Thanks…where's everyone? Is it okay to go out?" Val said and took the steaming cup.

"The governor gave us an ALL CLEAR and they've arrested more robots. Look, they've arrested Zag—he's the leader."

The monitors zoomed in on the wiry Zag, a Model 500 who stood shackled in a cage in front of the Capitol with swarms of police and National Guard surrounding him.

"Zag isn't talking, but his guardian found weapons in their garage and reported him missing from the premises," said the broadcaster.

"What a world we live in when our servants try to kill us. If you're looking for Dat, he's walking Tad with Arnold. Tad needed to go out. They wanted to survey any damage that had been done. But after I have my coffee, I need to run after being cooped up for days. Want to join me at the park for a jog? It's so nice to have another female around," Elise said, a huge smile on her face.

Val looked closely at this woman, who seemed older than her Mom, but looked young and chic with her green-streaked black bob, long floral robe, and black velvet slippers. Her mom never had the time to spend with her, and now this woman wanted to go jogging later. This woman was not in a hurry, didn't make her eat breakfast, or tell her what to do.

"Yeah…sounds good. We'll go for a run when they come back," said Val.

She sipped her coffee and joined Elise in eating a plate of French toast.

"That was so nice of you to come here for Dat. He really needs a friend right now. It's a hard transition for him," said Elise.

A short buzz on the intercom and the monitor showed a doorman and a woman.

"Ma'am, Ms. Landers, there's a woman here that says her daughter is staying with you, and she wants to talk to her. What should I tell her?"

Elise looked at Val, who blushed a deep shade of red.

"It's my mom…I'm so embarrassed. Please…I don't want to talk to her right now."

"Well…maybe she's worried from the alert and all. I don't mind her coming up."

Meredith's face appeared on the monitor.

"Honey, Val…I just want to see if you're all right. It was so scary these last few nights. Your grandma said you were staying with the Landers. Can I talk to you just for a minute?"

Val sighed and shook her head no.

"Hi Meredith, this is Elise. Your daughter is doing well but isn't able to speak to you now. Val is no trouble at all, and we don't mind her staying here with us. Can you call before coming next time? Thanks!"

The doorman appeared on the monitor.

"She's gone, Ms. Landers. Was crying but left a package to give to Val Tate."

"Okay, just bring it up. Thanks, Edgar."

"See what I have to put up with…and I'm almost eighteen…in just two weeks. Thanks, Elise, for taking care of that."

So pushy…just came right here. Elise must think I'm a real baby. Maybe Mom will understand that I don't want to talk or see them. I'll have to send her a message to bug off.

Just as Val finished her second cup of coffee, the doorman knocked on the door. Elise took the package and handed it to Val.

"I'll leave you alone. Arnold and I have a conference call with the governor and will be tied up for a while.

Val took the package and stared at it for a minute. A part of her wanted to open it, and the other part was afraid. At least Elise understood how she felt and gave her some space. She needed a break from her parents. But curiosity got the better of her, and she opened the small box. In it was her Pooh Bear with a note.

> **"Dear Val,**
> **Here's your favorite toy. It always brings back good**
> **memories, doesn't it? We need to make things right.**
> **Your grandma assured me that you're all right for now.**
> **But this latest alert makes us terrified we' ll never**
> **see you again. The RRG has invaded the Capitol, and**
> **everyone is being threatened. Please come home, it's**
> **not safe now. The Landers are probably busy with their**
> **own affairs. Dat will understand if you want to see**
> **your parents, plus he has his guardians. We could**
> **make you come home, but we want you to have some**
> **freedom to make your own decisions.**
> **Love, Mom"**

What is she thinking? I'm almost eighteen. They don't even realize how important Dat is to me. I can't even address the elephant in the room—that I'm in love with Dat. It makes me so angry. And I'm probably safer with the Landers; at least there's a wall around the Guild District.

She quickly fired off a response in a hologram.

"Why did you come to the Landers? You embarrassed me so much, and you don't even know why. As you know, I'm turning eighteen and will be an ADULT. So, I will be able to make my own decisions from now on. Dat and his family have been wonderful to me and said I can stay as long as I want. Even Grandma supports me and says I need to stay away and get my head straight for now. Please try to understand."

"You and Dad are hypocrites. Dad says he believes in equality for robots, but then when I want to see Dat, he forbids me. And you will do anything the governor says. I expected more of both of you. I'm so disgusted right now. I just want to live my life and handle things my own way."

"Please, stop calling me. I really don't want anything to do with you. I am beyond hurt, and you will never understand it or accept it," she shouted.

Val's outburst scared Tad as they walked in the door. Tad barked and jumped on her. Dat stepped back and looked at her strangely. Arnold patted her shoulder and hurried to the kitchen.

"Are you okay? What's wrong?" Dat asked.

Val started to cry.

"My parents and I got into a big fight while you were getting healed, so I went to stay with my grandma. I don't want to see them, and my mom showed up this morning and left a package. I'm so MAD, and I can't get over this. They wanted me to stop seeing you, and I won't," Val said.

CHAPTER 5

Why don't they like me? Val's mom cared when I rescued her at the Gala. Now they don't understand our feelings for each other. We'd die for each other. Is it because I'm a robot and we're less than human? Dr. Tate doesn't realize how our human brains have affected how we act and how we feel. How Tony is a part of me, not just as a chef but his emotions as well. We have the ability to love. I guess it scares them.

Dat's sensitivity trackers adjusted as he gazed at Val's puffy eyes and clenched fists. Was she angry or sad? Maybe both. He wanted to protect her from her pain, even if it was her parents. Outside his neighborhood remained untouched and still beautiful, but just beyond, he noted the dirt and rubble of older neighborhoods and armed police barricades. The carbon graphene walls protected the Guild Tower District island's 3D printed light gray plastic apartments, according to Arnold, who said they were built in early 2040. His acute senses picked up blood and the smell of burnt metal and rotting bodies below. A continuous alarm hammered in his brain, and the painful cries gave him chills. Dat turned to Arnold for answers.

Arnold said the reason was a misunderstanding of the robots and humans. Both wanted a better society, but robots were going about it in the wrong way. Humans created them, so the robots needed to respect them just like he and Elise did. They cared for Dat and had him fixed instead of sending him to the junkyard. Dat agreed with him, but he was still angry. Angry for his kind that were terminated and now for Val's mistreatment by her parents and their sudden dislike of him. Dat needed to do something.

His circuits electrified, and his sensors blazed. If he didn't calm down, he would overheat. Little Tad tugged at his leg, and Val pulled him close to her. Then an idea came to him.

"Let's find Grace Noble. She'll tell us the truth," said Dat.

An incoming message alerted Val. Her face brightened, and she looked like the beautiful young woman he was first attracted to.

"Whit told me there's a meeting at noon today underneath the old overpass just outside the City. Grace plans to be there to discuss her plans to fight the injustice. We should go now since the Landers are busy placating the governor."

⟶✦═◉═✦⟵

Haze and dust filled the air, but the atmosphere was devoid of sound as they marched toward the Skytrain's platforms. Dat took a seat, and they whizzed by the devastated Thompson High's South campus, watching it disappear from sight. Whit said to get off at the old Highway 210 ramp. They passed tall weeds and some tents. His acute senses picked up the scent of humans, but mostly metallic.

"Get off here," said Dat.

They turned the corner and were met by Whit, who waved them down and guided them to the center of the rally, as Grace Noble spoke from a wheelchair her staff set up for her. The crowd numbered five hundred and stretched along the arch of the former overpass. Some old rusting SUVs from the 2020 era were parked strategically close by in case of a quick getaway.

Whit hung back and blended in the background with his torn jeans and dirty sweatshirt that hid his green face.

"Hey, I'm covering for the GNet so I can't be seen, but secretly I believe in their cause. So, pretend you don't know me," Whit whispered.

"Don't worry, we've never met you before," Val joked.

Dat nodded and moved closer. He still didn't understand their friendship and right and left brains fought to keep calm. Grace's purple hair glistened in the sun, and her voice was strong and clear.

"Today a robot has been singled out and convicted before evidence has been gathered. Zag has been convicted of a crime because of planted evidence. His guardians told police he was stashing guns and ammunition, but the story is that he wanted independence. He trained to be a gardener, but they had him rebuilding and fixing things 24 hours a day without any rest periods, which is against Robot Role Rule #571. Zag got fed up and left for a midnight run.

Police picked him up at 12:02 a.m. and then caged him per Robot Control Enforcement (RCE) policy. He never put up a fuss and was not belligerent. And Dr. Tate, the famous robots' designer and scientist, has chosen to testify against one of the models he has created. We need to do something about the evil RI and their next plans. But it is this rush to justice by Governor Thompson. What are we going to do about that?" said Grace, her voice booming over the crowd.

"The Great Divide strikes again, now targeting us mechanical folks. I say RRG is not effective and maybe too militant," shouted a robot, his arm dangling and an eye socket exposed.

"We need to protest the curfew that has been in effect for over a year and demand our freedom," said another robot, his silver-banded arm-waving.

Others echoed words of protest and held up signs and photos of mutilated robots. Dat lingered on the fringes of the rally, not wanting to be seen, but to pledge support for Grace Noble. Val hung on his arm, and Tad wrapped his body around his legs.

"Later this evening, we will be forming a chain in front of the Capitol, even though it's a bad omen for me. We need everyone's support, both human and robot, to form this blockade around the perimeter so no one can get in or out. I also have an effigy of the governor, and I want to make a statement," said Grace.

The rally ended as Grace's nurse, and caregiver held up their hands to the mob.

"Grace needs her rest before tonight's rally. We ask that you leave now and meet at RI at 7 p.m. Thank you," said her nurse.

"I want to go to the rally tonight…but now security is watching my every move," said Dat.

"I'll talk to the security guards and the Landers, and you can slip away, but first…I want to talk to Grace," said Val.

They pushed people and robots aside, stepping on toes and angering some in their frenzy to leave. Val flagged her entourage down, yelling her name and finally made their way to the front. Grace was being led to an old battered SUV.

"Wait. Grace Noble…wait…I have a suggestion," said Val.

Grace Noble looked up as her bodyguards congregated around her with hands on their weapons, forming a barrier.

"Let her talk…oh, it's the Tate girl. Are you a messenger from your father and the governor? I really don't want to hear this," said Grace.

"Not at all…I'm not speaking to them. It's because of him…my boyfriend, Dat. I'm against the horrible treatment of robots, and I want to help you," Val said, breathing hard.

Grace wheeled her chair past her bodyguards and stared intently into Val's eyes.

"For some reason, I believe you. Why are you willing to do this? Are you crazy?"

Val took Dat's hand in hers.

"Crazy…in love…with him. He's a Model 500, but I don't care. Us— we deserve a chance to be together," said Val.

Dat's left and right brains struggled, and his head ached. What did she say? Love and as in a couple? But his sensitivity tracks triggered, and he recalled his feelings the other night—his senses and circuits burning. Was he becoming more human? He searched his memory tracks to see if Tony had answers.

They had a connection, and he wanted to protect her. And she cared for Tad. He couldn't define love, didn't know what it meant for robots. But with Val, it felt special, and he liked having her around. Important enough to fight for robots and humans to be together.

Grace looked a little skeptical, frowning, and ready to turn her wheelchair around.

Dat and Val blocked her from leaving.

"Okay, and your parents don't approve? I get it. What's your plan?"

"Break in after the rally…I know how to get into RI. Maybe you can find the answers you're looking for."

Grace's eyebrows shot up, and suddenly she was beaming.

CHAPTER 6

Her mind raced. Meeting Grace was a real rush to Val, and she could barely contain her excitement over this upcoming evening. As they walked in the door of the apartment, she found Elise waiting for her with presents. Her mind diverted from saving robots to just being a teen girl.

"Val, I'm so excited that we're going to run together, that I picked up some outfits. Let me show you," said Elise.

Elise dumped out Nike shoes, jackets, VS pants, and tops on the kitchen table.

"Not sure what colors and styles you like, so I bought several. Your choice."

She smiled at Val and gave her a big hug.

Val was overwhelmed by this woman's generosity and lacked any words to express herself. She hadn't received anything new in a long time and marveled at the sheer volume of outfits to choose from.

"Like this one—let's change and go now before dinner. Besides with Dat's cooking and all those calories…we need some exercise," said Elise.

They discovered they liked a pink and gray combination and laughed at their similar styles.

"We both have good taste," said Val as she adjusted her pink headband.

Val kissed Dat before departing out the front door. He gave her a thumbs-up as he glanced at her outfit.

"What about Tad? I'll start dinner while you're gone…" said Dat.

The little bulldog jumped on Val with a leash in his mouth.

"Be careful…you may want to take a security guard with you. Still not safe out there," yelled Arnold as he watched the news on the wall monitors.

"We'll be just fine…we have a feisty dog to protect us," shouted Elise, winking at Val.

Both women checked each other out in the mirrored elevator. Val never did casual things with her mother, who was always preoccupied lately with work. Now it was just two women sharing a moment together. Out of the elevator into the gated park area near the Metro Apartments, they took off slowly as Elise tried to keep up with Val. But they developed a rhythm and talked about Dat. Val recognized this area near the tunnel and heard the swoosh of the Skytrain nearby. But she concentrated closely on Elise's shocking comments.

"We never had children of our own, and Dat has become like an adopted son. He's smart, kind and of course quite a cook. Never thought he could have a girlfriend. Do you mind that he's...a robot?" said Elise.

"Uh...it's not a problem. He's more considerate and fun than other boys I've hung around with. Totally fine," said Val.

She wasn't sure if she wanted to share her true feelings for Dat with this woman. She seemed open-minded, but she couldn't really trust Elise. Even though she treated Dat like a son, he was still their chef and someone who worked for them.

They ran in unison together, and Val was impressed with how Elise kept up with her, with her e-shoes in low gear. Sometimes they slowed down to a quick walk and then speeded up again to skirt around people in the neighborhood. Val received a bleep on her watch and looked away. She was being tracked and wanted to avoid contact.

"Hey Elise, let's go along the shore for a better view," said Val.

"Val, honey, is that you? I need to talk to you," said a female hologram that sounded close behind.

Val took a sharp turn to the left, while Tad split off to the right.

"Slow down, someone's calling you, and your dog just went in the opposite direction," said Elise, running after the dog.

Val stopped to face her mother.

Stupid technology—how did she catch up with me?

"What's up? Why are you following me? I just want you to leave me alone," said Val, her face red from exhaustion and irritation.

"It's good to see you—just happened to be in the neighborhood and tracked your location. Glad to see that you're all right after that RRG attack. Dad is home and resting. Will we see you for your birthday?" said her mother.

Her mother embraced her, but Val stiffened at her touch. She smelled the lilac perfume and felt the soft embrace.

Her eyes scrutinized her mother's casual leggings and sweatshirt, her hair in a tight bun. For a minute, Val felt homesick, wanting to hug her mother and ask about her father. But she held back now that she was with Elise. This other woman made her feel like an equal and not a child. She saw her coming toward them out of the corner of her eye. But these two women facing each other was almost too much to handle.

"It's nice to see you again. Sorry we couldn't talk the other day about your birthday celebration," said Elise.

Elise wiped her brow and held Tad firmly in her grip.

"Yeah…Mom, we're kind of in a hurry. And my birthday is no big deal, so I probably will just have dinner with Dat. But say hi to Dad for me," said Val.

Her mother gulped and stepped back abruptly. Her eyes never left Val, ignoring Elise.

"Oh…well, I think you forget that I'm still your mother and that we worry about you. We've said things we shouldn't have, and now we regret what's happened. We understand you want to be on your own, but we want you to experience life and not do things hastily. And Elise—thank you for taking her in," said Meredith, her voice trembling.

Elise looked at Val and then her mother.

"There's definitely a resemblance…same auburn hair and hazel eyes. Your daughter is a joy to have around. And she's helping Dat to adjust and back to his old self," said Elise.

Val bent down to fix Tad's leash as he wagged his tail at her mom. She desperately wanted her mother to go away. It was extremely uncomfortable to deal with her mom and Elise at the same time.

"Please come home soon—I love you," said her mom as she crouched down to pet Tad at Val's eye level. Her eyes begged Val to connect with her.

"I can't, and I won't. C'mon Elise, let's go," said Val, avoiding her mother's face.

The three jogged off toward the beach area, leaving her mother standing alone.

"Val—your mom seems very concerned about you. Maybe you should go home to check on your Dad. He suffered while the rest of us escaped that terrible attack. What do you want to do?" said Elise.

She stopped Val and grabbed her arm as she spoke softly to her. The words weren't accusing or probing, and Val appreciated Elise's advice.

"Um…I know, but Mom forgets that I'm an adult. If my dad was hurt or failing, I would go home. But he's recovered now. I'm still upset that he didn't give Dat a chance because he's…I don't respect him for that. My parents are against me having a robot for my boyfriend…we're not even serious. It's my life, and I want to stay with you guys," said Val.

Elise smiled and took Val's hand in hers.

"I respect your reasons, and of course, you're welcome to stay. Now let's get back before it gets dark," said Elise.

⋄→══◯══→⋄

It was so easy sneaking out of the apartment after dinner. I talked the security guards into taking the night off, and I'm glad Elise and Arnold aren't the snoopy parent types thought Val as they meshed into the crowds. The human-mech-chain gained momentum as supporters; mostly robots joined the barrier around the city, past Thompson High, the hospital, and then gathered at the Capitol's platform. Robots in silver armbands waved signs that said, *Life, Liberty, and the Pursuit of Happiness for All…and Robots.* A huge ballooned head of the governor bobbed in the breeze.

Val and Dat, both dressed in drab clothes and hats that covered their features, kept out of sight, close to the edge of the protesters. The little bulldog, afraid of the noise and shouting, lay buried in Dat's chest with Val clutching his arm. Grace Noble was nowhere in sight.

"Release Zag. Release Zag," they cried.

A trail of silver-lit armbands rushed around a figure in black, his steel arms and legs exposed. Their light provided a soft glow around a grungy-looking man in ragged clothes.

"Hey brother bots, stand up for your fellow models, demand equality and respect. All Models Unite. Look at me—part chrome, part flesh due to fighting in the Great Divide. Live free," he yelled, his face half-metallic, half-human.

"Don't Let Big RI Control You. I'm standing up for Zag," said a younger Model 300 with his baby face and mechanical body.

Then he threw a flare into the courtyard, followed by some snaps that exploded upon contact with the ground.

"Hey, we don't want you here in our neighborhood. Go do your jobs," said a voice from one of the high rises above.

"Get out of here, let us have some peace," boomed another voice into the night air.

Red laser lights flashed on the disrupters.

The crowd roared as the police arrived.

"Won't go till we're free," they shouted with a loud clanking of metal.

Val's watch vibrated. Grace's hologram appeared.

"Stay under the radar and meet us at RI's back parking lot D. They're using the protests as a diversion so I can complete my mission. Can you get us in?"

Val was stunned and awestruck. How was she going to get past these crowds? Didn't Grace know that RI was guarded 24 hours a day?

"Uh...yeah...have access. But *you* may run into guards," she texted Grace.

The square grew chaotic, and the platform swayed as the police attempted to control the protestors. Many were arrested, and barricades were being set up. Val pulled on Dat and squeezed past the oncoming stampede.

"Grace needs our help. Need to jump on the Skytrain to RI asap," she said to Dat.

Her body tensed as she observed the mania below from the Skytrain. The robots had built a steel wall of metal with their figures around the police barricade. Their shouts echoed in the darkness. Val knew it was getting late, and they were in danger of being exposed and arrested. She hoped Grace knew what she was doing.

Dat took her hand, pulling her back to reality.

"Are we going to RI? Don't like this. We've got to hide Tad, so he doesn't make any noise," said Dat.

They reached a wooded area behind the building per Grace's instructions and found her flanked by her bodyguards. She looked like a doctor in her lab coat and tan trousers, her purple hair hidden by a curly blond wig.

"You still want to help me? I know both of you could get into deep trouble…banishment, and school expulsion. If you're willing, let's see if we can enter without an issue and see if they're hiding anything," said Grace.

Her eyes focused solidly on Val.

Val exhaled. "Yes…if it will help the cause…I'll risk it."

She entered a secret entry, hidden by tall polyethylene bushes. Her father had taken her through this way many times on weekends. She used a simulation of her dad's eye imprint to part the bushes and revealed the hidden wall. Then she punched in the key code, and a transparent door opened into a dimly lit hallway. Val remembered that only key administrators had access, and the entrance was not heavily guarded.

"Stop…don't go any further," said a Model 500 in a security uniform with a taser in one hand, the other under a desk.

Val knew the guard could press the alarm any minute.

"But I'm Dr. Stone…forgot some paperwork earlier. These are my associates and Val, Dr. Tate's daughter, who's assisting me tonight," said Grace, moving ahead of the group.

The Model 500 seemed to scan their faces. His eyes lit up as he recognized Val. But then he zoomed in on Dat.

"Hi, Von, nice to see you," said Val.

"You're all okay…but the dog…is not permitted," said the guard, his eyes focused on the squirming bulldog.

Val tightened her grip on Dat, whose fingers curled into fists. Her stomach formed knots. The situation could move to a standoff if not handled properly.

CHAPTER 7

His eyes narrowed, and his sensors triggered to the breaking point. He let go of Val and stepped forward nose to nose with his rival Von.

"The dog is coming with us. He's not staying behind," Dat said, eyeballing the Model 500.

"Rules are no animals allowed," said Von, his muscular arm attached to a taser. Then numerous doors opened, and a parade of Model 300s descended upon the group.

They rushed the small party, weapons engaged and baring down swiftly upon them. Val sucked in air and looked for the closest exit. Tad jumped down, barking wildly and growling, showing a mouthful of sharp teeth.

Grace's bodyguards sprang into action, taser guns set, and ready to defend Grace's vulnerability.

"Reverse direction and stand down," commanded Grace as they advanced toward the group.

"Woof, woof," said Tad, biting one Model 300 on its leg.

The 300s stopped in mid-step and turned around, heading for the open doorway where they emerged, except the one bitten by Tad, who spun around and fell down.

"I created that command, and it always works. Knew it would come in handy," said Grace.

Val stood in awe. Not even her dad used that order.

Then Grace's bodyguards stood their ground and advanced swiftly toward Von, who picked up his weapon, aiming at them. They overpowered him, knocking him down as the gun hit one of the bodyguards in the shoulder. The bodyguard shook his shoulder in pain, then snapped back to grab the taser as the others deposited the mechanical man into a nearby closet as Grace, Dat and Val moved toward the development areas.

"Close call, just keep that dog quiet. Don't have much time, need to get to R & D," said Grace.

Dat contained himself, uneasy about being back in places where he shouldn't be. This was unauthorized territory. Did he really want to discover something about his birth or origin? And Tad didn't belong here—he needed to go outside. Wasn't it time for him to pee? The little dog struggled to free himself as the group advanced toward the lab area. Dat vaguely remembered this large open section with exposed ceilings and multiple levels. Only glass walls separated the rooms filled with computers, wall monitors, testing areas, robotic parts, and even the various models.

"Do you remember how they programmed you? Can you recall the process?" Grace directed the question at Dat.

Dat stood there, speechless. They turned off his sensors, so he couldn't recall any of their actions. His memory banks failed him at this moment.

"Uh…much was kept from me during my reconstruction…just like a human operation. Sort of like sedation," said Dat.

"Let's see if my code still works and if I can get into the system," said Grace, her fingers flying over the keys.

The system hiccupped at her touch as she tried different passwords. Grace became frustrated as minutes turned to an hour.

"Extremely frustrating. I know you've been here before. I want the Genealogy secrets and to stop this project," said Grace, glancing at Val.

Dat sensed Val's discomfort as she trekked through the huge lab to his office. The world-renowned Dr. Tate was the mastermind on the new Model 500s. Only he knew the secret of brain-to-robot implants. Many celebrities donated their brains upon death after hearing his talks on "Robot Realism."

"Um…I'll try to use his code, but not sure if it will work. Dad may have changed it. However, I can take you to Reconstruction," Val said.

They followed her down a long, transparent hallway, the offices lighting up to reveal their interiors. Their footsteps echoed through the still halls. Dat was surprised there was not more security, but his keen eyesight picked up the tiny bug-like cameras on the walls. By tomorrow everyone would know the group had entered the building. His identity and security were at risk again, and if Elise and Arnold found out, he was doomed.

The rooms contained a massive number of cubicles and stations, marked by numbers on the tall columns separating them. It would be almost impossible to find Dr. Tate's office or the Reconstruction area. And he couldn't recall anything since they turned off his mind when he was in the repair phase.

He watched Val press up against a wall that opened into a lab, filled with tables, monitors, and carts. It shocked him to see various Model 500s scattered throughout the area in various states of disrepair—arms lying next to bodies, heads poking out of sheets, others posed in chairs, or at desks. A monitor appeared to be on, displaying a series of memory sequences with robots hooked up to them, draining them of their histories.

"I don't feel comfortable being here. I think we should leave before they find us. The 300s probably will alert the police," said Val.

Dat focused on those scenes, mesmerized by the human emotions displayed, the passages of uninterrupted scenes like a plot to a story. His brain banks remembered bits and pieces of his own restoration time and sickened by how they took away some of his memories. His sensitivity trackers emitted sadness for these 500s who, like him, were still controlled by their human creators. Even though Dat cared about his guardians, he still wanted more, believing his destiny to be the greatest chef of all time. With Tony's genes and experiences, he could accomplish his dream. But were they destroyed after this recent reconstruction? Was he fated for the junkyard if they found him here tonight? His circuits shuddered at the thought, hot electrical impulses surging through his body.

"Keep moving...you promised to help us. Don't freak out now," said Grace. Her eyes smoldered, and her lips curled in disdain.

Dat sensed a presence and took Val's hand.

"What are you doing here? No one is allowed in this area at this time. And is that you Dat, my buddy? Why are you with these humans?" said a male voice.

The figure stepped out of the shadows and revealed himself. Thin, with thick chestnut-colored hair, freckles, and stone-gray eyes, a young man faced Dat. Their eyes met, and Dat gasped at his friend, built at the same time, and looked like a male version of the governor.

"Uh...helping Dr. Stone," said Dat.

"Don't recognize Dr. Stone. We met during your last Reconstruction, but I'm here being cloned. The governor also wanted sons but couldn't have any, so she created my brothers and me. Our brains came from the Thompson descendants," said the young man.

Two more of the governor look-alikes joined the group.

"What a narcissist—if this gets out, the governor and her clan will be run out of town. I'm appalled at what's going on here. Cloning your own genes goes against program procedures. We need to document this. All the more reason to win this rebellion," Grace said, taking snapshots with her watch.

Dat's sensors burned as his right and left brains collided. Confused and repelled, he felt the urge to leave immediately. Was he still original, or had he been altered like the governor's son? He held the writhing Tad tighter and glanced at an alarmed Val. Her eyes mirrored disgust and horror. He turned and took off back down the dim corridors with Tad whining in fright. Tad wiggled his way out of Dat's arms and jumped to the ground, leading the way out of the building. They both took off in a frenzy, not believing what they had seen.

"Wait, don't leave. We need to talk," yelled the cloned Model 500.

But he raced through the building, shadows leaping along the walls, lights going on and off as he passed through the rooms. He focused on the back entrance and breezed past the security area since the Model 500 security guard had been silenced. Outside, the air felt muggy and dense, as if a depressive curtain had dropped. But Dat kept running for miles, hoping that he would not get caught, never looking back or wondering if Val was right behind him. Obviously not with that disturbed look on her face.

CHAPTER 8

An ominous tone settled over the area as Grace and her bodyguards hurried to record their findings. Now in a state of shock, Val wondered how to handle this new piece of information. Cloning? The governor's robot sons? She wanted to cry and laugh at the same time. Maybe they'd already cloned Dat, and she didn't know it. Her dad would never approve.

Val was still angry about her last meeting with her parents, but she knew that her dad would never put the program in jeopardy. He told her he wanted to create robots to be like humans and not be altered in any way. Her dad showed her the results of his work several weeks ago before his accident. Didn't Val need to defend him?

"Hey, why did Dat run away? What's going on, and how did you get in?" said the Model 500.

He advanced toward Grace, his movements, and grand gestures similar to the Thompson family.

"This cloning must have shocked him. I'm Dr. Grace No...uh Stone. I work here and was called in to monitor these robots. Is there anything else happening here that we should know about?"

"Name's Trig Thompson. Uh...just had a memory cleansing. They said I behaved badly, and a correction needed to be made."

Val stared at him in awe. Her mind raced, and her head started to throb. So overwhelming and confusing.

"I messed up...I stayed out past curfew too many times to see my girlfriend. So, they erased it from my memory tracks. Now I don't even remember her name."

Val's pulse quickened. Would that happen to Dat? Maybe Elise and Arnold would send him back here if that happened and create another clone, a more obedient one.

"Wait…this isn't right. My dad would never allow this. It doesn't make sense. He always said he wanted the Model 500s to make their unique contribution to the world as per their donors' wishes," said Val.

Grace laughed.

"You're so naïve. Why do you think we're fighting for mechanical freedom? The governor wants a series of slaves and warriors to fight against her enemies. I saw her directive and argued against it. But they silenced me, and I was fired. Now I need to get into your dad's office. I worked on the GP and want to see his project advances. You said you would help me. If you don't, I will pin this on your dad, but I really just want to ruin the governor."

Val wished that she had followed Dat.

I am being used by Grace Noble as she tries to demonize my Dad. All I want to do is run, but I just want her off my back.

They left Trig and the Reconstruction area, heading toward her dad's office.

"Open his desk and get into his computer. I want specifics on the brain implants and experimentation."

Val pretended to pry the desk open but instead set off a voice-activated alarm.

"STOP now. Confidential material. Break-in recorded."

Grace flipped on one of his monitors and tried to initiate a password. The keyboard locked up, and a series of words appeared on the screen.

Do not enter. Do not enter. Do not enter. Do not enter. Do not enter. Do not enter. Do not enter. DO NOT ENTER. DO NOT ENTER. DO NOT ENTER.

DO NOT ENTER. DO NOT ENTER. DO NOT ENTER. DO NOT ENTER.

A screeching alarm sounded.

Grace's bodyguards moved swiftly to search his office but stumbled against the walls closed in on them, and the room temperature climbed to one hundred degrees, and smoke spewed from the vents.

Val slipped under her dad's desk, hiding from the intruders. She curled up into a ball and held her breath, hoping she wouldn't be heard. She knew there was a secret tile under his desk where he hid a secret drive, breathing heavily from the heat.

"Geez—the room's fighting back. Did you know about this? Let's go before we get caught," said Grace, coughing and sweating profusely.

"What about the robot in R & D? Won't he talk and say he saw us? Also, the girl—can we trust her?" said a bodyguard with a resist tattoo on his arm.

Would they harm her? She needed to exit quickly. Where was Dat? Would he even help her? She wondered how this scenario had gone so wrong. Val thought she believed in Grace, but the activist turned on her. The alarm pierced through her ears, and red warning lights flashed off the walls. Her heart pounding and her body unable to move, Val feared they would discover her hiding place, or she would suffocate from the smoke.

"Forget her, let's get out…of here now. Can't breathe. Got photos and a recording from the clones…enough to blackmail the gov," said Grace.

The bodyguards picked up Grace, hoisting her on their shoulders and leaving Val behind to fend for herself. Squad cars raced down the streets, their sirens blaring. Val was trapped.

Her desire to be on her own and be with Dat backfired. Abandoned, scared, and totally alone, Val panicked. Lightheaded, sweating, and ready to vomit, she thought about hiding in this vast building. But she knew someone would find her and she would be caught. Embarrassed to call her parents and tell them the truth, she avoided contacting them. She fell to the ground and rocked back and forth, then settled down to think. She covered her eyes and sat with her head on her knees. Tears flowed from her eyes, blinding her from objective solutions.

What am I doing? Grace wanted revenge; her motives were not pure. Did Dad know about the clones? All I wanted to do was to help robotkind, and I messed up. My life is a wreck, and no one is around to help me. Even Dat left me here to handle everything. If I contact Grandma or Lucy, they'll know where I am and track me.

The sirens stopped with only the sounds of police dogs barking. No one had rushed into the building, and Val could only hear her breathing. Curious, she got up slowly and peered out the window. Police cars surrounded Grace and her bodyguards. Officers handcuffed them and shoved them into their vehicles. Val could barely make out the figures, but it looked like Grace was yelling, and her bodyguards were holding her back. In a matter of minutes, the police would find Val. She needed to pull herself together, stop crying, and vacate immediately.

Val remembered a secret exit when she was here with her father a few weeks ago. He used it to avoid security hassles and running into unwanted employees. She ran out of the office, looking both ways for any police. Unfortunately, the alarms still echoed through the building, and some overhead lights flashed on and off.

Val remembered her Dad's instructions:

Down the hallway to pillar 505, make a left past the bathrooms toward a utility closet where there's another door. The door to an emergency stairway, down twenty floors.

She heard voices as she opened the door and bounded down the stairs, almost tripping over her feet. Val pushed herself to go faster, knowing Grace had probably revealed her presence. Her legs burning, adrenaline flowing, and her lungs about to burst, she made it to the ground level, opened the door, and took off running into the night.

Her watch vibrated. It's got to be Dat.

"Grace Noble has just been arrested at RI and revealed your presence. Tracked your com watch. Stay hidden, and I'll be there in less than a minute…"

She breathed a sigh of relief as Whit drove up on his Turbo Z. Val hugged him and hopped on. In ten seconds, they flew above the chaos, the RI building far from sight, but the space copters still circling above.

"I've contacted your grandmother. She wants us to stay with her until this blows over. I think you will be exonerated since you are a minor, and Grace coerced you, right?"

"Technically, no—my 18th birthday is today."

"What the hell? This scenario mucks it up. And hey…where's Dat? At the Landers?"

Val muddled through her response, not knowing how to answer. He just ran off, and it really bothered her. Abandoned by the one you love was so painful—Val wanted to scream. She gave up everything for him, even her family.

"I don't know where he is…he was at RI with me, then just took off."

Val bit her lip and held back her tears. Instead, she got angry.

"I'm so done with him right now. Let's get to Grandma's fast. She'll know what to do."

They flew above the heavy smoke and fires below. Val gasped in awe at the charred hills, toppled buildings, and shallow lakes. Had the RRG done this, or were humans to blame?

CHAPTER 9

He ran like a maniac as he heard the police sirens hoping not to get caught and carried the little dog into his arms for what seemed like miles. Racing through the Capitol, Dat struggled to hold onto the whimpering, squirming dog who clawed at him to get down to the ground. His left brain kept him on track, logically focusing on getting away, escaping and reaching safety. Whatever that might be. Dat wanted to believe he didn't have a clone and was truly unique so carefully crafted by Dr. Tate and implanted with Tony De LaFleur's brain and skills. Seeing Trig's alter egos freaked him out.

OMG. How could I leave Val? She probably hates me. But I can't deal with her right now. She made me feel like a human, but yet all I am is a mechanical being that can be cloned. Tony gave me my identity, but are there others like me that exist? And Grace is not my hero anymore, using us to get what she wants. And how can I face the Landers when they gave me a second chance? I'll never be the chef that everyone admires.

His sensors adjusted as the sounds of wailing sirens stopped, and the sun began its ascent. Dat slowed down to catch his breath. The destroyed neighborhoods shocked him. The RRG leveled many poor homes, and the streets smelled of feces and rotten food. Garbage littered the shores, and blood-stained sidewalks alerted him to the current devastation. Tad looked up at him with round, frightened eyes as Dat unclasped his strong grip.

"Woof. Ruff...ruff," said Tad, as if talking to Dat.

Dat stared at the bulldog fondly, then looked around. No one was after him.

But this world wasn't home, far from the gold and glitter of the Gild Tower District's Metro Apartments. But he was finally on his own. Free for now with his dog, his companion. A world without rejection and discrimination. And that was something to be happy about.

"Whoa. Ha… I'm alive and can do…what I want," Dat said aloud, but no one answered him.

He wandered for a few blocks, then jumped on the train as a bright morning sun was breaking through the haze of the City. Surprised to see a packed train, Dat took the last remaining seat and kept the little bulldog close by. The train was unusually quiet, with passengers checking their com watches, listening for their stops, and focusing on their journey.

A man with slicked-back gray hair entered his section. His wild eyes perused the area, having found no available seats. He started spewing atrocities, harassing anyone in sight, a guy on a bicycle, a woman in a red suit drinking her morning coffee, and even the man standing next to him.

"Geez…what the hell. Never a seat for an old man. Make room for the elder. Get out of my way Bike Man. Look at me, lady, and stop drinking that coffee. Do you know who I am? The world now is full of bottom-feeders. Taking up space."

They all scrambled to escape his vile language. No one was free of his criticism and cruel tongue.

A seat opened up, and he planted himself next to a petite woman he described as "Mother Theresa," who was dressed in black with a veil. His heated language turned from English to Spanish as he ranted and raved at this poor woman. Tad fidgeted at his tone, but Dat stayed silent, not wanting to be exposed. He feared being exposed, escaping from RI.

But the man continued to taunt and badger the woman as she tried to answer his questions. The poor woman looked terrified and stared back at Dat, her eyes begging, "please help me." Dat sensed her panic, his sensitivity trackers engaged, and he noticed she was trapped in her seat by this bully. Tad whimpered and felt his anxiety. The bully's rantings became louder and more intense, and the woman continued to look for relief. No one moved to assist her.

No one's willing to stand up to this monster. I may be risking everything, but I won't let him hurt this old lady. It's now or never.

Dat exhaled with his circuits imploding. He tapped the woman on the shoulder.

"Do you want to move?" Dat asked.

The bully turned around, got up from his seat, and lit into Dat with a litany of accusations.

"Don't you dare touch her. You violated her. Leave her alone. Don't bother her," the bully shouted, his eyes penetrating Dat's.

The old woman trembled and moved quickly as a passenger offered to give up her seat. The bully continued his rage, directed his taunts at Dat.

"Who do you think you are? I'm a POLICEMAN, DOCTOR, BIOLOGIST. I wouldn't hurt a fly…just having a conversation, and you interrupted me. You're just the scum of the Earth."

Tad growled.

"Stop. I was just trying to help…not harm her," Dat said.

No one interfered as the bully pushed Dat to his limits.

"You're just a low life…dirt on the ground." He demonstrated as he stomped his foot.

Then the train's monitors relayed the late-breaking news stream.

"Grace Noble and her bodyguards broke into Robot International last night, stealing valuable information and disabling the security guard on duty and other Model 300s. Police say she had help from Val Tate, daughter of a scientist, Dr. Rod Tate, and a robot friend. Camera surveillance picked up these images. No one knows the whereabouts of the girl or the robot. If you see these individuals, please contact the police at this number. The robot had a tracking device and was also identified by a Model 500 who spoke to him."

The monitors showed Val and Dat's faces. The bully's eyes turned black, and words spit out of his mouth as he connected Dat with the monitor's image.

"Wow, you're a damn bot. A traitor who conspires with Grace Noble. You're even worse than a worm crawling along the ground. Disgusting mechanix–how dare you ride with humans. You make me sick. I'm gonna report you now. Look, everyone, this creep is that bot that broke into RI. He's with RRG. Get him!"

A group of humans sprang into action. Dat felt a hand grab his shoulder.

"We have a terrorist on this train. How did he get on?" yelled a man in a suit who pushed a button on his com watch.

The bully lunged for Dat as passengers started to scurry off at the next stop. The old lady screamed, and the woman in the red suit dropped her coffee.

"Woof, Woof, Woof." Tad barked and jumped at the bully who tried to kick him as he lunged at Dat.

Dat heard the space copters overhead as he jumped off at the next stop and ran in the opposite direction toward the outlying neighborhood. Police vans swarmed the area, and he could hear the screeching sirens. Tad let out a yelp as police tried to ambush Dat. Adrenaline pumping through his sensors, he ran with lightning speed, zigzagging through the dumpy modular homes, almost bumping into strangers and mothers seeing off their children to school.

Three policemen descended upon him. Agitation and fear built up inside him. His system went haywire as his left and right brains collided with confusion.

"Stop, we have you cornered. We'd rather not terminate, so give up now," said a voice from the space copter.

The police immediately tackled him, and the bulldog howled. Pulling his hands behind his back, they handcuffed him. Dat felt like his head was going to explode as his circuits overheated. They pushed his head into the back seat of the space van.

Now I'm screwed. Elise and Arnold will never let me back home. I ruined my chances of being like Tony.

A crowd gathered at the scene with the crazy old man at the center of it. The bully winked his twitching eye at the Sergeant and directed an evil, crooked smile at Dat.

"The big hero is nothing but a lowlife bot. You bots are all the same— stupid and predictable. You should have minded your own business, and that lady would have been fine. But you interfered, and all she'll remember is that you're a loser. Know that humans are in control and always will be. Thanks, officers," said the bully.

Dat gulped. He'd never be special. Where was Val? Did she turn him in?

As they shoved him in a space van, they promised him that this would be his last day. No time in jail, just a trip to the junkyard. And once he got there, the police took him to a secure room, showed him the surveillance tape, and threw him against the wall. He recognized the officer, another Thompson, brother of RI's CEO, who warned him of complete dismantlement. And supporting Grace Noble in the break-in was almost as serious as treason.

"You piece of junk… assisting that Noble woman and then trashing the RI building and Dr. Tate's office. If it was up to me, I'd disengage you right now and sell off your body parts. It says here that you're a chef for the Landers. Why can't you just stay home and cook for them? Instead, working with a traitor and that teen rebel—Val Tate. Another ungrateful, spoiled teen."

Dat hung his aching head, his circuits shutting down, his senses fearing mutilation and despair. He shuddered, remembering their threats and little Tad being tied up in another office. No one was coming to his aid.

CHAPTER 10

They huddled inside her grandmother's panic room, gripped with fear. Red alert warnings echoed throughout the city, even reaching the safe haven. Alerts on their com watches showed the two still at large. Val felt like a criminal. She never realized that she would be caught and now charged. Her life was a series of unfortunate circumstances since she met Dat. Was she really a robot advocate or a silly teen? Whit held Val's hand, and her grandmother smothered her with comforting words.

"Be strong and don't give in. I know you only wanted to help the mechanix cause and then got tied up in Grace's ugly scheme. She's a menace, and now you're blamed for her dirty deeds. I will back you all the way, even if your parents or the police don't. Your mother gave me holy hell, but I told her you were trying to do the right thing. She may never forgive me for defending your actions."

The panic room appeared insulated and soundproof. The guards protected her grandma's place like a fortress, but soon the police would find her. Hopefully, she would get off on a technicality. Whit stayed by her side even though Dat didn't. She believed that he was captured and maybe off to the junkyard.

Val shivered, and she wanted to vomit. But held her head up and asked for her grandma's advice.

"What should I do? I thought Grace just wanted access, but then admitted she wanted the GP's secrets and Dad's formulas. At that point, I knew it wasn't right. But then we discovered some clones—the governor's robots infused with her family's genes. Who is right?"

Her grandma smiled.

"Neither and that's what makes a strong activist to determine the right action. Defend your cause, but fight for your values. Don't you have influential friends? You'll have to organize and may have to take a different tactic. You'll figure it out, and this young man will help you. And don't give up on Dat—he's still out there and defenseless."

Her grandmother showed her a thirty-year-old relic—a digital photo of herself as she marched for equality for women and gay pride, leading the way across the San Francisco Bay Bridge.

"They called us millennials and said we just cared about ourselves. But we stood our ground and showed our acceptance of everybody."

Val laughed at the photo of her grandmother in a T-shirt that said, *We're Not Entitled; We're Committed.*

A basement monitor beeped, and one of the guards appeared on the screen.

"We're surrounded, and they know Val is here. Do we surrender her?"

Her grandmother gave Val a tight squeeze. "It's time, and my lawyers can help you."

"I'll handle it myself. I need to….face the consequences and make it right for the real Robot Rebellion with or without Dat."

"Let them in, and we'll be there in a minute. I'm so proud of you and don't worry if your parents don't agree with you. We had to fight our way to prove to our parents that we weren't the losers they always thought we were. Don't worry– it's your 18th birthday and you'll still be receiving your inheritance from me."

She hugged her grandmother tightly and whispered her thanks. Then the three took the elevator to the top floor where the police waited for Val. This birthday was the hardest and longest day of her life.

A flurry of space vans gathered in the driveway, and the officers pushed aside Whit and her grandmother in a hurry to handcuff Val.

"C'mon, get into the police van. You have a lot of explaining to do, you and that robot friend of yours," said one of the officers.

Whit flipped out his media credentials.

"I'm Whit Johnson from GNet covering the arrest of Val Tate. Nothing has been concluded, and I'm here at Dr. Simms's residence, Val's grandmother and former activist of the Great Divide."

"Hey, we didn't know that GNet would be covering this, but we have surveillance cameras putting Val Tate at the scene of last night's break-in at RI with Grace Noble and her cohorts. Very incriminating!" said Officer Nichols, his eyebrows arched and his hand close to his gun.

Val started shaking, as her grandmother looked on.

"Can't believe you're taking my granddaughter to jail. Is this really necessary? Is it because she's related to Dr. Tate's daughter and me? Grace Noble used her as a pawn to break into RI. Sounds like a win for the governor who wants to make a political statement and not for justice."

"With no disrespect, your granddaughter is not entirely innocent, and Grace Noble said she helped them get in and past the guard who knew her. That's her testimony when we picked Grace up at the scene," said Nichols.

Whit recorded everything, and it was only a matter of time, and her story would be circulated around the Internet. But it looked sympathetic toward Val with her grandmother's statement.

Val's watch vibrated, and a hologram of her father appeared.

"The governor told us you just got picked up by the police. And just saw the news flash. It's got to be mistaken identity. We'll come right away—you must be terrified. Glad you were with your grandmother. Not a good way to celebrate your 18th birthday," said her Dad.

Val ignored the call and stole a look at Whit and her grandmother. Besides, her hands were firmly behind her back as she was whisked hurriedly to the police station. The flight seemed endless, and her wrists hurt. In less than a minute, they landed, and Val was shuffled inside the station. She put on a brave face to meet Elise and Arnold, standing there waiting for her. She sighed in relief.

"We paid the bail sweetheart, and we'll have you and Dat sprung in a matter of minutes. The Police Chief has an apartment on the 29th floor, and we know him well. He informed us of this mishap, so we came right away," said Elise, giving her a hug.

Val buried her face into Elise's shoulder and mumbled a thank you.

"Take off those handcuffs, or we'll have your badge," said Arnold, sauntering up to the young officer.

"No can do...sir. Get out of my way. She goes to jail. Deposit your things here, miss. We go by procedures," said the officer, walking briskly past Arnold and holding onto Val's arm.

A tall man in a designer suit and tie with wingback shoes stepped out of his office. He looked directly at the young officer, smiling broadly at Elise and Arnold.

"Officer Nichol, let me handle this. I know you're just doing your job, but I will take over now. Unhandcuff this young woman," said the Police Chief.

"Uh…but, we were just informed that Ms. Tate showed up in the footage and was also confirmed by Grace Noble," said Officer Nichol.

Val stood stiffly beside the Landers.

"Yeah, and Grace is being held here on bond. According to Dr. Simms, her grandmother, Ms. Tate, was a minor at the time of the RI break-in, probably coerced and then kidnapped. She's been staying with the Landers, and they can vouch for her," said the Police Chief.

Several minutes later, Val was led into a room with Elise and Arnold. All charges were dropped because of her grandmother's influence and the Landers' status.

I see how the powerful get their way, but I'm not complaining. I'm safe for now, but what about those robots outside? Now I understand what they're saying about equality. The world favors humans, especially those making their own rules. I'm lucky, but is it justified?

They were waiting for Dat to be released so they could go home. Val's head ached, and her body slumped down in the chair. Her eyes started to close, having been sleep deprived, but her mind focused on Dat. Was Tad here as well?

"You must be exhausted. Did that horrible Grace drag you and Dat into her little cause? I admire her tenacity, but recruiting minors is a crime and using our Dat. Breaking into Robot International—what was she thinking? We heard you were taken from the esteemed Dr. Simms's house and treated like a criminal," said Elise, rolling her eyes.

"Ruff, Ruff, Ruff."

Val heard the little bulldog and wanted desperately to hold him. He must be so scared, and where was Dat? Even though he ran off, she wanted to see him, make sure he was all right. Plus, she better keep her mouth shut. No need to tell Elise what really happened.

"The dog's been released, and an officer has it in the lobby. You need to pick it up—making too much noise," said an officer.

Tad sat in a corner with a forlorn look in his eyes. At the sight of Val, he jumped up to greet her, his tail wagging furiously. Just then, her parents rushed into the lobby, out of breath and sweating.

"Honey, are you okay? We're so worried. And it's your birthday, and we want you to come home to celebrate. You're our little girl. Remember we went to Maxwell's last year and..." said her mother.

Val straightened up and scrunched her face with the dog in her arms.

"That was your memory, not mine. Always about you, isn't it? I'm fine—thanks to Elise and Arnold. They got me out, and I'm planning to celebrate with them. And of course, Dat—remember him? Yes, we're still together. Now...if you don't mind...we have to go soon," said Val.

"Woof, woof," barked Tad as if acknowledging her statement.

Her parents' mouths fell open, and they looked like someone hit them with a brick wall. Her dad hobbled up to her to plant a kiss on her cheek, but Val turned away. Her mother's eyes filled with tears. She knew she hurt them badly, but she really didn't care. If it wasn't for the governor, her parents wouldn't be here now. Maybe she'd been a little harsh, but they didn't practice what they'd preached. Part of her wanted to hug them and go home now after all she had just endured. The safety of her home, her comfy room, and their devoted love still meant something to her. But she still believed they didn't really treat her like an adult, and that bothered her. And their disrespect for Dat and their relationship. Even now, her parents didn't ask about him. Val believed they only wanted to control her. Her place was with Elise and Arnold, her new guardians as Dat called them.

"Oh...I'm sorry I didn't know it was your birthday and it's Val's choice where she wants to spend it. We'll let you alone if you want to speak with your parents now," said Elise.

The Landers crouched in a corner away from Val and her family. Val stared at her bewildered parents with disgust.

"We're your parents, and we'd like to sit down and talk to you. Why can't you just come home right now and discuss this? You owe us that— Mom's met you a few times and written you emails. We don't understand why you can't..." her dad said.

"No...I'm done here and ready to go, once Dat is released. I'm tired of being controlled, and the Landers don't tell us what to do. See you around

Meredith and Rod," she said as she brushed them off with a wave of her hand.

But her words sounded hollow as the Police Chief came out of his office and made an announcement.

"We're keeping Dat for further questioning. He left the scene and caused a disruption on the train. We have reason to believe that he may be the leader of the Robot Revolt Group."

RETRIBUTION

CHAPTER 1

A month later

"Hey, Pretty Boy, what's your deal?"

Dat looked around the dark, gray walls of the basement structure to find the guy with the attitude. He'd lost track of time and still couldn't believe they actually threw him in this robot prison. He thought the Landers would help him, but the Police Chief had another idea. Without Val's recording of this conversation via his com watch, he would never have known the truth. The words boggled both his right and left brains.

"With evidence from Trig Thompson and also from his neck ID, we have put him at the scene of the South Thompson High attack. He looked like he was rescuing Val, but he was actually escaping from the scene. Val found him beaten up by students, and they should have left him to be picked up for trash, but instead, she saved him. This bot has manipulated everyone, including you. He tried to leave again after the school incident, claiming to see Val, but again planning his next attack," said the Police Chief.

"What about the initial raid? He was an innocent bystander at the Gala and saved Ms. Tate. You're now saying he was the Mastermind all along?" said Arnold.

"Yes, he's very clever and takes after his donor, Tony De La Fleur, who fooled his fans and nearly ruined his reputation in the Cupcake Scam. Tony apologized, but it left a "bad taste in everyone's mouth," so he donated his brains to the Genealogy Project for good will," said the Chief.

"This is ludicrous. A case of revenge and false accusations. Our Dat is fine and upstanding and had nothing to do with his donor's actions," said Elise.

"I'm sorry to say…we have reason to believe and evidence that we can't disclose right now that would implicate Dat. We don't want to terminate him just yet, so we need to hold him longer for questioning. We're putting him near another instigator…Zag, who we picked up last week. Their cells are being bugged, and we'll be monitoring their every move. Just trust me on this," said the Police Chief.

"Get him out of here before I rip him apart…lying bot," said Arnold. Elise nodded in support.

"I don't believe this about Dat. Let me just see him before he goes away," said Val.

That's how he ended up in this predicament.

⊷══◯◯══⊷

His sensors froze as he tried to make sense of his situation. But after being here for thirty days without any contact beside Val's message, he really thought this was the end, that he'd be broken apart and thrown into the junkyard or robot dump.

Without the comforts of his own room and his dog Tad, jail was a place of boredom, despair, and unlimited time. It reminded him a little of RI when he was in Reconstruction, feeling isolated and worthless. Maybe if he was allowed to cook, he could prove himself. The shadows danced along the walls in this large room filled with steel-barred cubicles, each with a bench and wall monitor. Slivers of light filtered down through the 100-foot ceiling. Dat peered through the bars of his cell, searching for the deep voice.

"Yeah, what do you want?"

His anger rose up, and he was ready to snap, having been transported from interrogation, whisked away blindfolded through underground tunnels to an unknown location, put in a space copter, and swooped down to a helipad atop a 1000-story building. Human cops hustled him into an elevator down to the first level of a concrete warehouse and registered him. The humans tore off his blindfold and let him see the stark, bleak walls of his destiny. The holding cell was a huge metallic cage surrounded by thick metal walls. The masked guards stood outside and surrounded him with terminator guns, ready to shoot if he made a wrong move. Only the bright spotlight shined down on Dat as he endured the humiliation.

His senses were raw, and he knew his rage would crush them, but his left brain convinced him that sometimes the only way to win was to concede.

"What's your deal? Use your status with the Landers to orchestrate attacks throughout the Capitol? Brilliant, but we caught you and thinking you could gain secrets from RI? But heard you ran when confronted by Trig, the gov's bot," said a scratchy-voiced investigator, hidden in a black hoodie and dark glasses, flanked by Model 300s and their weapons.

He sat silent under the spotlight, not knowing how to answer.

"Speak up, and we'll free you…back to your gal pal. Pretty little thing who was the only one to take your side. Got her fooled with your bot charm," a younger voice sounded above.

Confused by more voices bombarding him with questions, he twitched in his seat with flashing lights, electrical impulses to his brain, and buckets of water thrown in his face. He endured weeks of pain until he thought he would break, but Dat never uttered a word.

Dat's rage grew as he was stripped of status, clothes, identity, and given a silver-striped jumpsuit. They shackled him before he could fight back, his circuits exploding, and his sensors shuttering. Then he was relocated via an elevator to a secured floor to his own private misery, a place for maximum security robots. Two grim Model 300s ushered him to his new home, a steel pit with transparent walls and no privacy.

The inmate kicked up against one of the hard surfaces and uttered a throaty laugh.

"Greetings to you…my brother 500. We've got to stick together—zone out. These other grunts will be terminated soon, but we got value. Seen your face before…you protested with Grace," said a scruffy-looking robot with a half-metal, half-human face.

As daylight filtered through, Dat gasped at his fishbowl existence, cells above and below him, separated by hard plastic and suspended on top of each other. Only a corridor with an elevator led the way out of this glass prison. He viewed hundreds of robots in similar cells all stacked on top of each other. He heard faint rumblings.

"Whew…what the hell?" said Dat.

Vertigo kicked in, and he thought he would drop to the next cell below. The maze of cells and enclosed robots almost blew his sensors, and he started shaking. He'd need a friend right now. But everyone had abandoned him, even his bulldog. He could still hear Tad's whimpers as they tore him from Dat's arms. Even his dog could feel his pain. His right brain ached to hold Tad, but his left brain wished Tad would never see him like this.

"You'll never get used to it, so just hold on to your senses. Don't worry, it's solid Ultra Plastic, totally unbreakable. I figure you're the only one to get us out of here—that celeb girlfriend or those rich guardians. Even if they're pissed, they'll never believe that you did it," said the half breed.

Dat steadied himself and gazed to his right. The other robot looked familiar, but suddenly he placed him.

"Who are you? Were you recently picked up after jogging for false pretenses?" said Dat.

"Righto…good memory, Zag it is. I got caught, and I'll probably be terminated after they use me. But you have a way out of this dump…Val Tate. The word trickled down from the top that she's still staying with the Landers, and they are the only ones who can spring you. And she's got their ear. Estranged from her parents because of you. Do you think she can get you released?" Zag said.

Dat wanted to call her, tell her that he was sorry and that he wasn't guilty. The governor's robot Trig had it in for him. Also, apologize to his guardians and try to win back their trust. Their faces and anger tugged on his right brain responses, but he didn't understand why they let him go. They rescued him before when he got beat up by that bully, but he knew the Chief sealed his fate…for now.

Dat's watch vibrated. It was a miracle they let him keep it.

"Listen—I know you have your doubts about me, but I'm on your side. Val believes in you and has a plan and way to get you released. She will visit you here tonight at 6 p.m.," said a muffled voice.

The call ended quickly. Dat's acute hearing picked up the tone and cadence of the caller and was shocked to realize who it was.

"I just received a message…Val will be here at 6 p.m. Not sure what she wants," Dat said.

"Suck it up, and sweet talk her. It's your only chance to convince the Landers. Here come the guards," Zag said.

The same Model 300s that locked him up were now about to release him. They punched in a code, then handcuffed him in silence and led him back to the elevator. In a matter of seconds and multiple floors down, the doors opened. They quickly ushered him down a pitch-black corridor that only his acute senses guided him through. A Model 300 pushed a secret panel, and a bright light spilled out, temporarily blinding him. Dat squinted and found himself in a comfortable living room with chrome furniture, monitors along the walls, and a large bay window, overlooking the city. He found it hard to believe.

I'm at Robot International—in another area.

He noticed the room was bugged with small cameras in the corners. The Model 300s gestured for him to enter a glass box with a bar stool. They exited, and a door opened with a wiry man in a gray suit with Val.

"I'm Warden Blackstone. Val Tate has agreed to meet with you. Don't try anything out of the ordinary. I'll be watching your every move," the warden said and disappeared behind a secret wall.

Val stared at him for the first time in weeks. She sat across from him in one of the black chairs and touched her earring. He noticed her thin figure, sad eyes, and hair pulled back in a ponytail. Her designer jeans and black cashmere sweater hugged her body, and her glossy lips parted in a smile. He wondered how they would communicate so far apart.

"Hello, how are you?" she said softly, adjusting the pearl in her ear.

Her eyes locked with his, and he realized only he could hear her.

"Adjusting…it's hard. I didn't do it, and I'm not who they think I am. I'm a chef," he said.

She licked her lips and looked like she might cry. Dat wanted to take her hand, but he was stuck in this transparent box.

"I know, and I believe you, but I'm not sure if they do…the Landers. They trusted you, and now you've…let them down. You were more than a robot…to me and them," Val said, her eyes looking downward.

Dat wanted desperately to explain, but he was confused. The police accused the wrong guy, and someone else was guilty. Robots really had no power. It didn't matter who your guardians were or their status. And forget about Grace Noble. But he wanted to change the subject because his sensitivity trackers picked up her depression level. His smiling eyes caught her attention.

"Val…how is Tad? Are you taking good care of him?"

Her face brightened.

"Yeah, he's fine, and the Landers love having him around, especially Arnold. Just so you know…they miss your cooking. The bananas flambé, cinnamon pancakes, and the Chateaubriand."

She laughed so hard the tears came.

"Oh, that's great. I miss cooking…creating meals like Tony De LaFleur. Do you think they'll want me back? Do you?"

His eyes shone brightly at the compliment. He wanted to create something for her at this moment, but he was locked away.

She took a deep breath.

"Uh…I'm not sure if they do. Do you want to come back? I want you to be released."

Dat looked surprised.

"I want to be a chef, and I like working for them. But I want to be with you. What about your parents? Are you going back home? I'm sure they're glad I'm out of the picture."

"Haven't spoken to them—we don't talk anymore. They still don't understand us. Maybe the Landers can work out a deal—I'll ask them."

Dat exhaled. He succeeded. Val was on his side, even after all that happened.

He had a chance now, and only Val heard him.

CHAPTER 2

Those romantic feelings for him rushed over her. The sight of his beautiful bronze face contrasted with that ugly jumpsuit unnerved her. She admired his strength and tenacity to live and be part of society, even as broken as it was. Was he just a robot or truly her soul mate? His life was in her hands. Her influence and status as a Tate could ultimately free him. She heard herself say those words about wanting him to be released, but did she mean it? Her life was just beginning, and now with her inheritance, she could do anything because she didn't need anyone, not her parents, the Landers, or even Dat. Her thoughts ruminated over her parents' last communication, and the words still stuck in her mind. But she was proud of her response.

"My dearest Val,

We've been so worried about you since we saw you at the jail two weeks ago. You looked so thin and tired. You didn't seem like yourself. And of course, we wanted to celebrate your birthday with you. We have some lovely presents for you.

I'm sorry for everything that's happened, and I would love to get together with you. It's been too long. Maybe we could have some one-on-one girl time together. We've always been able to talk and have had this special bond between us.

And your dad would really love to get a call from you, especially after the break-in of his office and your kidnapping. We've seen the news and now Dat's arrest for being the head of the RRG. Now you know what he's really like. You must realize all these

terrible things happened after you met Dat. It must
be so stressful for you living with his guardians. You
must be so distraught after the news that he was so
dishonest. The media said the Landers have gone into
seclusion. So, are you still staying with them?

Please come home, and let's talk about mending
our relationship. Life is short, and we miss our only
daughter so much. I'm sure we can figure this all out
and come to an understanding. We love you so much
and only want the best for you. Our house is always
open to you.
Love, Mom"

She couldn't believe her mother's message. They would never
understand the hurt and pain that she'd been through these past weeks.
She'd lost almost twenty pounds; her hair was falling out, and her mental
state was deteriorating. Her tears alone would have cleared up California's
drought. If it hadn't been for Elise's therapist, Val thought she would have
lost it. Her mother really had no idea what she'd been through. Her new
therapist advised her to stay away from her family at this moment to clear
her head and gain her sanity. But she didn't have to explain any of this to
her mother, but she wanted her to realize what they had done. Val's fury
caused her to quickly respond.

"Dear Meredith,
After listening to your hologram, it seems to
me that you do not really want to fix the ongoing
problem...STILL! Now you say you are sorry for how
things have gone. Instead of trying to fix the problem,
you complain this has gone on for "too" long.

We do NOT share a bond anymore. You want to
continue to defend your actions and Rod's, claim you
are good parents and place blame on others instead of
yourself. I can't make you change the way you want
to treat me and Dat, but I can change myself by not
allowing you or Rod to treat me and my boyfriend this

way. I know that he is not a terrorist, but he did leave me alone to deal with Grace's break-in of RI, but I'm in the process of forgiving him. It's the only way to get through this, according to my therapist.

To be honest, I don't want a relationship with you and Rod anymore. You have completely broken my trust, and you have not attempted to gain it back. I don't understand how you expect me to want to bring you back into my life. And my therapist agrees!

Goodbye, Val"

The warden appeared out of the shadows and jolted her back into reality. Val didn't want her meeting with Dat to end. She wanted to talk about their time together, their future, and her plans. Dat kept staring at her with those warm brown eyes, and now his dazzling smile warmed her heart.

"Love you," Val said, approaching the glass cage.

"Me too," Dat said.

"Hey, I hate to break up this moment, but Dat must go back to his cell. Visitor hours are over, and Dat got special treatment due to some important people on the outside. Ms. Tate, it's time to go," the warden said.

His lined face and blank eyes revealed a man of little emotion and stringent rules. He pointed to the secret passage. Two Model 300s magically materialized, ready to take Dat away.

Val choked back tears and felt the weight of her decision. Her legs almost collapsed as she rose from the comfy chair. She wanted Dat to fight back, show that spirit that first attracted her to him, but he complied and allowed the guards to release him from the glass box. She wasn't sure if he was ready for this, but now was the time to act.

"Wait…please. I need a private moment with Dat," Val said, directing her words to the warden.

But the Model 300s grabbed Dat, and he shuffled toward the elevator.

"One minute only—Ms. Tate. Guards, let them have their privacy, Remember the walls are watching," said the warden, dismissing them. They all disappeared beyond the secret wall, and Dat stood alone.

Val moved closer to hug Dat's stiff body and pressed her mouth to his ear.

"Listen carefully. Dead men don't die, they use the switch at 4 a.m."

He bent to kiss her and clasped her hand tightly. "Thanks," he mumbled with a puzzled look on his face.

Val backed away and put her hands over her eyes. She cried openly and loudly, falling to the ground.

"I can't bear to see him go. It's not RIGHT. He's innocent and won't harm anyone or anything. My heart is breaking..."

"Ms. Tate, pull yourself together. Get Ms. Fowler out here now. Guards take him away immediately," said the warden.

Val crouched on the ground, hugging herself and now crying uncontrollably. A young woman in a security uniform walked briskly toward her and yanked her up. She shook, pushing the woman away and watching Dat out of the corner of her eye. He winked at her as he was led away by the Model 300s.

Stretching her neck up at the tall glass building, Val looked at the top floor. He was there in a cell, but she helped in setting him free. She'd done what she came to do for Dat and the robot movement. Just like her grandmother, she had a part to play, her gift to the robot rebellion. Because Dat was a Model 500, he could figure his way out to independence. But Val was not sure the Landers felt that way.

A stern Ms. Fowler escorted her out of prison, part of RI's vast compound. The glass door slammed behind her, and Val shivered at this experience. Being an adult was not easy, with hard choices to be made. She wished things could have turned out differently between her and her parents. But her pride made her stand on her own, and Val was satisfied with her decisions. She looked around. A dented space van with blackened windows pulled up beside her. It was a Sport, one of the first space vans made. The night sky opened up, and a cold rain hit her shoulders, and she was grateful for the ride. The van's door slid open.

"Hurry...get in," said the driver.

Val recognized his eyes, but not the beat-up old vehicle. They had to be careful now because everyone was watching.

"Breakout is scheduled for tomorrow. Be ready," said the driver and then zoomed down to the Metro Apartments. The ride lasted five minutes in silence, and they could only communicate in sign language. As she stepped outside, Val heard a raspy voice.

"You think…you're special? Boyfriend is guilty, but you stay with the Landers. Lucky."

Val turned to see Rad, a smirk on his face.

"Leave me alone. Who are you, and what do you want?" Val said.

"Everyone…thinks I'm stupid…just a Model 100. I don't just…park cars. I know everything going on…here."

Val jumped and ran toward the elevator. She shivered as it climbed to the thirty-third floor. She opened the apartment door and was greeted by an excited Elise.

"Hi Val, good to see you. We were worried about you—it's past curfew. It's dangerous out there, and people know who you are. Are you okay? You look like you need a drink…maybe some hot soup. That's all I can make since Dat's been gone."

Elise gave Val a warm hug.

"I'm okay—just needed some fresh air. It's been so hard lately," said Val.

Tears rolled down her cheeks, and she wiped them away with the back of her hand.

"Here, baby. I know we haven't been here for you lately. Been trying to avoid the publicity and determine our next steps. Join us in a glass of wine, and Arnold will give you a cup of chowder," said Elise.

They gushed over her as she ate the soup and sipped on the Chardonnay. It was becoming her favorite. They truly spoiled her with their kindness.

"What are your plans when you graduate? said Arnold.

"Uh…not sure…too much going on. Maybe college now that I have an inheritance from my grandmother."

Elise smiled.

"Honey, you can stay as long as you want. We know that you're not getting along with your parents right now. And we think it's wonderful that you want to go to college."

Then little Tad appeared, barking and wagging his tail. He jumped on Val's lap and licked her face. She hugged him fiercely and scratched his ears.

"Look who's glad to see you," said Arnold.

"We have our family unit now—group hug," said Elise.

Val burst with joy for the first time in weeks. This was her new family because the Landers welcomed her. She had a home base, an inheritance, and just freed her boyfriend. But that was only the beginning.

CHAPTER 3

Midnight

Dat rose from his bunk, mulling over his last conversation with Val. Must have been a secret code, but for what? A switch for dead men? He was a chef, not a technician.

"Hey, buddy, did you get it? When is springtime?" whispered Zag.

Dat wondered if he should trust Zag. After all, they hardly knew each other. He turned the phrase over and over in his head. But he realized he needed help with Zag's experience to pull this off.

"Val only said something about dead men don't die if they use a switch...at 4 a.m."

Zag pressed himself against the transparent wall as Dat moved toward it.

"Let me think about this. A switch for dead men to be used at 4 a.m.? Well, that's our time to go, but....uh yeah...wait...a *Deadman switch* is used by humans to stop robots, mostly 100s and 300s, to incapacitate them. It's found at the back of the neck, near the shoulder, a small red button which will turn off their power for about sixty minutes. If we can deactivate one and then divert another. Brilliant clue only known by a scientist's daughter," Said Zag.

"There will be a cell check at 4 a.m. We do it at that time and then release everyone else for a major prison escape. I deactivate the switch on the first guard. You can be the diversion," said Dat, his eyes lighting up at their plan.

"Yeah...if I get the big one in a headlock and you take on the midget, we'll be set. But you also have to use his eye imprint to open the doors," said Zag.

"What about the other prisoners?"

"Don't worry, they'll follow our lead."

The hours ticked by slowly, and Dat awaited with dreaded anticipation. Tiny stars twinkled above, and his acute hearing picked up on every creak, movement, even the white noise. Then the elevators parted, and he heard the heavy footsteps of his captors. He wondered how they complied with the human's demands against their kind, but then these machines were programmed with no empathy.

They clomped past each cell, getting closer to Dat's area. They approached his cell and stopped.

"Here to check Dat's cell," said a Model 300.

Dat's sensors fired up as adrenalin took over. Then a crashing and banging on the cell next to him as Zag started whining.

Dat grabbed the smaller 300's arm and yanked him around.

"Come here, big guy—got a problem!" said Zag.

The big 300 started taking off for Zag's cell.

"Revolt…revolt…revolt," Zag started the mantra.

A chorus of chants echoed throughout the cells as each robot joined in.

The hefty Model 300 struck Zag in the face.

By this time, Dat had swiveled the midget 300 so that its back faced him. He struggled with his arm around the 300's neck, trying to locate the switch with the other hand. But he held on tightly and pressed it. The 300 froze, then crashed to the ground.

Dat mustered all his strength, his rage driving his sensors. He whipped the 300 around to face him and connected the lock with the guard's eye imprint. The entrance opened just as the other 300 encountered him.

Cries of "Freedom" grew louder. Zag's door was halfway open, having fallen to the ground, the human side of his face beaten.

Dat tripped up the second 300, pressed the deadman switch, and ran to free Zag.

"Get up, we don't have much time. Let's free the others."

Zag staggered as Dat pulled him up from the ground.

"Ow…uh…thanks. Let me show you how it's done."

Zag tore out the right eye from the midget and the left eye from the larger 300. Then he pressed them along the inmates' cell doors. They automatically slid open, and the robots howled at their instant freedom.

"Each robot must help another. Take an eye imprint and pass it on, then follow that Model 500," yelled Zag, pointing at Dat.

Each robot duplicated the other's behavior, and each floor was set free. Dat took off toward the elevator with alarms and sirens sounding in the distance. He heard the crashing of metal and click of cells opening as the robots were released. Because of the stackable cells, there was a rush to the elevators, but Zag urged them to fall in line.

"Orderly output so everyone can escape. Shield your leader. Onward with Dat," yelled Zag as he waited for everyone to depart.

Dat wondered how he could lead since he remained hidden from the world most of his short life. But his "Tony De LaFleur" charm guided him on the path to freedom and out to the free world. He turned around to see a line of robots following behind him.

"Let's fight and bring independence to all robots. Robots deserve to make their mark in this world. The future depends on us, and we are the next generation. Everyone with me?"

A crowd cautiously surrounded Dat in the elevator. The doors parted, and the war began.

"Freedom…FREEDOM…FREE..DOM," their cries resounding as they reached the first floor. They were greeted by guards with stun guns and terminators.

"Fire to stun, only terminate if challenged. NOW," ordered the warden.

Dat pressed on, hoping to avoid a barrage of shots. His instincts told him to advance, but his sensors indicated danger and warning signals.

Suddenly a wall of metal moved in formation to defend him, their fates instantly sealed.

Many went down, to be replaced by rows of others. Dat heard the pop, snap, and clank of metal as his defenders hit the ground. He continued to march forward as the elevators opened, and more robots rushed out, some hiding behind their fellow comrades, others rushing in unison.

"Robots Unite, *Robots Unite*, ROBOTS UNITE," said the inmates, their voices raised.

Many Model 500 guards defected and took up their weapons in offense.

"Knock'em down. Shoot to terminate," shouted the warden over the loudspeaker.

Many robots fell as rapid-fire hit them. As Dat reached the entrance, he realized it was locked, and they still needed to climb the steel gates and fence. His right and left brains wrestled, and he wondered how he would make it. The glass doors and walls revealed hundreds of robots outside with an unfamiliar front-runner leading the pack. His eyes popped in recognition. They came with their headlights and weapons. Their energy and persistence inspired him to figure a way out of this impossibility.

Dat signaled inmates beside him to grab the guards as shields.

"Proceed forward to freedom," he commanded as he pushed a guard's eye imprint into the door. It opened, and he stumbled out.

CHAPTER 4

Hours earlier

"What's wrong, Val? You seem distracted. Time to celebrate," said Elise.

"Uh, I'm actually very tired…need to rest," said Val.

Val gave her new guardians hugs, leaned down to pet Tad and headed for her room, formerly Dat's.

"Wait…what's wrong? Is it your parents? College applications?" said Elise.

She hurried toward Val and turned her around to face her.

"Let her go…she's had a long day and a lot to think about," said Arnold.

Val nodded and wished they weren't so worried. They were starting to sound like her parents.

She entered his room and plunked down on the soft pink comforter that Elise bought for her. A gray scarf draped over the desk chair, reminding her of Dat. Her jittery nerves and upset stomach bothered her as she waited for her new directions.

Do I want to go to college or be a part of this rebellion? It's selfish to just think about myself when everyone needs me.

She clasped her neck and felt the old charm attached to her necklace. Pulling it off, Val read the words, inscribed, "Everyone deserves a voice."

Her grandmother led the movement that brought the masses together, not realizing that someday a new class would arise. Dad helped to create the new class of robots so people could pursue better jobs. It was her turn to continue in their legacy.

Val's watch vibrated, and she smiled.

"Saw you were released from jail and exonerated; however, Dat is still there. I know that you will trust your heart and sort it all out. Is the robot cause worth pursuing, and what about the RRG? Being a leader is hard, but know that I have your back. I fight in spirit, but new blood is needed now in this chaotic world."

Her grandmother ended the hologram with a peace sign.

She ruminated on her grandmother's words as a hologram came through, but it was not who she expected.

Who would be calling me now while I'm waiting for directions?

> "Hey Val,
> Happy Birthday!
> You're streaming in the news right now. Whoa—my friend, the celebrity! And Dat is an RRG terrorist? I believe you if you say he's not involved. Probably set up.
> Anyway, no one is safe anymore. The robots are becoming more agitated, even in my neighborhood. They're watching the activity in the Capitol and playing copy- cat.
> Your mother just contacted me as a last-ditch effort. She told me that you both aren't talking, and I get it. Over a guy—of course, parents don't understand the real deal. And they're scared he's part of the RRG. We know he's not—I trust your judgment. But you can't stay mad forever.
> Reach out and tell them how you feel. I've never known you to hold a grudge, and besides, I think your parents have good intentions. Always have.
> Do it for me and let me know when we can get together.
> Your BFF,
> Lucy"

She wished Lucy were here to fix things. Like the time she became her science project partner when Chad dropped out at the last minute. Val needed her BFF around. There were too many elders telling her what to do. Her mother was getting desperate if she contacted her best friend. Once her life was straightened out, she'd contact Lucy.

Val thought about it but still could not forgive her mother. The anger and pain caused by her parents' rejection of Dat would not go away. They thought once he was jailed that Val would come running home. On the contrary, it made her more determined to enjoy her freedom and make her own decisions. An urgent beeping alerted her.

"Wizard here. I hope this is a secure line. I'm incognito for obvious reasons, so I'm laying low. Quickly—meet at the old Universal Studios theme park. Look for the sound stages, Jurassic Park Ride and neglected food stands at 3:45 a.m. I've gathered the forces, but you're in charge. But the RRG is still out there, and our guys don't believe in their tactics. So, we gotta be careful. Keep it under wraps, it's a highly sensitive mission."

Val pulled on her jacket and grabbed Dat's scarf. Checking out her reflection in the mirror, she saw a serious young woman with determined eyes, someone much older than she felt. Was she ready for this? It was definitely dangerous yet exciting at the same time. She could make a difference, and her grandmother and BFF supported her.

"Be good, Tad, I have to leave. Find Dat and rescue him," Val said.

At the sound of Dat's name, Tad whimpered but laid his head down on the carpet.

Val crept out of her room and tiptoed into the hallway, leaving the little bulldog behind. She locked him in the room with a little food and water and papered the floor. The apartment was quiet and dark, and she assumed the Landers went to bed. All she had to do was get on the Skytrain and avoid Rad, and she'd be on her way. At 3:15 a.m., the side elevator was empty, and she rode it down to the lower level in silence, breathing heavily. The world outside blurred as the elevator hit the ground in two minutes.

You can do this. Be strong and think of Dat. He's waiting for you to set him free. And Wizard has the connections and ammo.

The night smelled of melting plastic with little fires burning everywhere. Val felt a heaviness and veil of depressiveness settle upon her.

What's happening to the world? Is it slowly being destroyed?

She wrapped the scarf around her face, and the jacket warmed her in the unusually brisk early morning. No one stopped her. She feared the security guard Rad, but he must have the night off. She ran quickly and met the next Skytrain as it stopped at the platform. Just a few lone souls sat in the worn seats. Val breathed deeply, comforted by the strangers who were asleep or occupied by their com watches. Probably working the nightshift in their scrubs or security uniforms. Sitting on the train for thirty minutes, she realized there was no Universal stop, and her stomach tightened. Passengers got on and off the train. Her head ached, and she hesitated. Still dark outside, it was hard to make out her surroundings.

"End of the line—Downtown, formerly Universal Studios," announced the robotic train conductor.

❖❖═◗◖═❖❖

Her heart leaped when she saw him waiting for her among the dilapidated buildings abandoned stores and rusty rides. Then the group gathered around him, their silver armbands gleaming in the moonlight. His smile flashed in the darkness.

"I hate what the governor is doing to the mechanix, and I've switched sides. Leaving GNet and going underground was the right thing to do. We've been waiting patiently. I've convinced them to follow you. Listen to her," said Wizard, Val recognized as Whit.

Fired up and ready to fight, the warriors were hidden in a caravan of trucks ready to move near the prison walls. Their worn jeeps and lack of ammo reminded her of the protest groups from the Great Divide. With little weapons, but with strength in numbers, they were ready to fight.

"I've spoken to Dat and given him the tool to break free. We must resist and persist to make this raid happen. I know many of you doubt me because my dad works for RI and my mother for the governor. But I love Dat and believe in him. The cause is great, and we will win. "I'm not a warrior, so I need your strength and fighter power. Freedom for all," said Val.

They raised their arms in unison and marched toward her with Whit leading the group.

"The breakout will occur at 04:00, and we're waiting from a signal from Zag, a cellmate of Dat," said Whit.

Val knew the deadman switch was the secret to their escape, but not sure how it would all go down.

Whit checked his vibrating com watch.

"It's time. Val, stay close to Von and me. We'll protect you, but here's a terminator if needed. Von, show her how it works. Our plan is to break down the wall, sack the guards, and rescue as many robots as possible. Of course, the inmates will be told to protect Dat at all costs. If we have to surrender, then Val you'll need to be our spokesperson," Whit said.

Val sucked in her breath and gathered her courage.

"This is not a time for negotiations. All or nothing. Ready, now let's go!" said Val.

The group hurried past the dried-up Jaws ride and hid behind the Whoville stage. Val heard they once made movies here instead of virtual worlds. She stayed close to Whit as the mechanix followed them blindly to the prison. They entered the dark grounds and noted the barbed wire and high cement wall. They trudged past the towering Castle known as the Harry Potter ride. They reached the outskirts of Downtown and the backside of the concrete prison walls. She shivered, knowing that Dat was going to lead the pack, and she was actually going to be in the middle of a prison riot. Beacons of bright light illuminated the outside area.

Shots sounded, screams erupted, and sirens blasted. A rush of guards and inmates merged together. Overhead space vans whirled above, dropping grenades and smoke bombs. The warden's commands blasted overhead. Chaos broke out.

It's a warzone. I'm stuck. I'm going to be sick right now. What am I supposed to do?

Val stood frozen among the warriors.

"Move Val…NOW, shouted Whit.

A beam of light zoomed down in the area, highlighting Whit's group. They scrambled to various locations, ready to defend. Val heard shots around her and robots in RI uniforms advancing toward their little band of warriors. Val couldn't stand back and let the others protect her while other robots were being terminated. She wanted to help and not just be part of a movement. Other lives depended on her leadership.

Val moved cautiously in the semi-darkness as the fighting continued. She knew she was moving away from Von and Whit, but it was necessary to cover ground and attack the enemy. She heard the cries of robots in praise of Dat, and that fired her up. Her terminator was loaded and ready to fire, as instructed by Von. He urged her to shoot only when approached. Otherwise, any shots could call attention to her and their little band of soldiers.

Scrutinizing the area and crouching low to the ground, Val made her way toward the wall. She could see the inmates and guards surging forward. The sun peeked behind the clouds, and Val looked up.

An explosion lit up the skies as drones circled the area. Figures in black rushed the grounds and started shooting.

"Geez, what the hell? They're ruining our plan," said Whit.

A soldier dodged the shots, spotted Val, and pointed his gun at her. Her eyes registered his familiar face.

She pulled the trigger.

"Val, I'm coming, get down!" Whit screamed.

Grandma would be proud.

CHAPTER 5

The crowd of inmates rushed the entrance, some terminated, others freed. Their sacrifices were not in vain for the good of the pack.

"Robot Power!" Zag shouted.

"Dat rules!" said an inmate.

"Stop him, surround them," yelled an alliance of Model 300 guards.

They surged forward to recapture Dat and his protectors.

"Hey, we're up here. Come and get us," said Zag.

He gave a thumbs-up to Dat and the inmates from the rooftop. His gang of loyal prisoners surged toward the edge.

"You're surrounded, Warden. We outnumber you—give up before you become an embarrassment to the governor," said Zag.

A cadre of space vans hovered, dispensing mechanical dust and a shower of terminating bullets. Tear gas and flares dropped on the unsuspecting inmates.

"Drop and protect. Those who support us, fire your arms," Zag yelled.

Dat ducked for cover as his protectors flung themselves toward the gate. He jammed a robot eye into the gate lock, but it wouldn't open.

"Surge forward, attack now!" yelled Dat.

The wall of metal and silver armbands advanced rapidly toward the prison walls as grenades were hurled. But the space vans above countered with radar and explosives. Dat pressed ahead with his body, even though his sensors were on fire now. But he hadn't felt this alive since he had been created.

"Keep calm and move on! Don't give up. All for Robots' Liberty," he shouted at the top of his lungs.

"Freedom, freedom, freedom for all," chanted the crowd.

"Here's to Dat, our champion. He set us free!"

The air crackled with bombs, flares, and gunfire. The sky cleared to show a hint of dawn. The force of metal against metal erupted, and a pungent odor permeated through the screen of thick smoke.

"Ah, by my last breath, I salute Dat," Zag said.

A loud thump and a cry of horror rose as he fell with a crash to the ground. Dat turned to see his co-conspirator take his last breath after being terminated by a grenade.

Not Zag, he protected and believed in me. How will I survive? Who will guide me?

"Zag, a true warrior to our cause. He would not want us to give up," yelled Dat as he ran to say goodbye to his friend.

He reached him, Zag's legs severed from his body, and his face still stoic in death.

"Oh…my friend, what have they done to you?' cried Dat, burying his face into the warrior's shoulder.

The inmates fought harder, pulling the terminator guns from the downed guards. They rushed to break down the wall.

Then Dat realized who shot Zag. Was he fighting two enemies? Who was their leader?

The soldiers in black advanced toward the middle, shooting at everyone. Their tactics mirrored the Gala attack and Thompson High shootings as they dropped from their own space vans. Soldiers from both sides started to fall as the drones attacked. Dat's anger surged, his circuits electrified, and his right brain urges pressing him to act. He couldn't let these maniacs kill his comrades.

"What's going on—we have two forces working against us? Save the wall, capture those traitors." The warden's voice sounded loud and clear over the speaker system.

Dat got up from the melee and noticed her sweet face. It was Val. He longed to protect her and rushed to the wall that had almost collapsed.

"Get them before they reach the wall—NOW or be terminated," the warden announced over the loudspeaker.

A pack of guards raced to the crowd, violently killing off many of the warriors. But the soldiers in black advanced. The group scattered, and Dat saw Val's frightened face as he scrambled to save her. He brought this on and got her into this mess. Why had he gotten her involved? She's young and doesn't realize that she could be hurt or even killed. It was a selfish act on his part, worrying about the robot cause and not her life.

I have to get to her before they do. My precious Val, she's come to save me, but I must save her.

"MOVE, it's the RRG. They're the *enemy*," yelled Dat.

Dat heard a pop, pop, pop. He heard a female cry and immediately knew what happened. Her body lay on the ground, bloody, her breathing labored. She'd been hit in the chest. Beside her stood a warrior in black, his face revealed. Dat became enraged.

"It's been you all along. I should have known. I'm going to kill you," said Dat.

He stood still in defiance, waiting to be challenged. His group descended from their hiding places, ready for action.

"The 100s are being…replaced. No respect for us. I shot the creator's daughter. She deserves…to die. Rise up," said Rad with a crooked smile on his metal face.

"Destroy them before they finish all of us. Wipe them out," Dat screamed, his fist in the air. Dat pushed Rad to the ground before he could lift his gun. His sensors and circuits exploding, and his sensitivity tracks fuming, he smashed Rad's laughing face.

"You're gone. But what have you done to Val?"

Suddenly the inmates, guards, and warriors banned together, realizing their true enemy. They charged toward the group in vengeance. Instead of fighting each other, they pushed against the real enemy. Shots took down the drones. The unified group tackled the smaller band of black from all sides, but they surrendered now that their leader had been eliminated.

Dat covered Val with his body, protecting her from any more harm. Suddenly a torrent of tears flowed from his blackened, dusty eyes. He shook her gently.

"Wake up," Dat said.

Val's eyes fluttered, and then she groaned in pain.

"Is it over? Did we win?" she whispered.

"Shh…stay still, don't move. Help is coming. Stop worrying. We accomplished our mission. Hey, we need help over here," said Whit.

"We need an ambulance…for Val Tate. Hurry!" Dat shouted, his sensors on fire.

The smell of blood and burnt metal filled the air. Sirens and gunfire echoed through the early morning hours as an orange sun began its ascent.

A space ambulance swooped down beside the injured. Dat held Val in his arms, blood gushing from her chest wound. But her heart rate slowed, and her breathing became shallower.

"She's bleeding heavily and having a hard time breathing," Dat said to the medical personnel.

They viewed him with puzzlement and wonder.

"Let her go. We need to take care of her before..." said the young EMT.

He aggressively brushed Dat aside to put Val on a stretcher.

"Wait. Need Dat...I love...you. Protect...them," Val said, her eyes closing.

Her breathing stopped, and the medics scurried to take her vitals and apply CPR. They shocked her small body, and they pressed water to her lips. But she lay still.

"What happened? Why isn't...she moving?" said Dat, his voice fading as he collapsed on the ground.

The young medic worked desperately to revive her, applying CPR, injecting fluids, and giving her a shot. But Val didn't respond. Her head lolled to the side, and she was completely immobile and bleach white.

"I'm so sorry...we did everything. She's dead," said the medic.

"Val was so brave," Whit said, taking her limp arm for one last time. He placed his hand on a tormented Dat as he laid on the ground by Val's side.

Dat numbed to the sirens, metal against metal, and fighting around him. His sensors grew high alert as his sensitivity trackers experienced a pain so deep that he thought he would overheat, then explode. But his impulses slowed, and he succumbed to the realization of her passing.

The wall crumbled. The fighting stopped as the hovering space vans crashed to the ground. There was a hole in the side of the prison. The RRG had been crushed and eliminated. The robot warriors raised their arms in solidarity.

"We won. The fight is over..., but Val is no longer with us. It's a sad day," said Whit to the crowd.

Dat stood up, brushed himself off, and wiped his eyes.

"My heart is broken. I have nothing left to fight for," Dat said.

His dull eyes remained on Val's body until the medics took her away.

"Ceasefire. Halt the fighting. Stop the war. Enough is enough," echoed a strong female voice.

Dat looked up to see the governor standing on the battered rooftop with the CEO by her side. The space vans hovered nearby, setting up a protective shield.

"We get it. Let's negotiate. The battle has been won, and the real enemy has been defeated. Both sides united in RRG's downfall, and that is a victory for all," the CEO said, his voice boomed over the mayhem.

Dat's sensors inflamed. Then a woman with dark auburn hair appeared at the governor's side, her face ravaged by grief, mascara tears running down her face and quiet sobs. Dat wanted to tell her he was sorry, but she'd disappeared.

⋅⋙━◯⟡━⋘⋅

24 hours later

The few remaining prisoners were escorted back to RI for evaluation. Mostly rejects, these robots fell into line with nowhere to call home. Their frightened guardians refused to claim them, so they waited for a decision or declaration. And Dat was one of them.

He listened carefully to the monitors from his cell in the Reconstruction area, his sensors dulled.

"In honor of all those who have fallen in this terrible prison breakout, both robots and humans, I dedicate this memorial," said the governor, placing a massive wall of flowers and ribbons, covering the one destroyed by the rebels.

The governor declared a state of emergency, calling in the National Guard. Her brother, the CEO of RI, condemned the prison outbreak and closed it down for an indefinite period. Cleanup needed to be done after many of the robot and human population had been terminated. The devastation and horror of that night showed on his lined and puffy face as he stood by the governor's side.

"The governor intends to bring peace to the region and unite all parties, and she has declared a day of mourning. *The Great Rebellion* occurred on December 1, 2045, and has made a huge impression on the Capitol's leadership. They said no one involved would be incarcerated, locked up or banished," said Del, a robotic reporter. Dat noted he replaced Whit.

He knew his days were numbered as he stayed in RI's Reconstruction area. It seemed like a holding cell, but he didn't care because his precious Val was gone. His short life had been shattered, and maybe they'd wipe out his memory tracks. He asked if the doctors could put her back together, but everyone around him only laughed. He understood termination, but not death. Because robots still had life with reconstruction, but what about humans?

He watched the monitors closely and saw Meredith standing near the governor, dressed in black, her face masked by huge black sunglasses. Dat was told Dr. Rod Tate was hard at work in the Reconstruction area to save wounded robots. The governor had designated Dr. Tate to manage the Robot Healing Project in order to bring the two groups together.

The Tates must really hate me now. How can I forgive myself? They should have terminated me.

His sensitivity track surged with sorrow, and his sensors were in low gear. He was told he was on standby to assist with the reconstruction process, mostly surgeries, and mechanical fixes. But cooking was his thing. The Tony De LaFleur in him did best when asked to create the perfect dish, and his value would increase. But who would he cook for now? Not for Elise and Arnold, who released him from guardianship. He guessed they wanted nothing to do with him after the rebellion. Watching the monitors, he got his answer.

"How are you dealing with everything? Have you spoken to Dat?" asked broadcaster Del, running to catch Elise and Arnold as they walked out of their apartment.

Elise held up her hand as a shield.

"We're shocked and upset and wish to be left alone. We've been betrayed by Dat, treated him like our own, and not a servant. And he involved Val, a young woman who was like a daughter to us, and who had a future. She wanted to go to college and be free of this rebellion and finally be on her own. We've lost so much," said Elise.

Dat stared at the monitors as they zoomed in closely to Elise's face, noticeably thinner, and her mouth drooped downward. Dark shades covered her eyes, but his keen eyesight noticed tiny tears.

"Dat, if you're listening—you were a great chef…and son. We loved you, man, and your girlfriend Val. You should have been honest with us. We can't help you anymore," said Arnold to the cameras. His angry eyes pierced through Dat.

His right and left brains collided when he heard Arnold's words, and he wanted to explain his intentions. He wished he could turn back time and bring Val back to life. But they put him in prison, asked him to lead a rebellion and fight for the future of robots. And Val was part of it. He felt someone shaking his shoulder.

"We need to extract your memories from last year in order to rebuild some of our robots. If you agree to this procedure, the governor has promised freedom for you. You will be a major part of the restoration process for the robot race, but you may experience memory loss," said Dr. Tate.

Dat whirled around to face a man who could have been his enemy. But Val's dad showed no bitterness or contempt. He marveled at the man's composure and strength. Dat nodded. He had nothing more to lose. They could wipe his memory for all he cared. His life was ruined, and he would be the scapegoat for the new robot race.

"If it will help robotkind, then I agree," Dat said.

He lay on a bed, his brain hooked up to a computer and series of monitors. Dr. Tate attended to the process, carefully calculating and recording his sensations and all of his past experiences from the last year. Dat twitched as they poked and prodded his brain. Then he dozed off, dreaming of his early gastronomical creation. For the first time in several days, he experienced peace as his sensors slowed, and his circuits adjusted.

I love you, Val, and I hope you're in a better place. I would give up everything if I knew you would come back.

CHAPTER 6

My body no longer aches, and I feel energized. I move toward the bright light, but my eyes are not focused. Voices are calling out to me. Are they in my head?

"Breathe."

"Lift your arm. Bend your leg."

"Stretch your body."

Maybe I'm not dead. I'm no longer hurting. I've gone to a better place. I'm in heaven. I see Dat's face hovering over me, although I'm not yet awake. We're together again and maybe for eternity? But this isn't possible because he's a robot and they never die. Only terminated, never to function again.

The last thing I remember was being shot and blood pouring out of my chest and mouth. The bullet pierced my chest, and I felt like I was hit with a baseball bat. One minute I was moving forward, the next, flat on the ground.

Some people wanted me dead, but I heard others crying. Kind people started working on me, telling me to stay with them. But I knew it was my last day on Earth. I believe I was too young to leave this world, but I knew I wouldn't make it. Dat called out to me, but I could barely talk. He kept telling me everything was going to be alright. But I was too weak to answer. Then I left this world. I saw myself gazing at my bloody body. I saw Dat and the medic trying to bring me back. I shouted to them—I'm still hanging on...please save me. I don't want to die. They couldn't hear me and continued to try and bring me back to life. But my suspended soul vanished, and I fell back into my body. The intense pain overwhelmed me, and I blanked out.

"Wake up," says a soft voice. "Open your eyes."

I blink, and I can see. I sit up and look around. I'm on a stretcher in a room with computers and monitors. It's a new world. My mind still functions, but I notice I'm healed. My skin has no bruises, wounds, or even scratches. It's a miracle.

This place looks familiar. My memory can't process how I know these surroundings. A man hugs me and is crying. He's my Dad! He looks tired, and there are deep lines on his forehead and around the corners of his eyes. I must be in rehab because I'm not in a hospital. Everyone around me is extremely excited to see me, and it seems like I just came out of a coma. Can a person be brought back to life?

Then a woman comes toward me. A loose strand of hair touches her face, and black smears line her jade-colored eyes. Her perfume soothes me. The lady is my mom, and suddenly I want to see her. She stands a few feet away, but I reach out to her.

My mom hugs me tightly, and I feel her warmth. She whispers my name, and her tears are falling fast. Why is she crying? I just want to hug her and tell her everything is fine. I'm alive, and everyone I care about is here.

Dat reaches over, and he kisses me. He says I was so brave, and he thought he lost me. Dat takes my hand firmly and doesn't let go. He assures me that he will never leave me.

Whit and Grandma stand in the background, waiting for me to be released. I want them around me and see the relief in their faces. Lucy and Jen are here in their track uniforms and e-shoes. Do they want me to race? I feel like I could run one hundred miles. They want to help me up, and their smiles light up my room. Everyone is anxious for me to say something, but I'm at a loss for words.

"How are you? Baby, you're alive again because of the Genealogy Project. You died, and your brain was implanted into a robot body. It's what we have been working on for a while, and what everyone in this room wanted for you. Immortality," Dad said.

I didn't die, and I'm a robot. I'm in shock. How do I handle this new body? I guess my mind will guide me. There's a reason for me to be reborn.

"Honey, I'm so happy we're together again. I realized that life is not worth living if you're not with us. And we're all here for you. Please don't be mad at me. We can have a new beginning," said Mom.

If I was once angry, I feel no animosity toward her and appreciate her kind words. She means more to me now than ever before. I don't really understand what happened—maybe the ugly past was erased. With that thought, euphoria washes over me. Dat takes my hand and shows me the way out.

"Now we can be together forever and never age," said Dat, flashing that dazzling smile that spreads warmth through my body.

I get up and run to him with my new super-charged body. It's a new world for my generation. It's the circuits and sensors surging through me. I feel electrified and renewed. I want to race Jen and Lucy, and they take my hands, eager for me to join them. I'm lucky to be alive and want to try out my new abilities now that I'm a robot.

Immortality, the new normal.

⚜══◯══⚜

8 hours later

"Welcome back, Val Tate. We are ecstatic over your rebirth. I'm so proud of your strength and bravery in standing up for robotkind and defeating the RRG. I place the Medal of Freedom around your neck for bravery in fighting the war against our enemies, the 100s formerly known as the RRG. We've scoured the area and rounded up the remaining 100s for further investigation and possible deactivation," said the governor.

The presentation streamed across the state and country, and Val's parents beamed at their daughter being called a hero as the attendees stood on the platforms of the Capitol. Val focused her piercing jade eyes on the governor, so as to penetrate through her and plastered a fake smile on her face. She still distrusted the governor's intentions but held no animosity toward her. Her senses were heightened to a new level due to her advanced circuitry and perfected intuitive tracks. The governor's eyes twitched, and beads of sweat formed on her forehead. Val sensed her uncomfortableness as she presented her with the award. Her family and friends stood clapping in the background, including Dat, her parents, her grandmother, Whit, the Landers, Jen, and Lucy. Her track mates gave Val a thumbs-up sign, generating laughter onto a solemn moment.

"We celebrate Val's persistence and strong advocacy for robotkind. She had a great model in Dr. Ashley Simms, her grandmother, who was instrumental in ending the Great Divide and finding a cure for the Caucasian Mosquito virus. And we cannot forget her parents, Meredith, my right-hand and trusted publicist and Rod, Dr. Tate who created the

Genealogy Project, taking it to the next level with his daughter's new identity."

Val turned to see tears in her parents' eyes and her grandmother's loving smile. The governor coughed and paused for a moment.

She looks about to choke up over this. I hope she gives Dat credit for his heroism and strength for defeating Rad and the 100s.

"I'm going to turn the mic over to my brother, Robert Thompson, CEO of RI. He plans to give us an update of the organization and prison situation," said the governor.

Her brother staggered up to the podium, once a youngish fifty-year-old, now looking like a ravaged old man, his hair gone white with a gaunt face and trembling hands.

"I also want to thank Val Tate for ending this rebellion, which has taken a toll on the prison, RI, staff, and my family. We've lost many staff guards, security, our Warden, and the physical structure of RI was almost demolished. Except for the Reconstruction Area, which was saved and utilized by Dr. Rod Tate, who dedicated himself to the GP and, of course, the rebirth of Val Tate. I honor his tenacity and perseverance under such troubling circumstances."

Cheers and whistles sounded from Jen and Lucy and the rest of the track team. "Woohoo, Val Tate…Val Tate…Val Tate."

Val laughed, but the governor shot dagger looks at her friends for interrupting Robert.

"Yes…we commend her and let me continue. In a spirit of compromise, we have rehabilitated the prisoners by providing new job sources and upgraded their classes. We no longer have 100s but are producing a new class—200 domestics with simple conversation abilities and 300s to be the technical class, 500s, and 500 plus models like Val Tate. The plus models have been given greater intuitive and communication skills, more on equal footing with humans. We want to be partners, not adversaries," he said.

Then a monitor showed a virtual layout of the new RI with more labs, production areas, and robots in job-training stations. Val saw that the Reconstruction Area had been expanded, and her Dad's office moved to the Executive Floor.

"What about the clones? Why not recognize Dat who fought the RRG and also supplied his memory trackers for Val's rebirth? Where is Grace Noble?" asked Del from GNet.

The CEO stared at the governor, and they both shrugged their shoulders.

"Uh…the clones have been terminated. They were not authorized by the governor and those involved… were fired. Yes, Dat…he fought bravely and redeemed himself by offering his memory tracks for Val Tate. His actions have been… forgiven. And Grace Noble has been released and offered a new job…Robotic Quality Assurance Director…and she's accepted," said Robert.

The mixed audience of mechanix and humans clapped and shouted excitedly. Flags waved in the breeze, and the air no longer smelled of fire, sweat, and blood. A calmness swept over the crowd that longed for positive words and affirmations.

Val gave Dat a knowing look. Their eyes met, and they knew instantly that the CEO was lying.

What a bunch of crap, but it really doesn't matter now. I love you, Dat, and I hope we can be together soon. We need some time with our families, after all that's happened. I hope you can understand me. Please let me know if you do.

He nodded and winked at her.

CHAPTER 7

Dat surprised himself as he read her mind.

You're a robot now, and we are in sync with each other. I have to convince the Landers that I'm not a rebel. That I want to be a chef again. Maybe they'll forgive me.

Val waved to him as the Landers moved into the influential circle. The adults merged together, talking and laughing, leaving the younger crowd to mingle. Jen and Lucy found a spot near the window to talk to Whit, their former classmate.

"Hey, do you really have a Turbo?" Val says you took her for a ride…" said Lucy, her lips parting to show her dimples. Jen moved closer and batted her long eyes lashes. Whit's face turned a deep emerald.

Dat shuffled over to Val, afraid to put his arm around her in front of her parents. He just stared into her mesmerizing jade-green eyes. His sensors now electrified.

The girls are moving in on Whit. It's the most attention he's had since leaving GNet.

Val gazed directly into his eyes and moved closer to his side.

Yeah, I'm glad to see he's got a couple of girls interested in him.

I'm happy to see he's eyeballing them and not you anymore. Got someone else to focus on.

Uh-huh, never thought you were jealous. Not my type. Perfect for Lucy or maybe Jen, who likes the adventurous type and dated a skydiver last year.

Look at your parents and my guardians, sharing in our fame. Nice to see them getting along. Maybe they'll understand our love and let us just be.

Yeah, but we have to sort things out first. I'm different from before; the rebirth changed me. I think I acted badly—need to figure it out.

Yeah, I feel sorry too…my guardians were good to me, and I have to explain myself.

Look, grandma is coming by and wants to talk with us.

"You two are quite a couple, although Dat didn't get much credit for his part. But I recognize that you stood up for your kind and in the process brought the humans and robots together. There's still work to do, but it's a beginning, and an olive branch has been raised."

She clasped their hands in hers. Her gray curls shone in the filtered sunlight, but her luminous eyes lit up the sky. Dr. Simms's warmth spread over them like a protective blanket, and Dat felt rewarded for his part in the Rebellion.

"Thank you, Grandma, and I hope it doesn't bother you that I'm different now, but still related to you. I want your acceptance most of all… it's so important to me," Val said.

Dat recognized her pain at being different. She was not human anymore, and that's something she would have to deal with forever. Val was in a different class and part of robotkind. His sensors dropped to a lower level, and his sensitivity tracks experienced sadness.

"Of course, I will always love you. You're still the same precious Val. That you're alive is all that matters…when we thought we lost you. Life is about acceptance and forgiveness. I've endured so long because those were my core values. Your parents and the entire world are lucky to have you on this Earth. Remember, you are the future," said her grandmother.

Then she hugged them both.

The Landers and the Tates wandered over to the threesome. Lucy, Jen, and Whit already took off together, and Dat smiled at that thought.

"Hey, buddy, ready to go home? I've sure worked up an appetite. Those little canapes and fruit skewers don't cut it. How about making me your famous Chateaubriand?" said Arnold.

Never stops thinking about food. Good thing, he goes to the spa every day.

Val giggled.

"I just want everyone to know that we misjudged, and instead of going with our instincts, we followed the rumors. Who would have thought that Rad had revenge on his mind? I'm sorry, Dat, for the way we treated you. Will you come home with us? Tad really misses you. Howls every day around lunchtime," said Elise.

Everyone laughed.

"I never thanked you properly for saving our Val so many times, especially sharing your memory tracks. It took courage and strength to deal with all of this, and you proved yourself," said Dr. Tate.

He reached out his hand, and Dat shook it, his sensors and circuits intensifying.

"And…we welcome you into our family," said Meredith.

His sensitivity tracks elevated to extreme happiness, and his circuits surged. Dat experienced surprise and elation and immediately gave Val's mom a crushing hug.

"Thank you, I've waited a long time for you to accept me," Dat whispered in her ear.

Meredith blushed.

Dat quickly backed away, his mind a mixture of emotions. Was he accepted for his human qualities of grit and heroism or because Val became a mechanix, and they had to accept him? They all seemed sincere, and it took a major feat to change people's minds. He grasped Val's hand gently.

Never in my lifetime did I expect this. This is the second happiest day of my life. The first was your rebirth to a 500, just like me.

I still don't know why they wouldn't accept you. But it's time for me to reacquaint myself. I have some memory lapses and need to connect with my family.

They may have filtered out your negative thoughts. But we can start over.

Dat and Val looked at each other and understood.

⊷══◉═══⊷

"Woof, ruff, ruff," said Tad, jumping up on Dat and then licking his hand. He scooped the little bulldog into his arms and squeezed him tightly. He missed him so much, and it seemed like a lifetime.

Dat's eyes swept over his favorite place, his kitchen. Mora and Tron rushed from their corners toward him, bringing a bottle of champagne, glasses, and a cheesecake. Mora twirled around, and Tron almost tripped over her as they gathered around him.

"Geez, you got quite a fan club there. We've been totally ignored since you left," Arnold said with a smirk on his face.

"Let's celebrate now that our Dat is home. And make a toast to the new year," said Elise with a tear in her eye.

They all clinked their glasses and downed the sparkling wine. Elise cut and served the cheesecake. Arnold switched on the wall monitors.

"Look, we're celebs, now on the news stream, broadcasting the governor's speech. There are crowds everywhere around the Capitol, like it's New Year's Eve. People and robots holding hands—truly amazing," said Arnold.

"Hey honey—check out the balcony. Fireworks, flags, and people waving. Such a change from before when we're afraid to go outside," said Elise.

Dat followed his guardians to the balcony. Silver armbands and American flags merged together. A soft chanting and singing sounded, their voices growing louder.

"Humans and robots unite."

"We will never fight."

"Our world is now right."

"Liberty and love tonight."

Dat's senses awakened, and his right and left brains meshed. He believed justice and fairness had come to America on this final day of the year, December 31, 2045, and he was a major part of it. Killing Rad, helping Val back to her rebirth and finally accepted as a chef, and part of the family, overwhelmed him. His circuits and senses nearly overheated as wild emotions flooded his sensitivity trackers. But being a chef was still his dream.

Dat scurried to the kitchen to make the greatest feast of all—Chateaubriand, oyster pie, poached lobster tail, venison cannelloni with kale, black forest cake, and French meringues. His fingers flew in excitement and pride, happy that robotkind was finally free.

"I'm very happy…to be home with my guardians, my dog, and my friends. I'm sorry for all the trouble…I've caused. Just eat!" Dat said.

Everyone moved toward the kitchen counter and observed the spread of delicious food that was precisely laid out in between glasses and bottles of sparkling wine. Even Mora and Tron joined in, their sensors lit up and fully animated.

"Here's to our family, friends, and the dawn of a new world. Today wipes the slate clean and the reboot of 2045, a year best forgotten," said Arnold.

He clinked his glass with Dat's.

"We also celebrate the reuniting of beloved Dat, may he always be with us, now and forever," said Elise.

She gave Dat a hug.

The chandelier swayed, and some books fell off a bookcase. The room started shaking violently as if the walls were made of thin paper. Dishes and glasses crashed to the ground. Arnold and Elise stumbled and champagned spilled on the plush couches. Tron and Mora bumped into each other as they scrambled to prevent the food from sliding off the counters.

Screams and cries sounded from below as people rushed through the streets, avoiding flying debris. Dat ran to the balcony and peered down at the chaos. Huge waves brushed up against the buildings, drowning some animals and washing away people like helpless dolls. He heard their terrifying screams. Space vans circled the building and were jostled off course. Dat heard his guardians' high-pitched cries but only thought of Val who was probably dead.

CHAPTER 8

Three hours earlier

Her room appeared the same after all these months away. Val stared at the remnants of her childhood. A teddy bear lay amongst the pillows on the flowered yellow comforter. Wall monitors and virtual posters of her favorite band, *The Striped Dogs*, lined the room. Piles of books served as bedside tables, and a lamp emitted a soft blue light. A hologram of the winning track meet with Jen, and Lucy flashed on the closet door.

She pressed a button on the wall opposite her bed, and her modular furniture opened into a desk, bookcase, and chair. Only a math assignment appeared on her computer screen. Sunlight poured through a skylight.

Val checked herself out in the full-length mirror by her bed, stretching her new body. She surprised herself by performing some insane pretzel moves. Balancing on strong arms and flexible legs, Val switched from one pose to another swiftly. Barely sweating and breathing smoothly, she stood and faced herself, noting her new crystal eyes, dazzling smile, and lustrous auburn hair. No blemishes, freckles or scars marked her flawless skin. She opened her mouth wide to reveal perfectly straight teeth and laughed out loud.

Too good to be true. To live forever and look this way is a miracle. I have dad to thank for my perfection.

"Darling, are you okay? Just checking in with you."

Val turned to see her mother at the doorway, who was keeping a safe distance. There was still an unspoken shyness that Val did not understand. What had come between them, and why did they seem like strangers?

"Oh…hi, Mom. My body's so different, and I feel…," Val paused. Her left and right brains collided with conflicting thoughts—happiness and resentment. But this time, she would be honest with her mother, who stood there looking puzzled.

A frown formed on her mother's forehead, and she blinked back tears.

"I've been waiting for this day for a long time, so we could talk face to face. But it took a terrible turn of fate...and you died. I don't want to waste any more time..." said her mother.

Val strolled across the room to confront her mom. She sensed her mom's apprehension and distress.

"Did something happen between us? I don't really remember. My life did flash before me as I was dying, but some bad memories have been cut. It also seems different between you and Dat. My instincts are telling me that you and I had a misunderstanding, and we stopped talking. Is that right? I want to start over now that I'm...reborn," said Val.

She threw her arms around her mother, and her circuits lit up.

Her mother blushed, sighed, and looked directly into Val's eyes.

"So much has occurred since we last talked. The RRG nearly killed us and took over our world, and I associated Dat with those monsters. But he always fought for you even at the cost of termination. I couldn't accept Dat as your boyfriend, but now that you're...reborn, I understand that we are all family. I almost lost your father and then you. It taught me about acceptance and finding the truth. And we all have something in common...we love you. You're my daughter, and I will always love you."

Val's new sensitivity trackers surged to a higher happiness level, and her empathy soared. She realized her mother's pain and anxiety, having lived in both worlds. Pieces of her memory filtered through. She'd been unreasonable, hurtful, and defiant. Val never realized the sacrifices her parents made for her. And they just needed to know Dat better.

"I love you too...and I'm sorry that we grew apart. I never want it to be that way again," Val said.

They embraced, just as her father walked in, limping yet smiling.

"My two girls getting together...makes me so happy."

Her father joined them in a group hug.

"Look, Daddy, how I can move. It's a miracle, and you brought me back. I'm sooo happy."

Val went back to a half-frog pose then forwarded into a somersault to stand up between her parents.

Her dad examined Val's joints and spine. Her mother just shook her head in awe.

"Amazing. Those are the advantages of the 500 plus. And you won't break down because you're automatically upgrading your hardware and software over time. Our programming has become so advanced due to the Genealogy Project. You will probably never understand how lucky you are...due to the regeneration aspect. My love for you exceeds any prejudices I had previously. That is...you are still my daughter even if your physical makeup is different. You and Dat have changed my perspective. The world is a brighter place for me," said her Dad.

Her jade eyes glowed, and her smile expanded to its limit.

"My right and left-brain functions completely complement each other. There's a greater understanding of others' emotions due to the high level of my sensitivity trackers. I'm highly functional and aware of everything. I know we disagreed at one time, but we seem to have a greater connection. I'm no longer one dimensional. My viewpoint has expanded. In other words, the new Val loves you even more," she said in a robotic monotone.

They all laughed at her analysis. Their eyes shone. They were now in sync. The pieces of their lives fit together, and only Dat would complete it.

Hey, baby, I wish you were here to experience this family reunion. They understand why I love you. Respond when you receive my message.

The room started spinning. Val heard the crash of trees, thumps on the roof, and a sudden jolt. Outside a loud fluttering of birds, cats yowling and crows cawing warned of danger. The house swayed back and forth. Val saw the panic in her mother's eyes.

"Hurry, let's get to the panic room. No time to waste. I think it's the earthquake they have been predicting for years," said her father, pushing them out of her bedroom toward the living room.

He pressed on the wall that led to a door. With his eye imprint, her dad released the combination, and the door slid open, revealing a staircase. They hustled downstairs as Val paused, feeling the walls shuddering and the floor buckling.

"The house is collapsing. It's finally the Big One. I'm not ready for this," her mother screamed, almost tripping down the stairs.

Val's instincts told her that it wasn't the end of the world. Her curiosity as always got the better of her. Especially now that she'd gotten her life back and in robotic form. But she feared for her parents and wandered why Dat hadn't answered. Her sensors burned, and the current flowed rapidly through her circuits. Before, it would have been her heart beating faster and shortness of breath. Her advanced wiring and keen intuition moved her to act and protect her kind.

"It's all right, Mom. I'll secure everything, just be safe," Val said.

"No baby, c'mon right now. The room locks in ninety seconds, and you need to be here with us. You won't survive. You've never been in an earthquake before," yelled her father, his voice echoing from the chamber below.

She heard the floors cracking and the walls crunching. An heirloom vase was broken on the floor in a hundred pieces. The floor was soaked with water and debris. The heavy family room couch and newly bought chairs lay upside down like doll furniture thrown in a corner. Grandma's portrait managed to stick to the wall, the only solitary decoration that was untouched.

Val peered out the window. Polyethylene trees broke in two, and live wires lined the ground outside. Small fires sprouted randomly on her block, and surrounding apartment buildings appeared dark and abandoned. An outdoor pool overflowed with water and fallen leaves. A family of ducks sloshed down the street in a rapid current. A crackling wire shook above and threatened to come crashing down on the precious brown babies.

Horrified, Val ran outside to save them, her circuits as electrified as the downed wires. The world was still reeling, and she felt dizzy from the after-effects. As she rushed to grab the ducks, they were swept away in the rising waters.

The earth continued to move as the streets opened up with huge gaps, exposing the ground below. She heard the Skytrain crash and passengers screeching. A space van fell out of the sky, and Val ran away to avoid crashing wreckage. Dogs and cats were running around and whimpering in pain as the ground still shook.

Val's jaw dropped at the sight of crumbled apartment buildings, once tall and luxurious, now reduced to sand. She blinked away the floating dust and tasted the grit in her mouth. She heard the clinking of metal and the human moans. As she walked closer, the smell of feces and blood overpowered her as she approached large piles of plastic rubble. Drones circled overhead to indicate victims' locations. Then she spotted the mechanix work crews, mostly Model 200s and a few Model 500s directing their activity.

"What's going on?" Val asked.

"Careful miss…we're pulling out the survivors. Even found a baby. You shouldn't be here…only robots are authorized by Governor Thompson. No human help is allowed…too dangerous. But nobody cares that we've been hurt," said a Model 500 with a hard hat and hobbling on one leg.

"Nothing's changed?" Val asked.

"No…sent out on the front lines. So much for equality for mechanix. We were…told…stay here until you find all victims…humans only, of course. The governor just orders more crew if we break down."

Val looked closer and recognized Von, who fought with her in the Rebellion. The other crew members were operating with broken limbs, battered faces, and endless courage.

"Von, is that you? We fought together, and you deserve better. I'm calling Whit to expose this injustice. This is what we fought against, and it's happening all over again," said Val.

She sent Whit the ugly images from her com watch, and he quickly responded.

"How did you get there? Are you okay? Be there in a quick minute on my Turbo Z. This is outrageous. I'll broadcast this info on my own podcast," Whit said.

Von finally recognized her and grinned, a dark smudge covering one of his eyes.

"Are you going to free us again?" Von said.

Val steadied her feet on the firm ground. The sky wasn't spinning, and the air was still and humid. No space vans flew overhead. The Skytrain stopped running. Birds and critters had disappeared. Her quiet breathing comforted her. She had a mission. To save the robots.

CHAPTER 9

The panic room seemed like a palace compared to the destruction outside. Dat inspected the gaping holes in the city streets below and ragged skyline where many tall skyscrapers and the vintage Grand Old Capitol Hotel had once been. Only RI was still standing. His sensors almost exploded now that his dream of working there was gone. The Landers sent him upstairs to survey the damage and determine if it was safe enough to enter the apartment. Besides, Arnold was hungry again. That was the real reason to cook a grand meal before they perished.

He noted that the kitchen was still intact, and Mora and Tron hadn't moved since the Big One hit. Only Elise, Arnold, Dat, and Tad were allowed into the panic room, a luxurious, smaller version of their apartment.

"All clear, only a broken champagne glass," Dat communicated through his com watch.

It took them less than five minutes to leave the panic room with little Tad. He wagged his tail furiously, begging to go out. Dat led him to a mini, enclosed yard off the balcony where he could conduct his business.

"Man...the almost-end of the world made me ravenous. Can you hustle up some small plates and a little bubbly to celebrate our survival?" said Arnold. He quickly activated the wall monitors.

Elise sighed.

"Can't believe you have an appetite after our near demise. I can barely catch my breath, and Dat probably has other things on his mind," said Elise.

Dat wondered why Val hadn't picked up his vibes. He'd try again after making his first meal of the new year. His mind focused on the Landers' favorites and reached for some French champagne.

"Happy New Year, babe. Can't you wait until we've had our first toast of the year? Do you really want to know how many died or what was destroyed?" Elise said, planting a kiss on his cheek.

"I want to know everything, so I can assess the situation carefully. You never know the human race may be wiped out now. Love you, honey," said Arnold, gulping down his glass of champagne and grabbing a plate of chocolate chip pancakes.

The wall monitors flashed on the carnage and devastation. Drones showed that that Capitol City had been leveled except for the elite Metro Apartments in the Gild Tower District and the governor's mansion, situated on their own private island communities. Smoke and dirt polluted the air, blocking any way out or in the city.

"I'm Whit Green, formerly from GNet, now with UniverseNet with the workers at the Capitol. Where's the governor? She's ordered these Model 200s and a few 500s to clean up and find the bodies. Our sources say that millions of people have died…and the air alone," said Whit, choking violently.

Dat stared at the monitors while cooking French Toast, Eggs Benedict, and a skillet of sausage and bacon. Looking closer, he saw a familiar face in all the rubble, and his eyes lit up. The cameras switched to her as Whit placed a gas mask over his face. She pointed to the hole in the ground where a crying mother and child were being pulled to safety by a group of grungy robots, covered in dust and soot.

"I'm Val Tate—as you can see, these 300s and 500s have worked tirelessly to save these survivors, some not receiving a break for hours. Without them, more humans would have died due to the massive destruction and poor air quality as a result of this huge earthquake," Val said.

The mother turned her bloody face toward the cameras, her clothes in shreds as her child clung to her leg.

"My daughter and I are so grateful to be alive. We've been here for hours and thought it was our last moments on Earth. Then these saviors came… to rescue us. It was… a miracle," the mother said and collapsed. Her daughter started bawling.

Val picked up the child and held her close, caressing her hair.

"We've become immune to pain and suffering. Our society deserves more compassion and love. The government has let us down. If anyone out there wants to help, please contact my com watch at 5555220."

The camera zoomed in, highlighting Val's mesmerizing jade eyes. The tiny child in the tattered clothes and scratched face hugged her close as her mother lay unconscious on the ground beside them.

Dat gazed into those eyes, and his sensors burned with passion, and his sensitivity tracks burst with love for Val. She was truly his partner, and he longed to be with her.

"Look at your girlfriend, bringing people together in these tragic times. I truly want to help her, but I'm afraid. What should we do, Arnold?" said Elise.

The other wall monitors showed similar scenarios where robots uncovered other humans from disintegrated buildings, under broken bridges, in between road crevasses and in destroyed neighborhoods. Dat watched in awe how his kind dug through the rubble to find dead bodies and a few who were still alive.

"Special Report—some key leaders have died as a result of this 9.7 earthquake. Dr. Ashley Simms was found dead in her compound by her bodyguards of an apparent heart attack. Governor Andrea Thompson's space copter crashed around midnight. Her brother said she was bringing supplies and water back to the Capitol. More from Robert Thompson, her brother, and president of RI," said Whit.

He blinked back tears from his puffy eyes. His voice shook as he looked into the cameras with a grim expression. "The governor...my sister was a true hero." He started to cry.

"She was only thinking of her constituents. I begged her...not to go, but she wanted to leave...to bring back medicine, water, and needed provisions. But her space copter...went down...as a result of the earthquake. Our Capitol is in mourning. I can't go on..."

Then Robert fainted. A team of robots rushed to pick him up.

The monitors switched to decimated communities and a tsunami that had washed away the coastal cities. Dead fish piled up on the beaches as teams of robots combed the shore for any signs of life. Dat gasped and wondered if they were the only family still alive. Then, a wall monitor picked a plea from a concerned citizen.

"Everyone needs to come together, both human and mechanix. Our world has fallen apart, and many people are dead, and communities are gone. Our only hope is unity and the Genealogy Project that will extend our life...now I can see that. If you're still out there, Dr. Tate, please contact me. We need you at this critical time, and I'm willing to work with you," said Grace Noble, sitting in her living room.

Her eyes twitched, and her purple hair was tied back in a tight ponytail. It wasn't the fiery activist that Dat was used to and sometimes feared. She looked frightened as she clutched her tiny poodle.

Tad jumped and barked when he saw Grace's poodle. The little bulldog wagged its tail and scampered over to Arnold.

"Sorry, buddy, don't want to play now. Elise, I guess we're very lucky we're still here. Not many humans survived. Happy 2046!" said Arnold.

He put down his plate and headed for the bedroom.

"Wait, honey...should we contact Robert? What's the next step? And if we go outside, will we survive?" said Elise.

She ran after him with tears running down her cheeks.

"We're screwed baby, better think about the alternative."

He pushed a button on his com watch.

"Urgent news and special report: Robert Thompson just had a massive stroke and has died. He leaves no descendants behind. In addition, Meredith and Dr. Rod Tate were found dead in their apartment, which was crushed by the earthquake. Their only survivor is their daughter Val who was last seen on the front lines, assisting the injured. We have yet to catch up to her for comment. We've reached out to other government officials, but they have not yet responded," said Whit.

Dat stared at the apartment where Val once called home. His right and left brains converged, leaving him depressed, but wanting to act. His circuits fired up. His instincts said no more cooking for his guardians. They had retreated to their room and left him to figure things out. The world was not yet over for him, and he needed to find Val.

Are you okay? Where are you?

Down here. I'm ready to implode. Just found out about my parents.

Dat ran to the balcony with little Tad in tow. Below stood a disheveled Val with dirty clothes and rumpled hair with tears flowing down her sooty cheeks. Tad whined and barked.

Meet me by the tunnel exit. I'm leaving right now and bringing Tad.

Be careful. The air quality is poor—cover up Tad. I couldn't stand it if another family member close to me died.

Dat exited through his bedroom closet with Tad wrapped in his specially made cloth carrier. It covered his nose and mouth, only leaving his frightened eyes exposed. They blasted down the tunnel and ended up outside. Two bloodied security guards lay slumped on the ground, crushed from broken rubble.

"More deaths and devastation. I've witnessed a lot. Not many humans have survived. You can't believe how good it to see you and Tad alive," said Val.

Dat hugged her tightly, pressing the little bulldog to her.

"Ruff, ruff," said Tad, breathing fast and squirming in Dat's arms.

"The earthquake frightened me…not like when you died. I just saw you on the news monitors. Sorry about your parents…only can imagine what would have happened if you were with them," said Dat.

Val let out a scream and big sobs. She started crying uncontrollably.

CHAPTER 10

The three gathered around the apartment building's remnants. Val murmured a silent prayer and sifted through the garbage and graphene material along with Dat and Tad. The bodies were buried underneath all the dense debris. She realized they were all that was left of her family. Would immortality eventually remove the heartache? Her sensors were dulled, but her sensitivity trackers indicated high levels of pain and anguish. Maybe she could find a tiny keepsake to remember them. Ironically, she'd forgiven them, and as a family, they wanted to start over. They finally accepted who she was and her relationship with Dat. Now, this.

"Hey, I think I found something...fuzzy ball. No...a bear," said Dat.

Tad started barking as Dat grabbed a one-eyed yellow teddy bear covered in ashes. He brushed off the dirt to reveal a black nose and gold medallion around its neck.

"It's Pooh Bear...got him for my first birthday from Mom and Dad. That's what the medallion says. Always there for me when I was sad," said Val, giving the bear a squeeze.

Tad sneezed.

"You'll always have those childhood remembrances. We can make our own memories and save this planet...together," said Dat, giving her a hug.

Val heard a roaring noise in the distance and a violent vibration of her com watch. Were there still space vans around? A Turbo Z flew by, kicking up dirt and rubble.

"Hey, they're asking for you. People...uh, robots want to help. Not too many of us humans left, and I may be one of the few. I'm so sorry about your parents, and your grandmother...her spirit will always be with us," said Whit.

Then he coughed and sneezed several times in a row.

"Whew…better keep your mask on. Thanks for your kind words…but I'm not sure what I'm supposed to do. Everything we loved is gone, and the world has fallen apart. Not sure where to start," said Val.

Whit put on his mask and spoke loudly.

"Your grandma was an inspiration and a force, and I think she left that legacy for you to follow. You know what your dad was trying to do with the Genealogy Project. RI is still standing for a reason, and Grace just needs a little guidance. So, let's go—we can all fit on this Turbo Z. Never returned it to GNet HQ," said Whit, smiling.

◦◦═◦◯═◦◦

6 hours later

"The inquiries haven't stopped pouring in after the New Year's Quake hit. Many of you have asked about the brave young woman who solicited survivors' help in the midst of its after-effects. But I tracked her down. You may not know that she is Val Tate, the descendant of Dr. Rod Tate, and recently reborn as a Model 500 plus. She has a plan to unite all classes, races, and genders after the immense Quake that took many lives," said Whit.

Val and Dat held hands in front of the RI building. She desperately wanted him by her side when she made this major announcement. After all, he was her partner for life. She prepared herself for her live streaming over the new UniverseNet. Her life had taken a 360-degree turn in every way. Val lifted her eyes to the heavens and spoke slowly.

"Good evening. We are in deep mourning for all the lost souls, especially my parents. Our world has been turned upside down due to the Big Quake. But it's a perfect time to come together for humankind and robotkind. Grace Noble and I will continue the Genealogy Project for the purpose of preserving future generations. I appreciate her desire to work with me."

As she spoke, many appeared out of the trash and dust to convene onto the Capitol's platforms. Both mechanix and humans joined hands in harmony to give their support to their young leader. They brought tools, vehicles, and strength to begin the hard work of clean-up and rescue.

"We look to you…for guidance, remembering your father," said Dolli.

Val welcomed her father's nurse with outstretched hands.

"I stand by this strong woman who will lead us into the next century. I saw her die as a human, fighting for robotkind and now reborn as a Model 500. I believe in her," said Von.

Val and Dat ushered him up to the Capitol's steps.

"I'm honored to help Val, Dr. Tate's daughter, to improve this world and offer everyone a chance to live in this age of change. We will be the new inhabitants of this Earth," said Grace, her eyes bright with a gray streak in her vivid purple hair.

Val clapped, and then everyone rallied around Grace.

"Humans and robots, we have much work to do. First, let's revitalize our city and next create a robust plan for our new world," said Val.

In her new planetary diaries, Val documented the ordeals and growing pains of the next decade.

We endured many hardships these first few years. The Big Quake destroyed the landscape of Capital City and the other island communities. Millions of humans died from poor air quality and a lack of resources. Additional Tsunamis caused structural damage to roads and buildings. Millions of human lives and animals drowned or were washed into the ocean. The Mechanical race stepped up and initiated a new course. We were now the new majority, and we held fast to our new dreams of a stronger generation with concerns of integrity, unity, and civility.

RI was key to our growth. Grace took on the role of chief scientist in charge of the GP along with the original team that survived. Under her direction, many humans chose "to die," and then their brains were implanted into mechanical bodies. Grace lost a few souls, which she regretted, but it was a learning process.

The Earth continued to deteriorate with the extreme climate and atmospheric changes. Pandemics and even with the many advances and highly technological Model 300s, millions of humans perished. Although many people fled to Mars, others chose to stay on their beloved Earth.

The Model 500s redesigned the new infrastructure after the 2046 Quake, starting with RI. The Model 200s and 300s implemented their plans by dismantling the skyscrapers to build underground offices and tunnels. Transportation moved below, and the Skyway and Skytrain became historical relics and were no longer used. Because mechanix didn't depend on the sun or air quality. We thrived underneath the ocean and rebuilt an underwater world.

Our sensor and sensitivity trackers synchronized as my love for Dat increased. He continued to be the awesome chef that he was created to be, just some of the food was created digitally, not cooked. But his imagination flourished as the Tony De LaFleur lived within him.

EPILOGUE

Year 2065

"We thank the pioneers who created robotkind like Grace Noble and those who fought and risked their lives for our independence, especially Whit Green. Grace, one of the few humans who survived the Big Quake and extended life spans through the Genealogy Project, died from cancer five years ago. Whit, always a friend, succumbed to COPD. We are extremely indebted to them for their bravery during the robot riots of twenty years ago and compassion for robotkind's well-being.

"Also, to Dr. Rod Tate, who took our race to a new level. He bravely entered territory where no man, let alone father would cross," said President Val Tate, speaking at a State dinner in an underground facility below the now-demolished White House, now duplicated with its many paintings and statues of the past Presidents, elegant chandeliers, 19-century furniture, and red carpets.

She paused for a moment as life-size holograms of Grace, Whit, and Rod Tate emerged from the wall monitors into the audience, showcasing the work they had done. The audience gasped in awe as they relived their lives, even though it happened over decades ago.

"True innovators and warriors in the world of robotics with a keen sense of the future's needs," said Val.

Dat looked lovingly at his wife of fifteen years, now the "leader of the new Earth." Imagine a woman and a robot running not just the United States but part of North America. He preferred to just be the best chef in the world, his signature digital Chateaubriand steak served in the White House at least once a month because only he could prepare it.

He admired his wife and the way she turned the country around with robots serving in many higher-level capacities in administrative jobs, as technology experts, scientists, and writers. History reported on all their advances as humans died off, and their brains were replaced in Model 500 Plus robots. A deep sadness overwhelmed him as Dat's sensitivity tracks surged in memory of both Meredith and Don Tate, who died in the Great Earthquake in 2046.

It's a shame they're gone from this world as many other good people. The scientists and advocates believed in climate control, But it's too late since the animals, vegetation, and fish have vanished.

He bowed his head as he reminisced further, thinking of his cherished bulldog.

Poor Tad, he never had a chance. I wish we could have saved him from that tsunami. I hope we can apply the Genealogy Project to animals someday. He pulled up a hologram of their beloved pet.

"My father envisioned a world where robots and humans coexisted. After *The Great Rebellion* of 2045, the governor and CEO of RI tasked him to find a solution to bring mankind and robotkind together. I was reborn that night after I died in the Rebellion, led by my future husband, Dat. He provided my memories, and Dad fused them with my brain into a robot body. I'll forever be grateful to those individuals who forged a new generation. And remembering my mother, Meredith, who I received back into my life, realizing that she only wanted the best for me and showed me the value of forgiveness.

But I also want to recognize my grandmother, Dr. Ashley Simms, Revolutionists, and the elimination of the Great Divide who lived a long life mentoring young people, succumbing to a heart attack. She motivated me to be the person...uh...proud robot I am today," said Val.

The audience cheered and applauded loudly, the metal clanking almost deafening.

Dat looked at the sea of faces in the audience, not necessarily from foreign countries, but mostly Robot Nations. He recognized leaders of the Meccanoid, Cosmos, Cartesian, and Vector Nations, their features very human-like, but distinguishable by their lack of blood, which was no longer needed in this new world ravaged by wind, water and sun.

Robots have really advanced as a race and survived throughout the years.

He smiled at the couple at the next table, Elise and Arnold Sanders, who legally killed themselves and had their brains transplanted into new robotic bodies. Elise winked at him, and Arnold toasted to his new stature. They looked the same, only their eyes were brighter with a youthfulness that reflected their upgrades.

I've always admired Elise and Arnold, putting the past behind them and embracing the future.

He scanned the room and noted others that were motivated by the Landers and decided to become part of the robot race. Val's friend Lucy became part of the mechanix and joined Val's Cabinet as director of Health & Robotic Social Services. She waved at Dat.

Jen studied under Grace Noble and moved into her spot as Genealogy Project Administrator. Grace donated her brains, which were now part of Jen's new Model 500 DNA. She sat next to Lucy and winked at him.

Even Ms. Lee, Val's former teacher, looked the same with a reconstructed body and a cheerful face. Val talked about her stern demeanor and courage when she escaped from the Thompson High terrorist attack. Dat noted that she listened intently to Val's message.

"I never thought I would say this, but I'm glad we fought for our rights and have taken over the world. Our logic and intuition have served us well, making Earth a better place. We've eliminated war, chaos, bigotry, tyranny, and misogyny, and the terrorist RRG and radical 100s. With the end of the Thompson Government, a takeover of Robot International and removal of mechanical terrorist factions, the world is kinder and finally at peace. Praise to those who fought for respect, harmony, and justice. With the creation of our Automaton Nation, the human race is now extinct," said President Tate, who smiled broadly at Dat.

Dat never imagined the justice for all meant only robotkind. He joined the audience as they gave her a standing ovation.

CPSIA information can be obtained
at www.ICGtesting.com
Printed in the USA
LVHW031609090321
680995LV00004B/392